Love Finds You™
∽ *in* ⊱

MARTHA'S VINEYARD

MASSACHUSETTS

Love Finds You™
∽ *in* ∾
MARTHA'S VINEYARD
MASSACHUSETTS

BY MELODY CARLSON

summerside
PRESS™

Summerside Press™
Minneapolis 55438
www.summersidepress.com

Love Finds You in Martha's Vineyard, Massachusetts
© 2011 by Melody Carlson

ISBN 978-1-60936-110-5

The town depicted in this book is a real place, but all characters are fictional. Any resemblances to actual people or events are purely coincidental.

Cover Design by Lookout Design | www.lookoutdesign.com

Interior Design by Müllerhaus Publishing Group | www.mullerhaus.net

Photos provided by Melody Carlson.

Summerside Press™ is an inspirational publisher offering fresh, irresistible books to uplift the heart and engage the mind.

Printed in USA.

Martha's Vineyard, Massachusetts

MY PRECONCEPTION OF MARTHA'S VINEYARD WAS PROBABLY SIMILAR to that of the average American who's never been there. I assumed it was the highbrow vacation playground of the rich and famous. Thanks to a small number of well-known personalities, from songwriters to politicians, this is somewhat true. But the first time I actually experienced Martha's Vineyard, I was caught off guard by its quaint charm and natural beauty—and I never saw a single celebrity. That might be because I visited the Vineyard in the middle of winter—a time when the population of the entire island is about fifteen thousand and life there is sleepy, subdued, and slow-paced. But winter is also a good time to get around the island and see the sights—and it's not hard to get reservations at the last minute.

However, if you attempt to go in the midst of the summer, brace yourself. The population increases tenfold—up to 150,000 people inhabit the small island and traffic can be a bear (bikes are recommended). The full-time locals wisely maintain a low profile during the height of the season. They're said to tell their friends, "See you in the fall," as soon as June rolls around. They're also reported to say, "I'm going to America," when they board the ferry taking them back to Massachusetts. I suppose that's just how removed they feel, living off on their little island in the Atlantic.

Since I've always been drawn to seaboard towns (we have a beach bungalow on the other side of the country), I felt right at home in Martha's Vineyard. I found the local people to be helpful, informative, and interesting. And the scenery—whether it was windswept beaches, picturesque lighthouses, handsome boats moored in Vineyard Haven, or gingerbread houses in Oak Bluffs— was perfectly delightful, not to mention photogenic. Despite being there in February, with severe storms raging inland, the weather on the island was temperate and mild. All in all, it was a great trip. Even the ferry ride in and out of Woods Hole was enjoyable. In other words, I highly recommend Martha's Vineyard. I'm looking forward to going back there again myself!

Melody Carlson

Chapter One

....

Where was that lake-effect weather when you really needed it? A nice chilly breeze off Lake Michigan would've been most welcome today. Waverly felt weary and wilted as she slowly made her way toward the "L." Not only was she perspiring profusely in her best summer suit, but her new spectator pumps were torturing her feet. She should've known better than to trust the adolescent salesgirl who assured Waverly that "four-inch heels really can be comfortable." And to buy the old line that "Oprah wears these exact same shoes for hours at a time" was truly pathetic. Sometimes Waverly wondered if someone had secretly tattooed GULLIBLE on her forehead in a special ink that only showed up in department store lighting.

As she limped across the street, Waverly wondered if she might've permanently injured her feet as well. This morning she'd been so focused on her big interview today that she'd even forgotten to tuck her usual flip-flops into her oversized bag. Well, that was water under the bridge now. Waverly paused at the corner of Columbus and, waiting for the light to change, peeled off her limp linen jacket and folded it over her arm. She fished a hairclip out of her bag and sloppily stuck her long thick curls on top of her head. If the pavement wasn't so hot, she'd take off her shoes too.

She probably resembled a bag lady now, but her neck and back felt a tiny bit cooler. Even though it was nearly 6 p.m., the temperature on the bank's reader board declared it was still 98 smoldering degrees. Summer wasn't here yet, and Chicago had already broken several of this year's heat and humidity records.

That wasn't the only thing broken, Waverly thought as she hurried across another scorching hot street. A few days ago, her air conditioner had given up the ghost, and so far her building's super had not returned her call. Normally, Waverly didn't whine and complain, but today she felt like flopping down on the greens of Grant Park and sobbing loudly and pitifully. Nothing, absolutely nothing, was going right for her. On days like today, she wondered why she even tried.

"You're somewhat overqualified for this position," Mrs. Tremble had told her this morning. Waverly had taken an early lunch break to sneak off to an interview at a new art gallery opening on North Michigan Avenue—in search of her dream job.

"I realize that," Waverly had explained. "But I'd really love to work for you and I—"

"Have you ever worked in a gallery?" Mrs. Tremble peered curiously over her bifocals at Waverly. "I mean, besides art conservation, which is admittedly a very important field in the art world at large but altogether different from working in sales. Certainly, you can understand."

"No...I haven't actually worked in a gallery," Waverly said slowly. "But I'm a fast learner."

Mrs. Tremble smiled in a placating way. "I'm sure you are. However, selling art is different. It takes a certain sort of *savoir-faire*.

A special type of personality, if you know what I mean. Almost a gift, I'm inclined to believe. The ability to read people, to immediately assess them, to understand their tastes, know what they want… and how much they are willing to spend…and more." She laughed lightly. "I sometimes call it the sixth sense. Really, it's an art form in itself, dear. It's a lot different from the science of caring for and restoring art. Do you understand what I'm saying?"

"I think I do," Waverly assured her. "I consider myself a fairly intuitive person. Although I didn't mention it on my résumé, I'm not only involved in the science side of art, I'm also an artist myself." She smiled hopefully. "I am both creative *and* scientific."

Mrs. Tremble sighed. "Well, then…now I am certain you wouldn't be right for our gallery."

Waverly frowned. "Why not?"

"I would never hire an artist as a salesperson, dear. Too conflicting."

"Conflicting?"

"Oh my, yes. It is one thing to understand and appreciate art. It's another thing to have the gift for selling art. But to have an actual artist working here in a sales position." She held up her hands as if Waverly had offered her a poisoned apple. "That would never work."

"But I haven't picked up a paintbrush in ages," Waverly tried.

Mrs. Tremble smiled as she stood. "Just be thankful you already have an excellent job. Working in the museum at the Art Institute of Chicago is nothing to be ashamed of, dear. And in this day and age, one is fortunate to have employment of any kind, don't you think?"

"Yes." Waverly nodded helplessly as she too stood. The interview was clearly over.

"I don't want to waste any more of your precious time." Mrs. Tremble looked at her diamond-studded watch bracelet. "I do thank you for coming in, and I hope you'll stop by again when we are properly opened. Do watch for the announcement in the *Tribune*. And we'll be having a special show for Summer Solstice, less than three weeks away."

"Thank you." Waverly looped a strap of her bag over her shoulder with a very forced smile. "I appreciate your time."

Mrs. Tremble walked her out of the office and into the spacious gallery, where electricians were working on the lighting system that, even at a glance, was state-of-the-art. At the front door, Mrs. Tremble had given Waverly a weak handshake, saying, "Thank you, dear. Have a nice day."

Waverly politely exited the sleekly designed gallery. Then, pausing in the shade of a canvas awning over the restaurant next door, she'd let out a long, exasperated sigh. She could not believe that Mrs. Tremble had refused to even consider her for the sales position. It was as if the old woman had made up her mind from the very get-go. But, good grief, how hard would it be to sell art? After all, the salespeople worked mostly on commission anyway. What was that mumbo-jumbo about special gifts and a sixth sense? It seemed clear—Mrs. Tremble simply had someone else in mind. Waverly watched as a precisely groomed and well-dressed man paused by the door to the gallery. Checking his image in the shining plate glass, he smoothed his short hair, made a self-satisfied smile, and, holding his head high, went inside. Yes, he was probably the exact sort of person Mrs. Tremble was looking for. Well, good for him!

Waverly had tried not to show any signs of her disappointment as she returned to work. Not that anyone would notice, since her job was a fairly solitary one—one of the many reasons she was seeking something different. The place was even more quiet than usual since she was now working through her traditional lunch hour. As a result, no one was around to notice her tears as she meticulously cleaned a 350-year-old alabaster bust of a middle-aged Italian woman. The woman's expression, at first glance, had been pensive...thoughtful...even wistful. But the more Waverly worked on Antonia, the name she'd given the sculpture, the more Waverly realized she was wrong. Antonia was not meditating on her lover or pondering the mysteries of the universe. The woman was plain sad. Perhaps even clinically depressed.

Was it possible that Antonia, like Waverly, was disappointed in life? Maybe she too had lost her beloved husband at a young age. Perhaps she felt disillusioned about her future. Disenchanted with life. Hopeless. Or maybe Waverly had simply been superimposing her own emotional state onto this cold gypsum form.

* * * * *

As Waverly entered the shabby courtyard of The Hampshire, the apartment complex where she had resided for the past seven years, she wondered, not for the first time, what had attracted her and Neil to these dowdy brick structures in the first place. Oh, certainly, they had been newlyweds and filled with wide-eyed optimism and high hopes. Plus, neither had ever lived in a big city like Chicago before.

"We'll only stay a year," Neil had promised her. "Two at the most. Just until we figure things out and find a place to buy." A year had quickly turned into two and then three. But they had been happy years, and Neil and Waverly Brennen made several good friends at The Hampshire. Plus they'd discovered it was handily located close to the "L." And by keeping expenses down, Waverly was free to pursue her art. So, really, life was good. Then, shortly after their third anniversary, Neil had gone into the hospital for what was supposed to be a "routine surgery."

As many times as Waverly had replayed the four-year-old scenario, as many times as she'd blamed herself, blamed the doctors, even blamed Neil, she now found herself replaying it all over again. Maybe it was the weather or the disappointing day, but as she climbed the metal stairs to her apartment, it came flooding back at her.

"Just go in and get it done while our insurance is still good," she'd told Neil after his doctor had recommended a cartilage replacement in his left knee. Neil wasn't even thirty yet, but an old soccer injury had been making him walk like an old man. With summer coming on, Waverly had wanted to get out their bicycles. Plus, she knew Neil had been considering a job switch where the pay was significantly better but the insurance was not. So it had made sense. Or so it seemed.

Waverly had gone in with him for the surgery. Then she'd brought him home and followed the doctor's instructions regarding rehabilitation. But two days after the surgery, Neil had complained of a stomachache. Waverly had suggested the usual remedies, like Pepto-Bismol and TUMS, and she'd even made him a cup of ginger tea. Then she'd gotten lost in a painting, a seascape that was still unfinished. By the time she'd checked on Neil again, she assumed he was asleep, but on closer inspection, she saw how pale and cool his skin was to the touch. And she realized he was unconscious.

By the time the paramedics arrived, his blood pressure had dropped seriously low, and by the time he was examined in the ER thirty minutes later, he was in septic shock. He died the next day. The doctor was sympathetic, telling her such a reaction to surgery was statistically quite rare. But that did not bring her husband back.

She unlocked and opened the door to her stuffy apartment. Despite having left blinds closed and windows open, the space was even hotter than outside. She checked her landline phone to see if the super had called back—since he hadn't called on her cell phone—but no one had called. She stripped off the remainder of her interview outfit, replaced it with a tank top and shorts, then went out onto the terrace where, thanks to the shade of another building, it was only 88 degrees. She sat down in her favorite wicker rocker, which was starting to crack and disintegrate, thanks to the harsh winter it had recently survived. Rocking back and forth, she simply stared out onto...nothing.

It had been more than a year since the last of their friends had moved from The Hampshire. Not that she'd been terribly involved with either of the couples after Neil's death. Oh, the Picketts and the Garcias had tried to include her at first, but as time passed, it got harder and harder to pretend that nothing had changed. Or that no one missed Neil and his slaphappy sense of humor. In a way, she had been relieved when the Picketts had gotten pregnant and moved to the suburbs. It made things simpler. Loneliness had simply become a way of life. Work and loneliness, combined with a bit of house-cleaning and shopping—that was her routine.

Waverly noticed something tucked behind the decrepit old barbecue that Neil had gotten them shortly after they'd moved in here. She pulled out the warped piece of cardboard and stared at the faded images pasted onto it. Oh, yes, she remembered now. This had once been her "vision board." Rita Garcia had talked Waverly into attending a woman's seminar awhile back. One of their "exercises" had been to create a vision board. This visual image was supposed to help Waverly focus on her hopes and dreams for the future, perhaps even make them come true.

Waverly had reluctantly cooperated in the project. For nearly a year she had focused on the sweet images she'd cut and pasted onto her board. She'd study those slick magazine photographs of a happy-looking couple, several children (two redheaded girls and a little blond boy), a beagle puppy with a blue collar, a stripey cat with amber eyes, a farmhouse, and even a dreamy cook's kitchen. For a short time Waverly almost believed it would work.

But then winter came—one of those harsh Chicago winters that feels endless. When she was alone and depressed at Christmastime last year, she had taken the detestable vision board and, despite the howling snow and wind, had shoved it out onto the terrace, wedging it behind the barbecue grill with plans to torch it later.

The flimsy paper shredded easily, crumbling in her hands like sawdust as she dumped the whole mess into the rusty barbecue. She was just going into the apartment to search for matches when the loud jangling of the landline made her jump. She was tempted to let the obnoxious interruption go to voice mail, but thinking it might be her slacking super calling about her useless AC, she hurried to get it. "Hello?"

"*Waverly!*" gushed what sounded like her mother's voice. "I can't believe I caught you at home!"

"*Vivian?*" Waverly had been taught early on to call her mother by her first name, and anything else at this stage of the game would feel awkward.

"Yes, darling, it's me."

Now Waverly jumped to the worst conclusions—the natural thing to do since her mother rarely called and, as far as Waverly knew, she was out of the country. "Are you all right?"

"Of course, I'm fine. I'm over here in—" The line crackled apart and the words were lost.

"You're breaking up on me," Waverly warned loudly.

"Sorry. This connection is a little iffy."

"But you are all right? Nothing is wrong?"

"I'm perfectly fine," Vivian assured her.

Waverly was relieved but curious. "So what's up then?"

"Oh, it's very exciting. Aunt Lou and I have just—" Suddenly the connection broke up again, crackling so loudly that Waverly's ears rang and she had to hold the phone away from her head.

About to hang up, Waverly shouted into the receiver, "Why don't you call back later when you have a better connection and I can hear—"

"You don't have to yell at me." Her mother's voice came through quite clearly now.

"Sorry, but I couldn't hear—"

"Yes, yes, but as I was saying, Aunt Lou and I took the plunge and bought the gallery. It's so groovy."

"Huh?" Waverly tried to piece this together. "What gallery? Where *are* you?"

"*Martha's Vineyard!*" Vivian exclaimed. "Weren't you listening to a single word I said?"

"You were breaking up on me and—"

"*Anyway*, we were just talking over dinner. Oh, you wouldn't believe the lobster here. Delightful. Although this is a dry town, if you can believe that." She laughed. "I tried to order a bottle of cabernet and was informed that was not possible. Not a drop of alcohol can be sold here in Vineyard Haven. Can you imagine? And we're staying at this adorable little inn that looks out over the harbor and even has a cupola on top. You can walk all the way around it and—"

"You purchased a gallery?" Waverly asked for clarification. "In Martha's Vineyard, Massachusetts?"

"That's right. And we're sitting here making wonderful plans together, and Aunt Lou came up with the best idea just now, Waverly."

The phone connection fell apart again. While she waited, trying to decipher her mother's words, Waverly tried to wrap her head around what Vivian was telling her. It made no sense, so she suspected she'd heard it wrong. Had Vivian really said she was with her right-wing, polyester-wearing, Bible-thumping sister? Vivian usually avoided Aunt Lou like the plague. How was it possible the two were presently in Martha's Vineyard, where they were dining on *lobster* and buying real estate together? The last Waverly had heard, her free-spirited, tie-dyed, vegetarian mother had been visiting a guru in Nepal. Really, Waverly had to have missed something.

"So what do you think?" Vivian's voice broke through the static.

"*Think?*" Waverly tried to remember what her mother had last said. "Think about what?"

"About coming out here to give us a hand?"

"A hand?" Waverly frowned. "You mean you want help?"

"Of course we want help. That's what I told you, dear."

"Help with *what*?"

"With the gallery, Waverly. Weren't you listening to me?"

Waverly was about to remind Vivian of her bad cell phone connectivity but knew it was pointless. Besides, it was as if a light had just gone on inside Waverly's troubled brain. She got it. Her mother was inviting her to join them in this venture—*operating a gallery in a very desirable location*. What was not to like? Yet it sounded too good to be true. "So, what do you mean *exactly*, Vivian?" Waverly asked carefully. "You want my help? You want me to give you a hand with a gallery? I want to be certain I understand you correctly."

"Well, Louise and I aren't getting any younger, you know. We got to thinking how lovely it is here in the Vineyard. And Lou said, 'Call Avery.' And I thought, *That's exactly what we need—youth and energy.* So we decided to see if you could come out here for the summer. Or longer if you like it. I'd love to spend some time with you, honey. Aunt Lou and I just made a cash offer on a nice little bungalow, right on the beach and not far from the lighthouse. Absolutely charming. We'll find out if we got it or not tomorrow."

"Oh…" Waverly considered this. A *beach* house? "It's wonderfully tempting, Vivian. Martha's Vineyard sounds heavenly, but I don't know that I can get away from my job for the whole summer. Then there are finances to consider."

"We'll pay you fair wages, honey. Plus, we'll split the gallery's profits with you. I'll gladly pay your airfare. And you can stay in the studio apartment above the business, so that would be free. The studio is a very cool place…with some work anyway. But great bones and good feng shui. I can just imagine how nice it will be. All the buildings in this town are so quaint and charming. The studio has a delightful view. Right out over the docks and the water and—"

"It overlooks the water?"

"Yes, Vineyard Sound. Very beautiful. You can see the ferries coming and going, and the other boats, yachts, sailboats. It's so picturesque. I think a visit like this might inspire you to take up painting again, dear."

Waverly was seeing the whole scene in her mind's eye now. Like a beautiful picture slowly coming into focus: charming old building...art gallery on the first floor...studio apartment above...overlooking the water...on Martha's Vineyard...cool marine breezes...soft summer nights? It was like a dream come true. How could she possibly say no?

"I know it'll be work for you, honey. I'm not saying it'll be easy by any means. But you're young and energetic. And I think it might be good for—"

"Yes!" Waverly shouted into the phone.

"What?" Her mother sounded genuinely surprised. "Are you agreeing?"

"I'm in like Flynn, Vivian!" Waverly laughed at her rhyme.

"Really? You'll come then?"

"You bet I'll come. It sounds absolutely fantastic."

Vivian let out a happy yelp. "Oh, Waverly, this is going to be so wonderful! The three of us together, working on a project like this. So memorable. Oh, you've made me very happy, darling! I can't wait to tell your aunt the good news." But the connection was deteriorating again.

"I can't wait to come out there!" Waverly shouted over the noise into the receiver. Eventually the connection improved, and they both said hasty good-byes. Waverly promised to get busy on her arrangements and to let her mother know when she would be arriving.

"I hope it'll be soon!" Vivian exclaimed.

Then Waverly hung up the phone and stood there in amazed wonder and unexpected happiness. Was it possible that, at long last, her life was getting on track and was about to take a turn for the better? It really did seem too good to be true, and that worried her a little. But if she couldn't trust her own mother, whom could she trust? Even if Vivian had exaggerated the charms of the old building the gallery and apartment were located in, or even the view of the water, it was *Martha's Vineyard* for Pete's sake. *Martha's Vineyard!* Waverly was about to escape a hot and steamy summer in Chicago. Seriously, how bad could it possibly be?

Chapter Two

....

Blake Erickson stared out across Vineyard Sound and wondered if this was a huge mistake. What had made him believe that this kind of isolation was a smart move? Oh, sure, the island was crowded enough—especially with tourist season kicking into full gear. But catching a ferry, commuting to Boston's Logan International, and the six-hour flight to LA…well, it wasn't exactly the simplicity he'd been longing for. And yet he loved Martha's Vineyard. It was as if he'd always belonged here but never knew it. Now that he was settled into his house, he realized he'd never felt so at home.

He switched camera lenses and snapped some more shots of the Sound. Several sailboats were out this evening, and the misty ocean air and what was probably a layer of industrial pollution off the mainland were combining to create a rather spectacular sun-set. He wondered if he had time to go over to the other side of the lighthouse, in order to shoot it in the foreground. Or, perhaps, if he waited long enough, the entire sky would be awash with this peach-and-rose-toned light. Some might say these shots were cliché or even quintessential Martha's Vineyard, but he was still new enough on the island to appreciate this sort of thing. After nearly twenty years of the Hollywood rat race, this peaceful place was almost like a sanctuary and most welcome to him.

"Hello there!" hailed a woman's voice.

He lowered his camera and peered at the stout woman trudging through the beach grass toward him. With short gray hair, cut nearly as short as a man's, she was wearing lilac-colored sweats and sturdy-looking shoes.

"Greetings, neighbor." She waved heartily as she approached. Then he spotted, not far behind her, another woman. Walking more slowly, taller, thinner, the other woman wore what appeared to be a pale blue caftan, and her coppery hair was long and blowing in the wind. At first he assumed the second woman was younger, but as the two got closer he could see that they were both older. Probably in their sixties or seventies. And the coppery-colored hair was streaked with gray.

"Hello, ladies," he said politely, trying not to show how they were interrupting his quiet evening.

"I'm Louise Grant." The stout woman nodded to the woman who'd just joined her. "And this is my sister, Vivian McDaniel. We purchased that bungalow over there. This week. Got the keys today." She was still puffing from her short walk.

"I'm Blake Erickson." He smiled. "Welcome to the neighborhood."

"Thanks. We're very pleased to be here." Louise pointed to the small gray-shingled house across a section of beach grass from his place. "Cash purchase, but it came unfurnished. The previous owners moved to the other side of the island, took everything with them. Every last thing." She shook her head as if this were scandalous.

"Yes, well, we knew the house was empty, Louise." The taller woman spoke quietly. "But I thought we could rough it."

Louise let out a deep throaty laugh. "Yes. My sister is an adventuress. She thought it would be *fun* to spend the night here tonight."

Vivian sighed. "We're prepared. We have our sleeping bags and some food and things. We can get by, Lou."

"Except it appears we have no electric or water." Louise directed this comment to Blake. "I do not understand why they haven't been turned on yet, although I called about it this morning. I paid the bill over the phone."

"I've heard that things don't move too quickly around here," he explained. "I suppose it takes some getting used to…the slower pace."

"Which is exactly why we're here," Vivian said. She turned to look out over the Sound. "Just beautiful."

Blake followed her gaze, nodding. "Yes. I was just getting some photos of the sunset."

"How long have you lived here?" Louise asked him.

"Only a few months," he admitted. "So I'm pretty much a new-comer too."

"I'm from Boston," Louise told him. "My sister is from San Francisco."

"Well, there and many places." Vivian smiled wistfully.

"And you are sisters?" He looked from one to the other, thinking about how different they appeared to be in every way. "I'm sorry, but I've already forgotten your last names."

"I'm Vivian McDaniel." She extended her hand.

"Pleased to meet you." He shook her hand. Her fingers were frail and thin and cool.

"I'm Louise Grant." The other sister stuck out her hand, strongly grasping his and shaking it firmly, almost like a man. "McDaniel used to be my name too. My maiden name," she explained. "Vivian never let go of hers." She made a funny face. "She's one of those women-libbers, if you know what I mean."

He chuckled.

"I'm an independent woman," Vivian said in a weary tone.

"That's for sure and for certain," Louise said. "Vivian has owned several successful businesses and traveled the world."

"I've been a rolling stone." Vivian sighed. "But now it's time to settle down and gather some moss."

"I suppose a nice warm coat of moss might be comforting in one's old age." Louise chortled.

"So you're really going to camp in your house?" he asked curiously. He tried to imagine these elderly women in their sleeping bags on hard wooden floors. "With no water or lights?"

Vivian shrugged. "I was in Nepal last spring. This won't be all that much different."

"So we wondered if we might be able to borrow some candles and matches from you—and a bucket of water." Louise smiled hopefully.

"We'd go back to town," Vivian added, "but I doubt anything is open by now."

"Not in Vineyard Haven," Blake said.

"Although Oak Bluffs might have something open," Louise pointed out. "But I'm not supposed to drive at night, not until I get my cataract surgery next fall, and Vivian informed me she was not inclined to drive over there tonight."

"I would rather go to bed in the dark...without water." Vivian sounded tired.

"I don't think you'll need to do that," Blake assured her.

Louise laughed. "Anyway, this will be a first for me—at my age, that is. But Vivian got the idea we can hearken back to our Campfire Girl days. I just hope she's right."

"I told Louise we'd pretend to be on a scavenger hunt." Vivian's face lit up in a smile, making her look instantly younger. "I figured we'd start with our closest neighbor."

Blake smiled back at her. He'd hoped to remain outside until dusk to get some more photos, but he knew that wasn't terribly neighborly. And part of his plan for this reinvented life in the Vineyard had been to do things right—like loving his neighbor. This seemed a good opportunity. Besides, he'd have lots more chances to take photos.

"Come on over to my place," he said congenially, as if he entertained old ladies on a regular basis. "We'll see what we can find for your campout tonight."

He led them over to his house, telling them a bit about himself as they strolled through the tall grass. Explaining how, after more than two decades, he'd finally made his escape from the film industry.

"But it's quite a change," he admitted as he turned up his walk. He'd spent a painstaking week repaving it with used bricks he'd set in a herringbone pattern, and it still filled him with happy satisfaction to see what his two hands were capable of doing.

"Los Angeles and Martha's Vineyard are definitely worlds apart," he said. "I have to admit I experienced a little culture shock at first."

"But you're adapting?" Louise asked with a creased forehead, making him wonder if she was uncertain of relocating—or perhaps this was merely a vacation spot for the two sisters. That's what most of the homes around here were used for, although he hoped that theirs would be a more permanent arrangement. The idea of having neighbors throughout the long winter, even if they were elderly women, brought some comfort with it.

"Absolutely. I love it here." He opened his door. It was still painted a glossy red, though he planned to remedy that before long. "Come on in. If I'd known I was having visitors, I'd have cleaned up some."

"So you're a bachelor then?" Louise's brows arched curiously.

"I am." He nodded and waved to the casual-looking space. Several days' worth of newspapers, a pair of flip-flops, a T-shirt, some used dishes, an opened bag of chips, and a couple of soda cans were strewn about. The sort of things one usually didn't notice unless unexpected visitors popped in.

"Well, I'll have to introduce you to Janice," Louise said in a mysterious tone.

Vivian laughed, but he thought there was a slightly sarcastic edge to it. "Janice is Lou's daughter. She's running for the state senate."

"Massachusetts," Louise informed him. "My late husband, Vance Grant, was a state senator too."

"So it runs in the family?" He kicked a dirty sock under the couch.

Louise nodded. "Janice just turned thirty-eight, although you wouldn't know it to look at her. Women age so much more slowly these days. But then she's never married either. Perhaps that keeps a woman's youthfulness. Not that Janice hasn't had the opportunity. But she's been so career-minded, what with her legal practice and now this senate race, the poor girl just hasn't had time to meet Mr.

Right yet." Louise peered curiously at him above her glasses, as if gauging whether or not he might fit the bill.

"Excuse me," he said. "I'll see if I can find what you need." He rummaged through his kitchen drawers until he found a box of "emergency" candles that someone in town had said he would need, removing half a dozen. "This should get you through the night." Then he located a book of matches. "You know, I might be able to help you with the water," he said as he returned. "If your house is like mine, there's a valve outside that turns the whole works on."

"Really?" Louise looked impressed.

"How about if I walk back with you and check it out? If I find out I'm wrong about the valve, I'll return with some water."

"Sounds lovely," Vivian told him. "I suspect we'll want to adopt you before long."

He grinned mischievously. "Well, at least until you get to know me better. Then you might want to pretend you don't know me."

"Or else"—Vivian had a twinkle in her eyes—"you might decide to relocate to a different part of the island in order to escape us."

He laughed as the three of them went back outside to where the dusky light was growing thinner.

"You know, Blake," Louise said as they walked, "my Janice is coming out here the end of next week. Perhaps you'd join us for dinner one night. Hopefully we can get our household in order by then."

"We can always sit on packing crates and eat our dinner from our laps like hobos," Vivian said. "It's been done, you know."

"Well, of course it's been done. I'm just not certain I care to do it myself," Louise responded crisply. "Being a gypsy is fine for some people. But it's never been my cup of tea. Besides that, the movers are set to pick up and deliver my things on Tuesday." She sighed. "That means we'll be spending most of the weekend figuring it out and packing it up."

"I can hardly wait," Vivian said in a tired tone.

"Perhaps you won't need too much," he said to encourage her.

Vivian smiled. "You obviously do not know my sister well. She needs her porcelain teacups and sterling service...her 800-thread-count bed linens and Egyptian towels."

Louise made a *humph* sound. "I simply enjoy my comforts—even more so as I grow older."

"Do you think we'll wear a path through here?" Vivian asked as they walked through the lavender twilight. "Between houses, I mean...over the summer."

"Time will tell," Louise said. This time her voice sounded gentler.

Blake didn't really understand it, but for some unexplainable reason he liked these two ladies a lot. He was curious to hear more about them. And perhaps even interested in meeting Louise's daughter—Janice Grant.

"Here we are," announced Louise as she opened the door.

"Home sweet home," Vivian murmured.

The women went into the house while Blake set out in search of their water valve box amongst the tall grass. The last of the twilight was quickly evaporating, and as he noticed the flickering candle-light through the salt-crusted windows, he realized he should've brought a flashlight along. Fortunately, their valve was located similarly to his own, and after some strenuous twisting, the stubborn metal handle finally creaked and turned. Replacing the heavy lid on the box, he stood and brushed sand from his hands and smiled with satisfaction. For a city guy, he was learning fast.

Now he went over and stuck his head in the still open door. "I think you should have water now, ladies."

"Yes!" Louise called back. "I can hear the toilet filling."

"You are a miracle worker," Vivian told him as she came to the door. "I'd invite you in for a cup of tea or something, but as you can see we are rather Spartan just now. Still, you will take a rain check, won't you?"

"Absolutely." He pointed to the darkened fireplace. "I could build you ladies a fire to take the chill off of the place, if you like."

Vivian looked hopeful, then frowned. "Except we have no firewood."

"Give me five minutes and I'll be back with some," he said.

"You are a dear boy!"

He grinned, wondering when the last time was that anyone had called him "boy," as he hurried back towards his house. Then, feeling like a Boy Scout, he gathered kindling, newspaper, and firewood. Piling them into the canvas firewood carrier he'd recently purchased at the hardware store, he headed back.

"There you are," said Louise as she opened the door for him. "Our guardian angel."

He set his bundle on the hearth, using the mini flashlight he'd pocketed, then peered up into the dark chimney. "One thing I learned the hard way," he explained, "is to always open the flu *before* you start a fire."

"Yes," said Louise, "that's usually the best way to do it."

It took a few minutes and a couple of false starts, but he

eventually got the fire crackling and snapping. Then he turned around to see that the sisters had put together a nice little indoor camp, complete with two nylon camping chairs, sleeping bags, and a few other necessities.

"Very cozy in here." He smiled with approval.

"It almost seems a shame to ruin this ambience with real furniture," Vivian said sadly.

"You'll be singing a different song come morning," Louise said. "I know my arthritis will be screaming by then."

Vivian sighed. "Hopefully not."

Louise turned back to Blake, clasping his hand in both of hers. "Thank you so much for your help, Blake."

"Yes," Vivian agreed. "Please know you are welcome at our campfire anytime."

He smiled. "Thank you both. Now I will leave you ladies to your little campout."

But before he could leave, Louise asked him to write down his phone number. "Not that we plan to bother you," she assured him.

"No problem. You feel free to call if you need anything," he said.

"I do think I might adopt him," Vivian said to Louise.

"You and me both." Louise grinned at him. "In fact, I can hardly wait to tell my Janice about you, Blake Erickson."

"Pleasant dreams," he called out as he closed the door. Feeling amused, he cut back through the grass again. Vivian was probably right. At this rate, they would wear a trail between their houses. Perhaps he'd even cut the grass and make the trail easier to navigate for the older women.

As he went into his house, he wondered again about Louise's

daughter, Janice. They say you can judge a daughter by the mother... and Louise was nice enough, although perhaps not as attractive as her sister. But she certainly had energy and spunk—especially considering her age. He surveyed his messy "bachelor's pad" again. He'd enjoyed being a hermit, but maybe it was time to clean up his act now. For all he knew, he might even do some summertime entertaining before long—maybe even for someone beyond elderly women.

He was stuffing a pile of dirty laundry into the washing machine when he heard the phone ringing. He'd gone ahead and installed a landline as a backup to his cell phone. But only a limited number of people knew that number—and it was close to midnight. But perhaps it was Vivian and Louise needing help with another problem.

"Hello?" he answered curiously.

"Blake!" His ex-wife's tone was sharper than usual. "We need to talk."

"Gia." He kept his voice even. "What's up?"

"It's Sis," she said curtly. "You're going to have to take her for the summer."

"Take her?" He tried not to sound overly sarcastic. But it was ironic that Gia was acting as if he hadn't been pleading with her for weeks, even months, to have Sicily come visit him in Martha's Vineyard.

"Yes. Gregory is having a rough go with Alexandria and Victoria right now."

"Oh?" Blake controlled himself from saying "I told you so," but he had specifically warned Gia that Gregory's daughters might be a problem. After spring break the girls' mother had gone into a treatment program, landing them in their father's Malibu house.

"Alexandria and Victoria used to be such nice girls," Gia was saying. "But they've turned into these monsters. I don't know what's wrong with them. And having them and Sicily…well, it's a mess, Blake. I can't deal with it."

"It's called adolescence," he told her. "It can bring out the worst in a kid. Fortunately, it won't last for long."

He didn't mention that the last time he'd seen those two girls they were downright rude to their father. At the time he'd reasoned that was simply what happened when you ignored kids for too long. Exactly why he felt a Hollywood upbringing wasn't healthy for most children. And why he wanted to have his daughter spend more time with him—and why he'd agreed to this house swap with his director friend Lincoln. To get Sicily away from there. He and Lincoln had agreed to a two-year swap to start with. Blake had come out here with high hopes of having Sicily here for summers and holidays… perhaps full-time. At first, Gia had been completely amicable to the whole idea, even encouraging him to take the plunge.

But before long, his plan had backfired. Shortly after relocating, he regretted his hasty decision to trade houses with Lincoln. Gia's attitude drastically changed right after he made the move. She'd grown increasingly cool and aloof, not to mention difficult. One time she actually accused him of abandoning his own daughter and talked about pressing legal charges. Whether her bad temper was Blake's fault or symptomatic of her troubled marriage and dysfunctional life, he couldn't be sure. But he'd felt extremely concerned for his nine-year-old daughter. And tonight Gia seemed to be confirming that concern as she ranted on about how bad things were in Malibu.

"Now Sis is starting to act out," Gia continued. "She's acting like a spoiled brat. All week long she's been picking fights with Alex and Vic. She thinks she should have the same privileges as them. And she's always trying to compete with them. It's like she's nine going on sixteen. I can't take it anymore, Blake. You have to do something!"

"I'm perfectly happy to bring Sicily out here," he assured her. "Want me to arrange for her flight?"

"Oh, *could you*?"

"Absolutely. How soon can she be ready?"

"How soon can you book a flight?" Her voice oozed eagerness.

He looked at his desk calendar. "How about Monday?"

"That'd be great—if you can get it set up that soon."

"Do you think that'll give her enough time to get ready and everything? Don't forget, Monday's only two days away."

"If you can get a flight by Monday, I promise you she *will* be on it." Gia made what sounded like a relieved sigh. "And I didn't mention it before, Blake, but I just got a small role on a TV pilot—it's a cop show. They start filming next week and I thought the girls would help watch Sicily while I'm at work. But then the three of them got into it this afternoon. And when Gregory got home, late as usual, Alex and Vic threw these dramatic little hissy fits. Obviously for their father's sake. Let's just say, it got pretty ugly around here." She lowered her voice. "Gregory's girls are so spoiled, Blake. Gregory gives in to everything. He doles out money and gifts like that'll fix everything. But it only makes them act worse. Talk about entitlement. And I'm afraid Sis is going to end up exactly like them."

"Oh, I'm sure Sicily won't be overly influenced by them, Gia." He remembered the last time he'd spent time with his daughter: Easter weekend, a couple of months ago. Sicily had been a little lady when he took her to church with him, and then she'd had nearly perfect manners afterwards when he'd taken her to dinner at a friend's house in Laguna. It had been an amazing day, and he had the photos to prove it. "Sicily is a sweet and thoughtful little girl," he assured his ex-wife. "Her bad-mannered stepsisters can't change that."

Gia let out a jaded-sounding laugh. "Just so you know, Blake, your little darling might not be the same angel you thought she was. Don't forget, you haven't been around Sis these past couple of months."

"No…no, I haven't." He wished she wouldn't talk like that. He hoped Sicily wasn't listening.

"All right then, let me know about the flight. And don't forget to let the airlines know she's a juvenile traveling alone. My best friend Cynthia sent little Leo to visit his dad in Connecticut last month and the poor kid messed up his connection in Denver. He ended up in Cincinnati instead. It was a total disaster."

"I'll have my travel agent handle the arrangements," Blake assured her. "In fact, if we can't get a direct flight, which could happen since it's summer, I'll fly out and meet her at her first connection and see that she gets safely—"

"Oh, you don't need to do that. Sis will be just—"

"I *want* to do that, Gia."

"Okay," she snapped. "Fine. But it's a total waste of money."

He wanted to tell her it was his money and he could waste it if he wanted to, but this was getting too close to sounding like an argument. He didn't need that. "So I'll let you know then," he calmly told her.

"You won't let me down, will you, Blake?"

He wanted to ask her when he'd let her down before. At least since the divorce anyway. He knew he'd let her down a few times during the marriage. Workaholics did not make good spouses. "No problemo, Gia," he said lightly to her. "And, hey, congrats on the new pilot. A cop show sounds like fun."

"Oh, it will be," she gushed. "It sounds like a network is already serious about picking it up. Judging by the script and the cast, I'm guessing it'll be a hit." She continued with industry talk for several minutes. Once again, he was reminded of what he'd left behind... what he did not miss. Even so, he pretended to listen patiently as he turned on his laptop and started preparing an e-mail to his travel agent, explaining what he needed and when.

"Well, I gotta go now," Gia chirped at him. "Thanks for being so willing to do this for me, Blake. I really appreciate it."

"Happy to help out." He inserted a smile into his voice. An act, perhaps, but an act he would gladly put on for the sake of Sicily's well-being. Because, as usual, the conversation was mostly about Gia, and he knew the best way to keep Sicily's life smooth was to simply play along. If his forced congeniality helped get Sicily out of LA and out of harm's way, it was well worth it.

His heart ached to think of his little darling being corrupted by the influence of those two teenaged girls. He felt sorry enough for the older girls, but there wasn't much he could do about their situation, other than to pray for them. He'd been praying for that whole family for a while now, ever since he'd finally returned to the faith of his boyhood last winter. As he turned on the washer, he realized that God really must've been listening, because it looked like he was about to get his daughter back—even if only for a summer. He just hoped that Sicily wouldn't be too upset about being plucked from her home and getting shipped off to the other side of the country.

Chapter Three

. . . .

With her letter of resignation in her bag and high hopes in her heart, Waverly walked into the Art Institute, still rehearsing the little speech she'd been preparing in her head during her commute. Her plan was to go directly to Geoff, present him with her letter, and honestly explain the situation. At first she'd been reticent to give up her job. She knew it was unwise to let the security of tenure and benefits go. But just as she'd lit a match to her shredded-up vision board last night, she decided it was time to burn her bridges here as well.

Her goal was to get out of Chicago, once and for all. Hopefully she'd prove herself to her mother and aunt in Martha's Vineyard and would carve herself a place to stay. Before long they would discover how much they needed her to run their art gallery.

It was the first time since losing Neil that she'd felt this certain about anything. Maybe she was delusional or desperate, but she felt confident she could do this.

"Very interesting," Geoff said quietly after she'd finished her spiel.

"Interesting?"

"Yes, it sounds like a wonderful opportunity for you, Waverly."

"Oh, yes…it is."

"But the interesting thing is that my niece is just graduating, and she approached me for a job in this department."

"Really?" Suddenly Waverly felt a little concerned. Was he already filling her job?

"Yes, but I told her we had nothing. And you know I had to lay a couple of people off last summer."

"I know." She nodded, remembering how thankful she'd been at the time that her name hadn't been on that list.

"So, if you're really serious about this change, maybe I'll give Darcy a call." With her resignation letter still in hand, he peered over his glasses at her. "I see that you gave two weeks' notice in here, but would you want to make it just one week?"

"One week?" She blinked.

"I'm not trying to rush you," he said quickly. "Feel free to take two weeks if you need it."

She thought hard. "No, no...one week would be fine."

He stood now, reaching to shake her hand. "It's been great having you here, Waverly. You're a diligent and hard worker. If you ever need a letter of recommendation, please feel free to ask."

She smiled nervously. "I don't think my mother and aunt will be needing anything like that."

"No, of course not." His expression turned thoughtful. "Say, what about your apartment? Any plans to sublet that?"

"I had hoped to find someone...or somehow break my lease."

"I wouldn't be surprised if Darcy might want to look into it."

Waverly brightened. "That would be wonderful."

She quickly wrote down the terms of her lease, the address, and some other details, along with her phone number.

"That's a handy location," he said as he looked at the paper. "I suspect Darcy will be very interested."

* * * * *

So it was that, by the end of the week, everything had fallen neatly—or somewhat neatly—into place. Darcy was thrilled to get the job and the apartment. And the super promised to get the AC fixed, although he was taking his sweet time about it. However, Waverly was distracted by her long to-do list. She spent the next five scorching evenings packing up her things, sorting out what she wanted shipped to Martha's Vineyard, which would be picked up on Monday, what she wanted to store, and what she wanted to donate to charity. By Saturday night she was nearly finished—and exhausted. And by Sunday morning, Chicago's record-breaking heat wave ended. Naturally, it was that afternoon when her air-conditioning unit finally got fixed.

"Leaving the Windy City to run off to Martha's Vineyard, are you?" the super asked as he put the metal faceplate back over the AC unit.

She smiled. "Yes. My mother made me an offer I couldn't refuse."

He nodded. "Yeah, hard to turn down a mother."

She pointed to the miscellaneous boxes and bags of things piled near the front door. "All that is for Salvation Army to pick up," she explained. "I'd like to put it outside my apartment on Monday, if you think it would be all right."

He frowned at the stuff. "Giving *all that* away?"

"Yes. I already stored a lot of things. Everything else in my apartment will go into the moving van and be shipped to Martha's Vineyard." Of course, even as she said this, she felt nervous. She hoped it wasn't a mistake to do this. But then she reminded herself, this was like taking a step of faith. God had opened a door, and it was up to her to walk through it.

"Looks like a lot of good stuff in there," he said, still studying the piles.

"Help yourself to anything you like," she told him.

He bent down and started to pick through her old things as if on a treasure hunt. "Tell you what." He slowly stood up. "Why not let me take care of it for you?"

"I'd love that," she admitted.

"I'll take a few things, give a few things away, and then I'll see that Salvation Army gets what's left. *Deal?*"

She nodded eagerly. "Deal."

"Well, you have a good time in Martha's Vineyard," he said as he shook her hand. "Always heard it was a swanky place. Didn't the Kennedys live there?"

"I'm not sure," she confessed. "I haven't had time to do much research on the area yet."

"I 'spect you'll learn plenty about it once you get there," he told her. "When do you leave?"

"The moving van comes on Monday, and my flight's on Tuesday."

"The new renter's scheduled to come in the end of the week. That'll give me just enough time to do a little painting and cleaning in here." He peered around. "Although it looks like you kept the place pretty clean." He grinned, exposing a gold front tooth. "Pleasant surprise too. Most people leave these apartments in a mess. 'Spect I'll be giving you most of your deposit back."

"Well, you have my forwarding address," she reminded him.

He gathered up a couple of the bags and promised to return

directly to get more. After he left, she looked in wonder around the room. It was still hard to believe she was actually doing this. Even harder to believe how quickly everything had fallen into place. Almost as if God truly were putting His blessing on it. At least she hoped so.

She sat down on the old leather club chair that used to be Neil's favorite and wondered what he would think of her hasty departure. Knowing Neil, he'd be asking her what had taken her so long. No doubt she would have his blessing too.

Now she began to wonder about Martha's Vineyard. What would it be like? What would the people be like? Suddenly she realized how much she wanted to fit in. But when she thought about her no-nonsense working wardrobe, she instantly knew it would never do. Why hadn't she thought to get rid of that too? Hurrying to her bedroom, where most of her clothes were already packed in boxes or ready to go into her suitcase, she quickly began to cull through the pile. Finally, she took most of it and placed it by the door for the super to sort through and probably send on to charity. She didn't really care where her dowdy old work suits wound up...as long as she never had to see them again.

And now, she told herself, *it's time to go shopping.* When she landed in Martha's Vineyard, she planned to hit the road running. She wanted to look like the manager of a successful, yet beachy, art gallery. As she rode the "L" into the city that day, she imagined herself in classic linens and other casual but stylish garments. Maybe even some dangly earrings, colorful scarves, and beaded necklaces. She would finally get to dress like a creative soul again—return to the person she once was, the person she hoped to be again...only she would do it better this time.

As she shopped, she knew it was a bit foolish to deplete her savings like this. But she remembered what her mother had promised—free rent, a salary, and a percentage of the gallery. What more could she want? Well, besides a bicycle. She planned to get a retro sort of bicycle when she got there. A fat-tired girl's bike with a basket in front. She couldn't wait to ride it around on the island. She would go to grocery stores and open air markets, filling the basket with fresh produce and other good things. Yes, her new life was going to be good. Very good. Perhaps in time she would get used to this strange feeling—what was it anyway? Anticipation? Optimism? Perhaps it was simply hope. Whatever it was, it was welcome. It had been a long time since she'd experienced any real sense of hope.

Chapter Four

As it turned out, the soonest flight Blake could get was on Thursday. But that would allow him some time to fix up Sicily's room. He wanted everything to be perfect. For that reason, he had scoured the island, bringing home an odd assortment of things. Now he didn't have the slightest clue what to do with all the stuff. Consequently, the small bedroom looked more cluttered and chaotic than charming.

"Hello the house?" called a woman's voice.

Blake came out and peered through the screen door to see Vivian standing there with a brown paper bag.

"I brought you something," she told him.

"Come in," he said, opening the door.

"I got carried away at the farmers' market." She held out the bag sheepishly. "It probably has to do with having been in Nepal all those months. But when Louise saw how much produce I bought, she couldn't stop laughing. Can you use some?"

He peered into the bag to see a colorful assortment of fruits and vegetables. "As a matter of fact, I can." Then he told her of his plans to meet his nine-year-old daughter tomorrow. "She has a connection in Atlanta. I'll meet her flight; then we'll fly together to Logan. I made a ferry reservation, and we should be here in time for a late dinner. So it will be great to have this on hand." He smiled. "Thank you."

"Well, you must be quite busy then," she said. "Don't let me keep you."

"Actually, I am. I'm desperately trying to get Sicily's room ready."

"Desperately?"

"Yes, But instead of making it better, I'm afraid I'm only making a mess of the whole thing," he confessed.

Vivian looked curious. "How so?"

So he told her about buying some things. "I imagined putting it together to create a beachy sort of bedroom. The items I got looked good in the shops, but not so good here. I guess that's why I always worked behind the camera and not in set design. Anyway, I think I need to go back to the drawing board."

"Would you like any help?"

"Do you enjoy that sort of thing?"

She smiled. "I used to run several shops in the Bay area. Some people thought I had a knack for setting up interesting displays."

"If you can spare the time, I'd love to get some advice."

"I can definitely spare the time." She laughed. "In fact, it'd be a relief not to have to go back to the house just now. Louise is unpacking, and I only get in her way. Our design styles are vastly different. She wants everything to be proper traditional, and I suppose I prefer shabby beach chic."

"Shabby beach chic?" he said hopefully. "That sounds perfect."

She looked pleased now. "Let me see what you have to work with."

He led her back to the bedroom. Picking up a shell mobile, he held it up. "This looked like fun in the shop, but now I'm worried Sicily will think I'm decorating a baby's room. Do you think nine is too old for something like this?"

She ran her fingers through the shells, making them clink together. "I don't even think seventy is too old for this." She started to go through the things he had piled on the bed, studying them and sorting them. Finally she looked at him. "Can you trust me with this?"

"Trust you?"

"To arrange this room for you?"

"You'd do that?"

"I'd love to do it."

He grinned happily. "It's all yours, Vivian. Knock yourself out. Well, not literally. But do what you like in here. You can't possibly do any worse than I've been doing."

Her eyebrows raised as she picked up a fabric sculpture mermaid that someone had talked him into purchasing. "This is interesting."

"So, anyway, I'll leave you to it." He stepped back, eager to escape this impossible task. "Seeing that produce you brought over is a reminder that I still need to stock up some groceries and things. I don't have too much around here that a kid would want to eat. I should probably get some DVDs too since I don't have cable."

She waved at him. "Be off then. I'll happily amuse myself here."

He thanked her and went into the kitchen, where he attempted to make a shopping list, then left. It took him a couple of hours to locate everything. But he was determined not to give up until he finally found some photo frames. The one thing he really wanted to do for Sicily's room was to print out some photos he'd taken with her at the beach last Easter. She'd had on the sweetest pink and white gingham dress and a white straw hat. He knew the shots would look perfect, enlarged and framed and hanging on her walls.

When he got home, his front door was locked, so he assumed Vivian had either finished the task or, more likely, given up. After a couple of trips of unloading the car, he went to peek in the bedroom. But when he opened the door, he blinked in surprise. Was Vivian a magician? Because the room looked simply magical. Somehow she had taken his motley assortment of sea treasures and placed them perfectly. Shells and glass balls and sea animals and mermaids and even the ship in the bottle were artistically arranged in a way that was neither childish nor expected. Not only that, he knew just where he'd hang the enlarged photos once he got to that later tonight. The room would be perfect!

He wanted to run next door and give Vivian a big hug. But first he needed to put the milk and other perishables away. If he was going to succeed at being a full-time dad, it would probably help if his daughter didn't perish from food poisoning on her first day here. But as soon as he closed the refrigerator, he headed off to thank Vivian.

"You are absolutely amazing," he told her when he found Vivian out on their front porch repotting some geraniums into flower pots.

"Amazing?" She stood and smiled. "Now, am I?"

He hugged her. "Thank you so much for working your wonders in Sicily's room."

"Thank you for letting me." She set down her spade. "I had such fun, Blake." Now her smile faded ever so slightly. "You know, I never had a grandchild, and I suppose, if the truth be told, I was never much good at mothering either."

"Maybe I can recruit you for an honorary grandmother for Sicily," he told her.

"It would be my pleasure."

"What's this?" Louise said as she came out onto the porch. "Do I hear that Vivian is getting to play grandmother to your child, and I'm not even invited to the party?"

"I'm sure Sicily would love to have *two* grandmothers next door," Blake assured her. "Sicily only has one—my wife's mother—and that woman doesn't particularly enjoy playing the grandma role."

"So when does the little princess arrive?" Louise asked.

Blake explained the plan. Then Louise declared that he and Sicily would have to join them for dinner on Saturday. "We'll have seafood and corn on the cob. It will be a welcome dinner," she said. "And Janice will be here too."

"Well, I don't know," he said slowly. He felt somewhat torn now. Partly because he wanted to keep Sicily to himself for the first few days and partly because he was curious to meet Janice.

"You must come," Louise insisted. "I will not take no for an answer."

Blake looked at Vivian for support.

"I think Blake needs to determine what's best for his young daughter," she said quietly. "It might be that she'll need some time to adjust to her new surroundings before she's thrust into any social settings."

"Oh, Vivian." Louise frowned. "Don't be ridiculous. The child is only nine. How much adjusting does she need to do?"

"Everyone is different," Vivian said simply.

"Come now." Louise shook her head. "Why don't you support me on this?"

"Because it's Blake's decision, and you shouldn't—"

"We'll come," he said abruptly. The last thing he wanted was to instigate a family feud, especially when Vivian had been so helpful. "Sicily will probably enjoy meeting our neighbors."

"See," Louise said triumphantly.

Vivian shrugged and returned to her flowers.

"I really do appreciate what you did for Sicily's room," he said again. "I think Sicily will like it too."

"Which reminds me, I need to finish up on Janice's room," Louise said. "She's decided to take an early morning ferry tomorrow, to beat the traffic. She'll be here before eight."

So they all said good-bye and returned to their various tasks. Blake felt unexplainably happy as he returned to his house. He knew it was mostly due to Sicily's impending arrival. But it was also partly due to having neighbors and feeling an odd sense of family with them. That was something he'd missed over the years. His parents had both died within a year of each other, shortly before his marriage had dissolved. For a long time he thought perhaps he was jinxed when it came to relationships in general. As a result, he had thrown himself wholeheartedly into his work, allowing it to devour his life. But now he suspected there was more for him. And he felt strangely hopeful.

* * * * *

Sicily wasn't only sporting an adolescent attitude when he met her at the Atlanta terminal, she looked like a punk rocker had picked out her wardrobe. But the worst part was that someone, she wouldn't even tell him who, had put a large purple streak into her otherwise golden hair. What was wrong with this world?

Blake tried not to show his disappointment in her appearance as he hugged her, lifting her high into the air like he used to do.

"*Daddy,*" she exclaimed in a scandalized tone, "put me down."

"Oh, okay." He nodded as he placed her black biker-style boots back onto the floor. "It's just that I'm so glad to see you."

"Duh." She rolled her big blue eyes.

"So, how was your flight?" he asked as he reached for her carry-on, a black backpack with purple skulls that matched her hair.

"I can get that," she told him as she tugged the backpack back, slinging one strap over her shoulder.

"Fine. Just trying to help, Sweet Pea."

"Puleeze, do not call me that. It's so juvenile."

"Right." He nodded, standing straighter. "So, do you want something to eat? I noticed a McDonald's near our gate, or we could—"

"*McDonald's?*" She made a disgusted face.

"You used to like Mc—"

"That was before I learned about things like *fats* and *calories* and *carbs.*" She spat out the words like she was describing arsenic, deadly nightshade, and hemlock. Then she started rattling off stats and numbers like an obsessed nutritionist.

"But you don't need to worry about those things," he assured her. "You're not fat."

"Oh, *Dad.*" She shook her head like he was hopeless.

Now he didn't know what to say. "Low-fat yogurt then?"

Fortunately, she seemed all right with that. But it took her a long time to decide whether to go with chocolate or orange, and the line behind them was growing.

"Why not get some of both?" he suggested.

She looked at him like she was about to roll her eyes again. Instead, she just nodded. "Okay."

He couldn't believe how relieved it made him feel that he'd gotten at least one thing right. He'd been with her for less than ten minutes, and already he was walking on eggshells. What would a whole summer be like?

"Do you want anything to read?" he asked as they were finishing up their yogurts.

She pulled a small handheld video game contraption from her bag, holding it up. "No, I've got this to do."

"All right then." He'd never been terribly keen on these electronic babysitters and was disappointed to see her so absorbed by one now—hunched over, pushing the buttons. When had she given up reading?

Finally, their flight was boarding, so she temporarily shoved the game back into her pack. But no sooner was she on the plane than she got it out again, continuing to play until right before takeoff, when the attendant announced that electronic devices needed to be turned off. Sicily then simply stuck her ear buds into her ears, connecting the other end to her armrest and tuning in to one of the airline's music selections. Some kind of thumping rap music from the sounds of it. And cranked up too loud as well.

Blake wasn't sure if it was possible to damage one's hearing from this sort of thing—it was what his own parents used to tell him when he'd listen to Michael Jackson's "Thriller" too loudly as a teen. He hated to start sounding like his parents. Really, wasn't he cooler than that? However, and as much as he hated to admit it, it appeared that Gia was right this time. Sicily truly was nine going on fifteen. It made him want to pull his hair out and scream.

Instead, he opened his paperback and pretended to be reading the latest Grisham novel. But out of one corner of his eye, he was studying his daughter, trying to figure out this stranger sitting next to him. He wanted to be a good father. He wanted to understand how his dear Sicily had been transformed from his adorable princess—Sweet Pea—into this obnoxious prepubescent punk rocker with the horrid purple streak in her hair. More than anything, he wanted someone to change her back. Please, change her back!

Chapter Five

....

Blake knew he should be grateful. Summer commuting was never easy, but despite a last-minute booking, and the usual oversold flights, the traveling part of the day was going smoothly. Other than a little turbulence over Virginia, the flight to Boston was uneventful. And Sicily's bags were intact and already rolling around the baggage carousel when they got there. He found the Audi with no problems, and the drive to the ferry was peaceful and quiet...rather, it was *stone silent.*

Thanks to Sicily's charger cord, which she promptly plugged into his car's outlet since her battery pack had expired, she was, once again, hunched over and glued to that confounded video game contraption. Blake wanted to curse whoever had bought her that stupid electronic nonsense. Probably Gregory, trying to buy her affections. Blake knew that if he could come up with a believable way to accidentally dispose of that thing, he would most happily do so.

As he approached Woods Hole to catch the ferry, he imagined standing with Sicily on the side of the boat. They would be looking out over the ocean—more likely, he would be looking out and she would be playing a silly game—and then, oops, he would accidentally bump her elbow and the whole works would tumble down into the waves below. Oh, he would be terribly, terribly sorry. He'd even promise to try to find her another one. But, alas, he would make certain that never happened.

Was he a bad father for imagining such things? Probably so. But desperate times called for desperate measures. And right now he felt like Daddy Desperate.

However, as fate would have it, Sicily didn't want to stand outside of the boat. She said it was too windy and cold. Instead, she hunkered down in a plastic chair by the snack bar where a TV was blaring loudly, and, sipping on yet another diet soda, she continued to play her video game.

Grieving for lost innocence and sacrificed childhoods, Blake tried to read his book.

It was past eight by the time they made it to his house. So far today, as far as he knew, the only thing Sicily had consumed was the chocolate-orange yogurt, a bag of peanuts, and several diet sodas, which she liked to point out rated a big "*Zero.* No carbs, no fats, no calories."

"How about I make us veggie omelets?" he offered after he showed her the house and finally her bedroom, which she had simply glanced at and shrugged indifferently as she tossed her bags onto the floor.

"*Eggs?*" she said, as if he really was trying to poison her. "Are you kidding?"

"No. Eggs happen to be a good source of protein and omega—"

"And *fat!*" She firmly shook her head. "No way am I eating an egg, Dad."

He thought hard. "What if I make yours with only the egg whites? I heard the white is very low-fat."

Her brow creased as if considering this. "What else would be in the omelet?"

"Veggies," he said cheerfully, opening the fridge and taking out the lovely produce Vivian had brought over. "Onions, spinach, tomatoes, peppers, and—"

"I don't like any of those," she informed him.

He blinked. "None of them?"

She shook her head no.

He thought hard. Well, to be fair, she had never been fond of those vegetables. But he figured with her new focus on nutrition, she should've been now. However, he was not going there. Not today anyway.

"Okay, how about an egg-white omelet with some, uh…" He considered his words. "Some *low-fat* cheese."

"Low-fat cheese?"

"Yes. Some cheeses are very low in fat." He was backpedaling now, digging in the cheese drawer of his fridge, hoping for a miracle. "Like Swiss," he proclaimed.

"Swiss is low-fat?" she asked a bit skeptically.

"Absolutely," he said with mock confidence. "That's what those holes are for."

She gave him a funny look. "Okay." Then she went back to playing her games.

Feeling like maybe he'd just won that round, he proceeded to make her a "low-fat" omelet. What was it with women and diets anyway? Who had been brainwashing her about this garbage—and how long would it take to unbrainwash her? Or was that even possible? He wondered if there was some kind of hotline for things like this: 1-800-DAD-HELP.

He finished the first omelet and, to his relief, she ate most of it, as well as the apple slices he'd put next to it. However, she turned her nose up at the chocolate milk. That was disheartening, because that had always been the one thing he could count on her eating before. Now she proclaimed it "full of fat and carbs."

After he finished his omelet, he began cleaning up in the kitchen, and she wandered out to the TV. But she soon discovered he had no cable and, minutes later, proclaimed his new collection of DVDs "childish." He was fearful she was about to return to her video games again.

"Maybe we can shop for some different movies together," he offered as he hung the frying pan on the pot rack over the stove.

"Do you even *have* a video store here?" she asked sarcastically.

"Sure," he said. "Martha's Vineyard isn't exactly the sticks."

"That's not what Mom said."

"There's a lot to do around here," he told her. "Beaches to explore and—"

"Does the video store carry games?"

He shrugged as he dried his hands. "I don't know."

"It figures. Alex told me I'd be bored out of my gourd here."

He chuckled. "Bored out of your gourd, huh?"

"Yeah."

"Has Alex even been here?"

"No, but her friend was here one summer."

"I see." Blake was desperately trying to think of something to say that would bring back that old sparkle in her eyes. "I made friends with the neighbors," he tried, "and we're invited to their house for dinner tomorrow night."

"Do they have kids?"

"Uh…" He thought of Janice now. "Yeah, one of the ladies has a daughter." Misleading, yes, but it wasn't exactly a lie. Mostly he simply wanted to pacify her, to assure her that they could do this… it would get better. Wouldn't it?

"Okay." She nodded like she was envisioning a young friend for her to hang with during the summer. "I'm kinda tired, Dad. I think I'll go to my room now."

"All right." He felt a mixture of relief and disappointment as he watched her turn and go into her room, firmly closing the door as if to tell him to "stay out." But to be honest, it was mostly relief he felt. He had no doubts that he was in way over his head. It seemed crystal clear: Sicily had no intention of making this easy. At this rate, he wasn't sure which one of them would give up on this summer first—her or him?

* * * * *

The next day started out as one of those delectable June mornings—a warm breeze wafting off the water, a few clouds wisping across a pristine blue sky. Perfect. As Blake leaned back into his Adirondack chair, gazing out toward the Sound, he stretched his long tanned legs out onto his porch and sipped a hot mug of coffee. Life was good. His daughter was sleeping in this morning. He suspected a better father would rouse her out of bed, invite her to walk on the beach and look for sea glass or shells, but he knew he wouldn't. Not today, anyway.

Despite the soft marine air drifting through his open bedroom window last night, Blake had not slept well. Instead of relishing the notion that his only and beloved daughter was finally safe and sound beneath his very own roof, the only thing Blake could think was that he'd blown it. No matter which way you sliced it, he'd messed up. The fact that Sicily was acting like a spoiled, bratty pubescent was his fault.

He'd tossed and turned, running the past ten years through his head with enough regret to make a grown man cry. He'd shed a few tears as he punished himself by replaying his many mistakes. If only he hadn't worked so much. If only he'd taken a more active part in raising Sicily. If only he hadn't moved all the way to Martha's Vineyard.

Or the biggie—if he'd somehow been able to keep his marriage together—which would've been a challenge since Gia had indulged in more than one affair during their relationship. Her rationale had been that "everyone did it," and it was the only way to secure a role. Not that she'd scored any big contracts from her couch sessions. But she did manage to hook Gregory. Not that she was happy with him now.

On and on he'd gone, torturing himself by the light of the moon until he finally saw the gray light of dawn creeping in. Then, feeling raw and hopeless, he got up and made coffee. The sun's rising, combined with coffee, improved his outlook. Some of his old optimism was returning. He and Sicily were merely going through a rough patch. *Give her a few days to get used to things, and she'll return to her old self.* Or so he was telling himself.

"Hello there," called a woman's voice.

Blake turned, looking toward Louise and Vivian's place, seeing a tall, unfamiliar woman coming his way. As she got closer, he could see her dark hair was cut short, curling around her face in a becoming way. She looked stylish in a turquoise polo shirt and bright-colored, madras-plaid capris. Waving toward him, she called out, "Hey, neighbor, I'm your neighbor." She waited at the bottom of the porch steps. "Mind if I intrude?"

"Not at all." He stood to greet her.

"I was sent over here by my mother to see if you happen to have a stick of butter we can borrow." She smiled brightly, revealing straight white teeth.

"I'm Blake Erickson," he said as they shook hands.

"So I've heard." She studied him closely now. Judging by her eyes, she liked what she was seeing.

"I'm guessing you're Janice Grant."

She looked slightly surprised. "You *already* know who I am?"

"Your mother, uh, may have mentioned you...in passing."

"Oh." She smiled wryly. "Well, now it makes more sense."

"What makes sense?"

"Why my practical mother was making hotcakes without a speck of butter in the house."

He frowned. "I'm not following you exactly."

She laughed. "My mother's way of forcing an introduction. Sorry about that. She's not the most subtle person on the planet."

"So do you need the butter or not?" he asked.

"Good question. I'll bet my mother *does* have butter somewhere, but she's tucked it out of sight, probably in a cupboard. I've got a mind to go back there and force her to dig it out, so I can rub her nose in it."

"Or I could just loan you some, which I do happen to have by the way. I put in provisions a couple of days ago. In fact, I got so much stuff, you'd think I was planning on entertaining a full house"—

he lowered his voice—"instead of one slightly anorexic daughter, who wouldn't touch butter with a ten-foot pole."

Janice blinked. "Your daughter is anorexic?"

He posed a forefinger over his lips now, tipping his head toward Sicily's bedroom window, which thankfully was closed.

"Oh." Janice nodded. "I see."

He continued talking quietly, feeling the need to unload his worries on someone. "I picked her up yesterday. She's only nine, but she's acting like a snotty teenager already. It's like an adolescent alien invaded her being and took over. The last time I saw her, a few months ago, she was a sweet, adorable child." He sadly shook his head. "Now she is...well, something else. And I blame myself."

"You blame yourself?"

He nodded, noticing that his coffee mug was empty. He held it up. "Care for some coffee?"

She appeared to consider this. "Maybe so. It might do my mother good to have to wait for me to come back. Teach her a lesson about honesty."

He opened the screen door. "Come on in." So while he made a fresh pot of coffee, she wandered through the kitchen and great room, peppering him with questions. He told her a little about his past and unfortunate marriage, even confessing about his addiction to work. "Which is one reason I moved here...to slow down." He handed her a cup of coffee. "I've discovered that being a driven workaholic comes with a high price, especially in relationships."

"That's one reason I've never married." She poured some cream into her coffee. "I knew that a husband would play second fiddle to my work."

"At least you had the sense to figure that out first," he said as they went back outside. "Some people have to learn the hard way."

"So are you *still* a workaholic?" she asked as she sat down.

"No. I'm recovering...hopefully." Then he explained about leaving the rat race behind. "So my buddy Lincoln took my condo and I took his house. We have a two-year agreement, though Lincoln is hoping it'll become permanent." He smiled. "It's a pretty nice condo...good location."

"And you'd give that up to live here?" She looked shocked.

"For now, and maybe longer. Mostly I just want to learn how to slow down and live my life differently." He looked out over the water and sighed. "I'm still getting used to the pace, but I think I like it."

She frowned slightly. "I like it for a while," she told him. "But I couldn't handle a steady diet of this."

"It's definitely not for everyone. I hear the winters can be hard."

"And they're not just talking about the weather either," she said in a warning tone. "This place empties out right after Labor Day. I was here once in midwinter, and it was a ghost town—or a ghost island. They say the population goes from fifteen thousand in off-season to a hundred thousand at the peak."

He nodded. "I've heard that too. Some of the locals go around saying, 'See you next fall,' because a lot of them go completely underground during summer, becoming recluses until the tourists go home."

"Where's the fun in that?" she said. "I like the idea of popping over here from time to time in the hopes of spotting some of the rich and famous. I've hinted to Mom that I expect to get invited to some of the exciting parties I've heard about. Now that she's a full-time resident, she could rub elbows with some big names." Janice laughed. "Although it's widely accepted that Republicans aren't terribly popular on this island." She wrinkled her nose. "Thanks to predecessors like Clintons and Gores. But it's a free country, and I'm not afraid to express my opinions in front of anyone willing to listen, especially if they have a vote."

"Yes, I hear you're running for state senate," he said. "Impressive."

"Don't be too impressed. I might not win. Not this time anyway. The first go-around is more about getting your name out there... again. My father was a senator, but it's been a long time. It's not that I'm trying to ride on his coattails. In fact, there was a time when I was certain I would never pursue politics. In a way, I think politics came after me." She finished her coffee and smiled. "Now, as pleasant as this has been, I think I better get back to check on those hotcakes."

"And the butter?" he offered.

"I think I'll force my mother to come clean about that." She handed him the empty coffee mug. "Thanks, neighbor."

"See you around," he called as she went down the porch steps.

"Yes, I hear we're having guests for dinner tomorrow evening. I suspect that means you."

He watched as she headed through the beach grass between the two houses, reminding himself to get some sort of grass cutting tool the next time he was in the hardware store. A path might be nice. Janice Grant seemed a pleasant woman—not hard on the eyes either. Perhaps she wasn't exactly his type—not that he knew exactly what his type was anymore—but she came across as intelligent, interesting, and energetic. Maybe he finally had time to investigate the possibilities of female companionship. Well, except that he had Sicily to consider now. He stood and stretched lazily, reminding himself that there was no reason to hurry anything along right now. No schedules, no deadlines, no pressures…at least for a while. And he intended to enjoy it.

Chapter Six

As she waited to board her flight, Waverly couldn't remember the last time she'd felt this exhilarated. Probably not since Neil was alive. The last time she'd experienced this kind of hopeful anticipation was probably the time they were getting on a plane bound for Mexico. Shortly after their first anniversary, they began planning a trip to Yucatan. It took a couple of years of frugality and penny pinching to save up enough for their dream vacation.

Waverly still remembered feeling cautious when the time came to book the big trip. So used to fretting over finances, she'd actually suggested they wait another year to take the trip. But Neil had remained steadfast, insisting they *had* to go. So they booked it shortly after the New Year. In late February, during a Chicago blizzard, they'd packed their bags and left. Once they made their escape from O'Hare, Waverly's regrets evaporated, and the rest of the trip turned out to be amazing and memorable—well worth all the little things they'd gone without to afford it.

Of course, there'd been no way to predict it would be their first and last big trip like that together. But looking back now, Waverly thanked God that Neil had convinced her to go.

Now—although today was completely different—she experienced a similar rush of excitement as she boarded the plane, found her seat, and buckled her safety belt. She was really doing this. No turning back. Every bridge was burned. Her nonstop flight to Boston would arrive in the afternoon. After that she'd ride a shuttle to the ferry, which would transport her directly to Vineyard Haven—her final destination. She felt like she was about six years old, like Christmas was just around the corner.

Vivian had been hard to reach this past week, plus Waverly had been distracted with packing and preparing for her exodus, but she had told her mother which ferry she'd booked and when she'd be arriving. Vivian had promised to meet her at the ferry. Waverly hoped she didn't forget. But even if she did, Waverly figured she could probably walk to town. According to the map she'd studied, the ferries were only a block or two from the center of the downtown area. Still, she hoped Vivian would remember since it sounded as if there was a lot going on there for them too.

"Janice just arrived," Vivian had told her during the weekend. "She's taking her vacation here, sharing Aunt Lou's bedroom, so it's pretty cozy in the bungalow. But you're welcome to stay with me in my room, if you don't mind sharing a bed. Otherwise you can start settling into the apartment. Aunt Lou had to store some things there. She had things brought over from Boston, but she'd overestimated on how much furniture our little bungalow can hold. It started feeling like a warehouse in here. But I'm positive she won't mind if you use her things."

Suddenly Waverly felt concerned—or maybe even territorial. Surely her mom and aunt would let her arrange the studio apartment herself. "My things are coming too," Waverly said with hesitation. "They should be here by the end of the week."

"That's wonderful, dear. As I recall, your aunt only had a sofa bed and a few other pieces stored there. If necessary, we can find someone who'll like them. We'll sort it out when you get here, darling. No worries."

Waverly was still trying to wrap her head around this new side of Vivian. She wasn't used to her mother being so congenial and easygoing. But she appreciated it. As Waverly stood outside now, leaning into the rail of the ferry boat and watching as it cut through thick, luminescent curls of water, she felt incredibly happy and free. The sea breeze against her skin, the summer sun on her head—everything seemed absolutely perfect. Picture perfect.

She took numerous photos, telling herself that someday, when she had the time, these very photos would inspire her to paint. Watercolors perhaps. Or maybe she'd break out the oils eventually. She stared in wonder at the vastness of the water and sky before her. So much blue—varying shades of blue around her. As they got closer to what appeared to be land, probably the island, she noticed more boats. Some sailboats, some yachts—nautical slices of pristine white cutting through the otherwise blue-scape. Fresh, clean, beautiful. She was going to be happy here. She couldn't wait to settle in.

During her flight, she'd decided that she wanted to move directly into the studio—no matter what shape it was in. The idea of sharing a bedroom with her mother—and a bed—wasn't going to work for her. As well located as their beach bungalow might be and as pretty as it sounded like they were making it, she was going to take a pass on staying there with them. She would rather "rough it" in the studio on her own.

She knew this decision was partly related to her cousin. Waverly had been surprised to hear that Janice Grant was there right now. Even though Janice was only there on vacation, Waverly felt caught off guard, and it had almost stolen some of the joyful anticipation about her new life. Of course, she'd convinced herself that it was silly to let Janice get to her. It wasn't that she didn't like Janice. Not exactly.

But she and Janice had never really hit it off as children. Maybe it had been related to their mothers, who were different as night and day, or maybe it was the girls' own unique personalities. Despite only being a year apart in age and sometimes thrust together at family events, the two girls never connected the way some cousins do. Janice had always been a little high-maintenance or, perhaps, simply goal-driven. When they were young, Janice was somewhat demanding, extremely competitive, and a little bossy, whereas Waverly had always been the dreamer, the artist, the girl who enjoyed silence, solitude, and a sketchpad. Sometimes Janice had even called her "boring." But Waverly hadn't minded. She'd preferred being labeled as dull rather than keep pace with Janice.

Of course, that was a lot of years ago. Hopefully they'd both grown up since then. But in case they hadn't, Waverly was determined to keep a healthy amount of space between them. Not having a car made her even more determined to stay close to town. No way did she want to be stuck out at a beach house, no matter how delightful, with her yammering cousin and no means of transportation to escape. Although Waverly did plan to go bike shopping as soon as she got settled. She'd even searched the Internet, locating several bike shops around the island.

Waverly felt a fresh surge of happiness as she sighted the island ahead. She felt almost giddy. Like she was going to a different country, a different life…a new beginning, doing something she truly wanted to do. The idea of operating an art gallery—in Martha's Vineyard— well, it was a dream come true! And each time she'd shared this tidbit with people during the past week and during her trip, she'd seen the interest and admiration in their eyes. Some of them even got a wistful look, as if they wished they could trade places with her.

For the first time in such a long time, Waverly felt as if her life was finally and truly blessed. As the ferry pulled into the dock, she whispered a prayer of thanksgiving. After these past few years of darkness and drought, God was finally shining His goodness down on her.

Knowing she'd be riding on a plane, bus, and ferry boat, Waverly had purposely chosen to travel light today. Just a carry-on that piggybacked on the same midsized roller bag she'd used for the Yucatan trip. The rest of her things would be here by Friday. She gathered these things and followed a few other passengers, who appeared to know where they were going, and disembarked from the boat. She was here at last—in Martha's Vineyard!

The parking lot was busy with cars and trucks loading and unloading, as well as a number of cars waiting to pick up passengers. She hadn't thought to ask Vivian what make or color of vehicle to look for, but it was so nice out that many of the cars had their windows down. But the more Waverly looked for her mother, the more she realized that Vivian had forgotten. Really, that wasn't surprising. Waverly had a long history of her mother forgetting things. Sometimes small things, like where she'd last placed her car keys when Waverly had been late for an art lesson, and sometimes big things, like the time and place of Waverly's wedding. She had arrived eventually, but because the church had more than one wedding that day, they had been unable to wait. However, she was very much present during the reception.

"*Waverly!*"

Waverly turned to see a red BMW coming toward her. And there was her mother, waving frantically with her head stuck out the window, orange scarf blowing in the breeze, and a big smile.

"Sorry I'm late," Vivian said as she pulled up.

"That's all right." Waverly opened the door, then wondered where to put her suitcase in the small car.

"I think there's a trunk," Vivian said as she looked around the controls.

"You think?"

Vivian laughed. "This is Janice's car. She let me drive it. Isn't it cute?"

Before she could answer, the trunk popped open and Waverly hurried back to put her bags in it, then back around just as a delivery truck behind them honked. "I'm going as fast as I can," Waverly called as she jumped into the car.

"He's probably trying to get onto the ferry," Vivian said as she pulled out. "I think I was in the wrong line. I'm still trying to figure this ferry thing out. Lou has it down, but I haven't been driving much."

"Do you have a car here?"

"Just one that we share." She turned, beaming at Waverly, as she waited for the stoplight. "You look beautiful, darling. How was your trip?"

"Wonderful. I loved the ferry. I'm so excited to be here, Vivian. Thank you so much for asking me…and paying for me to come."

The light changed, and Vivian pulled out. "I'm so glad you could come. And, don't fool yourself, we really need you." She shook her head. "I still don't know what your aunt was thinking, talking me into investing in The Gallery like she did. Certainly it was a great deal, good investment, but why she thought we could actually run something like that...."

"Well, that's why I'm here. Is there any art in it at all?"

"Art?" Vivian glanced curiously at Waverly. "I don't know." Just then a Range Rover darted in front of them, and Vivian stomped on the brakes. "This traffic! It gets worse every week. Lou and I got here before Memorial Day, and everything was moving a lot slower then."

"I hear the summertime crowd is really something." Waverly held onto the dashboard as Vivian jerked her way through the crowded street.

"But that's what keeps everyone in business," Vivian said. "So I guess we can't complain."

Waverly smiled. "I'm not complaining. Not a bit."

"Good." Vivian pointed to a side street, or maybe it was an alley, ahead. "This is where you turn to get into the back parking lot. It's kind of tight, but there's room to park one car back there. As you can imagine, parking is at a premium around here."

"I plan to get a bike."

"Smart." Vivian pulled up behind a wooden building and turned off the car engine. "Well, here we are. Home sweet home."

It wasn't impressive, but then Waverly reminded herself, this was the back of the building. What did she expect?

"It's kind of on the edge of the busy part of town," Vivian explained as they got out. "That's probably one reason it was such a good deal. That and because no else showed interest in running a business like this."

"Really?" This surprised Waverly. "I'd think a gallery would be quite popular in this town."

Vivian laughed. "Yes, a *normal* gallery would be." Now she was fiddling with some keys as if searching for the right one. "I think we'll have to go around front," she finally said. "I don't have the other key."

"That's fine."

Vivian pointed to some rather rickety-looking wooden stairs. "But in the future, you can enter the apartment from back here if you like. There's a backdoor at the top of those stairs. It's more private."

Waverly looked up to the shadowy structure above her. "Is that where the terrace is?"

"Yes." Vivian headed toward a narrow walkway that ran along one side of the big brown building. "Come along, and we'll go in the front door. I can give you the full nickel tour."

Waverly followed her mother around the corner. The building was situated just off of Main Street, but the traffic passing by looked as busy as the rest of town.

Vivian stopped and held both hands up, as if to point out something. "And here we are—The Gallery."

Waverly looked up to see a rather flashy sign with lights and big yellow and red letters that said THE GALLERY. "So that's the name? The Gallery?"

Vivian looked confused. "Yes, of course, that's what I told you."

Waverly forced a smile. "Right. I guess that makes sense. An art gallery called The Gallery. It's kind of quaint, and I suppose—"

"Did you say an *art* gallery?" Vivian's brows creased together.

Waverly nodded. "Yes. It's an art gallery…right?"

With wide eyes, Vivian slowly shook her head. *"Wrong."*

Waverly was having one of those moments now…kind of like slow motion, like the way it might feel to be in a car wreck, watching your vehicle tumbling over or leaving the road, or your life flashing before your eyes, or a dream going up in smoke. "Wh–what? What are you saying?"

"This is *not* an art gallery." Her mother spoke the words slowly, concisely, as if concerned that Waverly didn't understand English. "This is a video arcade. You know, for kids to hang out and play games. It's called The Gallery." She blinked. "Did you honestly think this place was an *art* gallery? As in we'd be selling paintings and sculptures and such?"

Waverly was speechless. Utterly speechless.

Now Vivian began to giggle. "Oh, darling, that's too precious."

"It's…not…an art gallery?"

"No, it's a video arcade. Complete with all the bells and whistles and machines. I've been told that some of them are collectable. And there are also a few antique pinball machines and some other old-style arcade games. Apparently it's been here for close to seventy years, if you can believe it."

"Are you serious?" Waverly bent forward, cupping her hands to peer into the front window now. Sure enough, the space was filled with hideous-looking machines. Like a bad sort of carnival—or a cruel joke.

Vivian was laughing loudly now. "Did you honestly think it was an art gallery, honey?"

Waverly was torn between wanting to sob and scream. Instead, she simply stood there, trying to absorb what was happening. She had given up her job, her apartment, even her work wardrobe…she had burnt her bridges…*for this*?

"You look like you're in shock." Vivian put a hand on her shoulder. "Maybe you can't see the humor in this yet. But I know you will…eventually." She gently tugged Waverly toward the door now. "Come on in. I'll show you around."

Suddenly they were inside what was most definitely a video arcade. Machines were banging and dinging and buzzing and making all kinds of loud, obnoxious noises—the kinds of sounds that reminded Waverly of a headache. A big, bad, blaring headache.

"That's Rosie." Vivian pointed to a brown-haired girl. "She's helping us for now, but she has to move back to the mainland by the end of the month."

Waverly said nothing as her mother led her down row after row of obnoxious, loud, flashing, blaring, repulsive machines. Hot tears burned behind her eyes; her head really was starting to throb now. Waverly had never liked these kinds of places as a child, and she liked them even less as an adult. What could her mother have been thinking to ask her to come and manage—*this*?

"This is the other way to get to your apartment," Vivian said in a calm voice as she led Waverly into a dim hallway. "I told Lou we might want to put another door here. Maybe with a lock, although everyone says no one locks doors in this town. But that would give you more privacy. I've noticed that kids sometimes wander up this stairway. It might be aggravating to have them knocking at your door." She chattered on obliviously until they reached the top of the stairs, where she slipped a key into the deadbolt, opening the wooden door wide. "Ta-da," she announced. "Isn't it great?"

Waverly swallowed hard against the lump growing in her throat and gazed blankly around the dull, dusty space. There, in the center of the room, as promised, were several pieces of homely furniture. A brown-and-tan-plaid sofa, mismatched end tables, an ugly gold recliner, and a dresser. Home sweet home.

"Oh, darling." Vivian's voice oozed with sympathy. "Are you disappointed?"

Waverly didn't know what to say. Disappointed didn't begin to cover it. Not even close. Try traumatized, devastated, crushed, ruined. But those were strong words and Waverly didn't want to hurt her mother's feelings. Not yet anyway. "I…uh…I'm not sure. I think I'm in shock."

"Because you thought it was an art gallery?" Now Vivian was starting to giggle again. "I feel completely clueless as to how that happened, Waverly. Perhaps our phone connections were worse than I realized. But I can't help but think it's terribly funny. Don't you? I can't wait to tell Lou and Janice about this." She laughed harder now. "Oh, my."

"This is not a joke," Waverly said quietly.

"No, no, of course not. But it is humorous. Don't you think?"

"Not particularly."

"Oh…"

They both stood in silence. Well, as silent as it could be with the sounds of electronic explosives and other noises that filtered through the floors and walls. Waverly wondered if this space was ever quiet. She knew tears were even closer now, but she didn't want to cry in front of her mother. "Maybe I should get my bags from the car," she said quickly.

"You're going to stay here?"

"Yes." Waverly nodded as she went toward the back door. "For now." She unlocked and opened the door, hurrying down the stairs to the car.

Vivian followed. "You're certain that's a good idea?" She looked dubious as she opened the trunk and Waverly tugged out her bags.

"Yes." Waverly nodded again. She was afraid to say too much, afraid she was going to completely lose it and start bawling like a three-year-old. "I *want* to stay here."

"Okay." Vivian smiled now. "Once you're settled in, I'm sure you'll see how amusing this is." She shook her head. "An art gallery."

"Thanks, Vivian." Waverly was lugging her bags through the gravel toward the rickety stairs now, wondering if they could safely support both her and her bags.

"I really do wish it were an art gallery," Vivian called out a bit sadly. "But this was the only business Aunt Lou and I could afford, and we felt we needed something to bring in some cash. I don't know, Waverly, it seemed like a good idea...at the time."

"It's all right." Waverly waved to her mother. "We can discuss it later."

"Yes, of course." Vivian opened the car door. "I'll call you. Aunt Lou wants you to come over for dinner. But maybe you'll want to get settled in first."

"Yes," Waverly called as she dragged her wheeled bag up the stairs. "I'll call you later...maybe tomorrow." And maybe she'd be calling from the deck of the ferry, informing her mother that she was on her way…where? Where could Waverly go?

At the top of the stairs, she turned in time to see the pretty red convertible exiting the tiny parking area below. As the scene fuzzed around the edges, she realized the tears she'd been holding back were spilling now. Perhaps she was being childish about this whole thing, not to mention foolish for daring to dream big. She took in a deep breath, pausing to look out farther, out to where the supposedly wonderful ocean view should be lurking, but all she could see were blurry shades of blue.

Waverly turned away, opening the door to the apartment, where she was greeted by the musty aroma of a neglected space. She knew she'd fallen for the oldest trick in the book. When everything had seemed too good to be true, she should've known better.

Chapter Seven

....

Blake didn't know if he'd been sending some kind of signal or if Janice was simply the type of woman who went after what she wanted, but they'd only met a few days ago and already she'd turned into an expected part of his day. It usually started with coffee. But then on Sunday afternoon she'd invited him to go on a bike ride, touring their side of the island. At first he'd made an excuse, saying he needed to find a bike for Sicily first. But Sicily, overhearing him, insisted that he and Janice go without her.

"I'm old enough to be alone," she'd assured him. Then Janice reminded him that Vivian and Lou were within shouting distance and even suggested that her mother would gladly come over to stay with the girl.

"I don't need a babysitter," Sicily had declared. "FYI, I can take care of myself."

Blake had suspected Sicily was already getting sick of him. He'd probably been smothering her with too much attention, acting too much like a parent, coddling. Trying not to look like his feelings weren't hurt, he'd gone off for a short ride with Janice, promising to be back in an hour. Then, only a mile into the ride, he'd felt guilty for leaving his daughter home alone. To Janice's disappointment, he'd cut the ride short. Of course, Sicily barely acknowledged his return. As usual, she was parked in front of the TV, where she'd hooked up her video game console and pretty much taken over the living room area. He wasn't ready to fight that battle yet.

After their morning coffee yesterday, Janice had invited him to drive over to Edgartown with her to pick up a lampshade for her mother. When he'd refused to leave Sicily home alone, Janice had informed Sicily that Vivian and Lou were baking pies and had invited Sicily to help. Apparently, that had sealed the deal. And Blake had to admit that riding across the island in the sleek BMW convertible wasn't entirely unpleasant.

Then on Tuesday, Janice had stopped by again, but he'd made it clear he didn't want to go anywhere. So they'd simply sat and visited for a couple of hours. Meanwhile Sicily had remained in the house and, no surprises here, played video games.

But today, when Janice asked Blake to join her in a beach picnic over near Oak Bluffs, he decided it was time to draw the line. "Unless Sicily comes along, I'll have to decline," he firmly told her. He knew that Sicily was in the kitchen, that the window was open, and that she could hear their conversation.

"Oh." Janice smiled stiffly. "Of course Sicily can come along, if she likes. But I got the impression she didn't want to."

Blake wondered how Janice could possibly know what Sicily did or did not want to do. First of all, Janice had barely exchanged more than a few sentences with the girl. Not that it was Janice's fault exactly. She'd tried a few times. Blake himself could barely get his daughter to talk to him. He had no way to determine what Sicily wanted to do—besides playing the hermit and her confounded video games, which were way beyond getting old by now. "Well, it seems reasonable that Sicily would want to go to the beach," Blake said rather loudly.

"Not particularly," Sicily had called through the open window.

"See." Janice shrugged with an I-told-you-so look.

He frowned. "But I can't leave her home alone...or even with your mother. The point of bringing her out here was so we could spend time together."

"My theory is"—Janice lowered her voice and stepped away from the kitchen window—"leave her alone long enough and the next thing you know she'll be begging for you to spend time with her." She winked at him. "You know, *reverse psychology*. Isn't that supposed to work on teens?"

"She's not a teen."

"Well, she's acting like one. So maybe that's how you should treat her." Janice checked her watch. "Come on, Blake. My mother already started putting together a picnic basket for us."

Blake sighed. "Sorry, Janice, but I'm going to have to say no."

She made a pouty expression. "But it's going to be a gorgeous day and—"

"If Sicily doesn't go, I don't go," he said, loudly enough that Sicily could easily hear him. "Sorry, Janice, but Sicily is my daughter, and I can't keep leaving her behind all the time."

"Fine." Janice nodded with a determined expression. "Then I'll have to see if I can talk Sicily into coming too."

Just like that she turned and went into the house. Even though Blake knew Janice was simply trying to help, he felt aggravated by her boldness. It was starting to feel like Janice didn't have many boundaries. As much as he liked the company of another adult—especially one who knew how to carry on an intelligent conversation—he was starting to resent Janice's intrusion into his life. Even if Janice did manage to entice Sicily to come along today, Blake wasn't certain he wanted to do this now. He was just thinking of a polite way to make this clear when Janice emerged from the house with a victorious grin.

"Sicily decided she'd like to come," she announced proudly.

"You're kidding?"

"No. She's getting her stuff ready as we speak."

Blake was flabbergasted. "So what did you do? Bribe her?"

"Not exactly. But I did tell her about my mother and aunt's new little business venture in town. Asked her if she'd been there yet."

"What was the business again?" He tried to remember what Vivian and Lou had told him about last week.

"The video arcade," Janice explained. "I promised her we'd stop by there on our way home from our picnic. And I promised her free tokens."

He let out a groan. "Why are you luring Sicily with something like that? Don't you understand that she's already addicted to video games as it is?"

"I know that, but at least this gets her out of the house for a while." Janice still looked quite pleased with herself. "That's a step in the right direction, don't you think?"

He thought it was more like giving an alcoholic a gift certificate for a liquor store. Still, he didn't know how to say no to her now. And Janice was right. It would get Sicily out of the house. So he decided to go along with this crazy plan. After all, it wasn't like he'd been having any success at this parenting thing. Maybe Janice knew more about it than he did. Perhaps he really did need some help.

Then, as they were gathering what they wanted to take to the beach, Blake pointed to the small black case that Sicily used to transport her video-game paraphernalia. "How about if you leave that thing at home today?" he suggested in a gentle tone.

She scowled at him. "Why?"

"Why not?" He smiled. "I mean, it's a gorgeous day, sweetie. What if you want to go swimming, and it gets wet?"

She wrinkled her nose at him. "It's not like I'd take it into the water, Dad."

"Well, what if you get sand in there and ruin your games and everything?" *That sounds like a good idea,* he thought.

"I won't." She tucked the video-game bag into her purple skull backpack, shoved a beach towel on top of it, then zipped it up and slung a strap over one shoulder.

As usual, Janice insisted on taking her car. Although Blake didn't really mind being a passenger again, he knew her pushiness would eventually get to him. Still, it was too late to do much about it today. Better to make the best of it. Figure it out later.

"So I noticed you have an Oscar," she said rather pointedly as soon as they were on the road.

"Oh, yeah...that." He glanced curiously at her. Had she actually gone into his bedroom?

"I wasn't snooping exactly," she said. "Just looking around. But I'm surprised you don't keep it on the mantel, Blake. That's pretty cool. What's it for anyway? I didn't look closely, but I assume it's not for acting." She chuckled. "Not that you aren't good-looking enough to be an actor."

Sicily made a snorting laugh from the backseat. It figured she was listening now. So much of the time she acted like she was ignoring him.

"It's for cinematography," he explained, "from a little indie film that turned out to be bigger than we expected. I was very privileged to be in charge of that particular film crew."

Now Janice grew extremely interested in his career—asking him about the movies he'd been involved with over the years. But the more they talked, the more he realized that she was more interested in his celebrity connections than the actual work he'd done on films. When he told her about working on a Sandra Bullock flick a couple years ago, saying what a nice person Sandra was, he could literally see the stars in Janice's eyes.

"Do you think Sandy will ever come here?"

"Here? To Martha's Vineyard?"

More backseat laughter.

"Yes. A lot of celebs come here, you know."

He shrugged. "I have no idea."

"But if she did come, and you heard about it, would you try to get together with her?"

He frowned. "Get *together* with her?"

"Yes. For drinks or laughs or whatever."

He laughed now. "Probably not. I'm fairly certain Sandra would appreciate me respecting her privacy. Do you know how hard it is for a star of her caliber to experience a normal life?"

"That's the price of celebrity."

"Maybe so. But in the film industry—if you want to keep working in it, that is— you learn early on how to maintain boundaries. Stars are no different from you or me, Janice. They need their space too."

He changed the subject to one that he knew would keep Janice occupied for a while—her political career, which sounded all-consuming. But he had to admire her enthusiasm, as well as her knowledge. And, unlike some politicians, Janice really did care about the issues.

All in all, it was a nice day. With temps in the low eighties and a gentle sea breeze to cool it off, he couldn't complain about the weather. And the food, as usual, was excellent. Louise really loved cooking and was thrilled to share her culinary skills whenever she got the chance. But from what Blake could tell, Janice didn't share her mother's passion for the kitchen. She'd said more than once that she'd chosen a career over domesticity. "I prefer hiring people who enjoy that sort of thing." He couldn't fault her for that since he was just learning to cook himself.

Being at the beach almost seemed to remind Sicily that she was still a child. Although she refused to play Frisbee, saying that it was a stupid game, he did entice her to go for a dip into the ocean. And when he caught her smiling, he was beginning to think that maybe this was just the ticket. Maybe the beach would break the spell of the video-game dependency and bring this nine-year-old back to reality. But it wasn't long before Sicily was dried off, sitting in the shade of her beach towel tented over her head, and hunkering down to play video games again.

"You know," he said as he peeked in under her beach towel, "I think if all you can do is play video games at the beach, you shouldn't get to stop at the arcade afterward."

She narrowed her eyes at him. "But you promised, *Dad*."

He shrugged. "*I* didn't promise anything."

She pointed to Janice now. "Well, *she* promised."

Janice looked uncomfortable. "It's true, Blake. I did promise."

"And I came to the beach with you," Sicily pointed out.

"But you're playing video—"

"You can't start changing the rules now," Sicily bitterly told him. "Just because you're the grown-up, you can't say one thing and do something else."

"She's probably right," Janice agreed.

He held up his hands now. "Fine. Have it your way. Two to one. I give up." Then he turned and ran back into the ocean's edge, waded out, and then began swimming vigorously. He was tempted to swim far out, but then realized it might make them worry about him. So after a couple of minutes, he turned around and swam back. No need to act juvenile.

Finally they packed it up and headed back toward Vineyard Haven, slowly working their way through the traffic.

"I think we'd make better time on bicycles," he pointed out as another pair of bikes moved past them.

"You'll have to find Sicily a bike," Janice said as she inched forward.

"I don't want a bike," Sicily said from the backseat. "Bikes are dumb."

Blake controlled himself from mentioning that video games were even dumber as Janice made her way into Vineyard Haven.

"I'm going to run a couple of errands while you girls go to the video-game place," he said as Janice finally managed to snag a parking place in town.

"Does that mean I need to stay with Sicily?" Janice asked.

"It was your idea to go play video games," he reminded her.

"Yes, but—"

"Then it's only fair that you go with her." He flashed a sly grin at her. "But I'm sure you girls will have a great time. I've got a book to pick up at Bunch of Grapes and something from the hardware store."

"Meet you back here in an hour?" Janice asked hopefully.

"Sounds good." He couldn't help but feel somewhat smug about how he'd gotten out of that. But, really, it was Janice's fault that they were here. Then, as he crossed the street, he wondered if he could really trust her to keep a watchful eye on Sicily. After all, she wasn't a mother. But she was an attorney. Surely she knew she would be held responsible if any harm came to his daughter.

Even so, he hurried to pick up his book, then decided to skip the hardware store altogether. He wasn't exactly paranoid when it came to his daughter, but town was so busy and, despite hearing that the island's crime rate was extremely low, he was a bit skeptical. As it turned out, it was probably a good thing because, upon entering the noisy arcade, he noticed that Janice was distracted in a conversation with another woman. Meanwhile, Sicily, completely unsupervised, was getting into an argument with an older boy over whose turn it was to play a particular video game.

"Is there a problem here?" Blake asked as the dark-haired boy looked like he was about to take a punch at his daughter.

"Who are you?" the boy demanded.

"I'm her father," Blake said in a tone meant to intimidate.

"Oh?" The boy stepped back.

"It was my turn," Sicily explained. "I was waiting. The other kid finished his game, and then this bully came up and pushed—"

"Fine," the boy snapped. "Take your stupid turn, *tattletale baby*."

Sicily looked hurt by his words.

"Don't pay attention to him," Blake said soothingly. "Guys like that don't deserve the time of day." He patted her head. "Especially from a pretty girl like you."

"Oh, *Dad*." She sounded exasperated, but he thought he saw a tiny twinkle of appreciation in her eyes. As pitiful as it was, like a starving man who was thankful for a breadcrumb, Blake felt relieved.

"Oh, there you are," Janice said as she joined them. "So what do you think of my mother and aunt's new business?"

Blake wanted to ask why any adult, in her right mind, would choose to purchase a place like this. But he didn't want to insult Janice or her family, so he kept his mouth shut. Instead of complaining about video games in general, he attempted to show some interest in his daughter's abilities to master this game. As he watched, he realized that it was slightly interesting. Although he'd been just old enough to avoid the video-game craze as a kid, he had to admit that graphics and special effects had come a long ways since the original Pong game he used to play at his neighbor's house in middle school.

All things considered, it was a fairly good day. But when Janice started talking about what they would do tomorrow, Blake knew he needed to make himself clear. "I have other plans," he said as he and Sicily got out of her car. "But maybe by the end of the week, I'll be available."

"Oh...right." She nodded, but he could tell by the look in her eye that she saw right through him and his phony-sounding excuse.

"Thanks for the picnic," he said as he reached for the basket.

"I can get that," she assured him as she got to it first.

"Well, thanks for everything," he said as he stepped back.

Sicily was already halfway home now, and he wished he was with her.

"Thanks for coming," Janice said crisply. "See you around."

"Yeah." He smiled, nodded. "See you."

Then, as he walked toward home, he felt uncomfortable. Not just from guilt either. Suddenly he wondered if he'd made a mistake to cut Janice off like that. Not that he'd meant to completely cut her off exactly…or maybe he did. But she did tend to overwhelm him a bit. Perhaps he needed to give her a hint that Blake Erickson was not a pushover. Maybe if she got this, and respected it, they could work it from there. If not…well, Blake didn't know that he cared that much one way or the other.

Chapter Eight
....

Waverly had never been one to give up easily. Oh, sometimes she fought her battles quietly, privately, but she did fight back. After recovering from her initial shock—and after a good, hard cry—she had emerged out onto the back deck and taken in a deep breath of fresh sea air, as well as a good long look at the amazing seascape scene before her, which was no longer a blurry shade of blue. Just like that, she realized that she wasn't going to surrender to self-pity. She wasn't going to tuck her tail and run. Even if it was totally crazy to stick around, she was determined to give this strange business venture her best effort.

"I want to apologize," she had told her mother on the phone, "if I sounded less than enthusiastic about helping with your business. It's just that I was caught off guard and—"

"I'm so sorry that you thought we were opening an art gallery," her mother had said back. "I never intended to mislead you, Waverly. After I got home, I could clearly see your point of view. You must've felt tricked."

"But I know it wasn't intentional," Waverly assured her. "And, like you said, I can almost see the humor in it now."

"I'm so relieved to hear that. To be perfectly honest, I questioned Lou's sensibility when she insisted that The Gallery was a good investment. Really, what do a couple of old women know about such things? I'm aware the business needs some work. We'll be lost when Rosie leaves. She's been managing everything for us."

"So I should probably schedule some time with Rosie." Waverly made a mental note to speak to the young woman tomorrow.

"Yes. It was her family who owned the arcade," Vivian explained. "Rosie's been working there since she was a teenager. But she'll be gone soon."

"I'll do what I can," Waverly promised. "For starters, I'm scrubbing down this apartment."

"Do you want me to come help?" Vivian offered.

Waverly remembered her mother's dislike of housekeeping of any kind. "No, I can handle it."

"Lou left some cleaning stuff there."

"Yes, I've already begun putting it to use." Waverly looked at the pile of dirt she'd already swept.

"I'm so relieved you're going to stay, darling. Most of all, I want to spend time with you. It's been too long."

"Well, I expect I'll stick around for the duration of the summer." Waverly had no idea what she'd do beyond that. Even as she made this decision, she reassured herself that she was not making a lifetime commitment. She would simply do whatever she could to help organize the place, attempt to make it the successful enterprise that her mother and aunt needed to stay afloat. After that, she would surely move on.

With this in mind, she continued to clean the studio apartment. Her plan was to simply carve out a space for herself up here—a place to sleep and hang her clothes—even if it was only a temporary one. With the floor swept clean, she went for the mop and bucket and started scrubbing the wood floors. To her surprise, the harder she scrubbed, the more the planks of wood began to come to life. She was so inspired by their natural wood beauty that she even started in on the windows that overlooked the water. But after a while, she realized it was getting dark. Washing windows at night was probably a waste of time and energy.

She'd noticed that the noisy arcade had gotten quiet somewhere around eight o'clock, which she suspected meant it had closed for the night. As she continued putting her space together, she located a plastic bag of bedding in one of her aunt's boxes. She put the grandma-style floral sheets and rose-colored blanket on the sofa bed, then slid the whole contraption closer to the windows, where she planned to enjoy the view. To make herself even more at home, she scooted a rickety side table next to the sofa bed and set a cracked porcelain lamp on it. Frumpy looking perhaps, but an improvement nonetheless. It would have to do until her own things arrived at the end of the week.

Satisfied that, at least, she had a semi-decent place to sleep tonight, she decided to slip downstairs to survey the state of the video arcade. She'd been too shocked at first glance to even remember what the space really looked like—although the sounds of electronic noises were still buzzing and ringing inside her head. She wondered if there was a way to turn the volume down on the machines.

She flicked on some lights and walked around the slightly eerie-looking space. With no one around, and the machines strangely silent, she thought it might make for a good setting for a creepy horror movie. Not that she was going to let her mind go there. Her plan was to start figuring this place out without anyone else around to distract her. What exactly made a business like this tick? What attracted customers to come and waste their money on these senseless games? And what might make this place even more alluring? What could she possibly do to improve something she really didn't understand? Well, besides throwing out all the horrid machines and turning it into a whole different sort of business, like an art gallery. Except she knew her aunt and mother could not afford to do that.

One thing she knew was that the whole place, not only the second floor, was in need of a good deep cleaning. And perhaps some better lighting too. Maybe a paint job would help. A more cheerful color than the drab beige, which looked like it hadn't been painted in ages, perhaps not since smoking had been allowed in places like this. The whole thing looked dark and dismal and depressing. Even the front windows were dingy and gray. She ran a finger over the surface of the glass to see that she left a clean trail through the grime. Hadn't the previous owners ever heard of soap and water? Or elbow grease?

Because, really, what sort of parent would want their children playing games in a filthy place like this? Of course, this made her wonder what sort of parent would want their children to play games like these in the first place. Or perhaps parents who dumped their kids here didn't really care. Maybe this was their way of having a break from their children. But unless she was mistaken, based on what she'd read about Martha's Vineyard, the tourists here didn't seem like that. Her mother had insinuated that the business needed help, and, as Waverly recalled, it hadn't been very busy today. Something was definitely not working here. She was determined to get to the bottom of it.

But not on her first night in this town. After all that labor, she realized she was ravenous. Heading out to Main Street to find someplace to eat, she walked a ways, finally stopping at a hotel restaurant called Zephrus, where she happily dined on delicious lobster cakes and seafood linguini. Then, thoroughly full and exhausted, Waverly ended her first day in Martha's Vineyard by returning to the studio apartment, where she crawled into her grandma-style bed and fell soundly asleep.

For the next few days, Waverly did little more than clean and scrub and spend time with Rosie, learning the ropes, as well as going over the books.

"As you can see, it's not terribly complicated," Rosie said to Waverly on Saturday. "I told your mom and aunt that they could probably run this place themselves, but I don't think either of them are too interested."

Waverly wanted to point out that she wasn't terribly interested either, but why bother? "I'd like to get someone in here to do some painting and help me move things around," she told Rosie.

"Why?" Rosie looked blankly at her.

"I want to see if I can make this place a little more welcoming."

Rosie just laughed. "Why bother?"

Waverly frowned. "Why not?"

"Because kids only come here for the games. They don't care what the place looks like."

"Well, I care."

Rosie shrugged. "I'll give you the numbers of a couple of guys who might be looking for work."

"Thanks."

Rosie was writing numbers on a scrap of paper. "I know I told your mom and aunt that I'd be here until the Fourth, but I'm hoping it'll be okay if I leave a little sooner."

Waverly felt worried now. "I, uh, guess so."

"You can easily find someone else to hire," Rosie told her. "I can give you some recommendations if you want."

"Yes," Waverly said eagerly, "please do."

Then Rosie had gone off on her lunch break, and Waverly was left on her own again. Not that this worried her anymore. Not like it had the first time Rosie had left Waverly alone in the arcade. By now Waverly realized that there really wasn't much to running the place. At least not in the way it had been run for the past several years. But Waverly hoped she could bring it up a notch.

She had just finished calling one of the guys Rosie had recommended, and he'd assured her he was a fairly good painter and happy to get some work, when a young girl with blond and purple hair approached the counter.

"That machine isn't working right," the girl explained.

"Which one?" Waverly asked.

"Road Warrior," the girl said, pointing to one of the games.

"Can you show me which one that is?" Waverly asked. Then she confessed to being new here and not that familiar with the games.

Suddenly the girl was explaining the whole thing to her in vivid detail.

"Wow," Waverly said as she looked at the game. "It sounds like you're a real expert when it comes to video games."

"I play a lot of games." The girl frowned at her. "Don't you?"

Waverly shook her head. "The truth is, I've never played once."

The girl looked shocked. "Never?"

"Never."

"And you could probably play for free here," the girl pointed out.

"Probably." Waverly handed the girl a token. "Go ahead and put this in and show me what's wrong."

So the girl put in the token and explained what the machine was doing and what it should be doing. Before long, Waverly slapped an OUT OF ORDER sign on it and repaid the girl her lost token, as well as a couple more for helping her figure it out.

"Will you get the game fixed?" the girl asked as she followed Waverly back to the counter.

"I guess so."

"Can I ask you a question?" The girl was lingering at the counter.

"Go for it." Waverly smiled at her.

"If you don't play video games, why do you work here?"

Waverly laughed. "That's a good question. I suppose it would be smart for me to learn how to play some of these games. But the truth is, I find them a little intimidating."

"Want me to teach you?" the girl offered.

Waverly blinked. "You know, that's not a bad idea. In fact, if you teach me, I would gladly pay you in tokens for your time."

The girl beamed at her. "It's a deal."

"My name is Waverly," she told the girl, sticking out her hand.

"That's a weird name."

Waverly laughed. "If you promise not to tell anyone, I'll explain how I got it."

"I promise."

"Well…" Waverly got a handful of tokens and put them in her

jeans pocket. "When my mother was pregnant with me, she got sick to her stomach a lot. All she wanted to eat was milk and Waverly Wafers."

The girl nodded. "I like Waverly Wafers too."

"And so my mother named me Waverly."

The girl laughed. "My name is Sicily," she told her. "My mother named me for the place she and Dad went to on their honeymoon."

Waverly smiled. "That's a beautiful name. And a great story too. Much better than being named after a cookie."

So her video game lessons began. It turned out that Sicily was a good teacher. But after about an hour, Waverly was concerned. "Are your parents in town?" she asked.

"My dad is doing errands," Sicily explained. "He said he'd be back to get me at one."

"Well, it's getting close to two," Waverly told her. "Do you need to call him or anything?"

Sicily just shrugged. "He knows where I am."

"Right." Waverly felt sorry for Sicily now. What kind of father left a young girl alone like this for nearly two hours? "Hey, can I get your opinion on something?"

"Okay." Sicily turned away from the video game.

"I'm going to have these walls painted, and I wonder what color would be best. Since you obviously love video games, maybe you'd have a suggestion." She pointed to the counter. "The color samples are up there."

They went to the counter, and Waverly spread out the color wheel that she'd been studying. "I really have no idea."

"You should paint the walls *all* these colors," Sicily said as she ran her hands over the wide array of colors.

"All these colors?" Waverly blinked. "Really?"

"Well, not all of them. But how about a rainbow of color?"

"A rainbow?" Waverly considered this. "Or maybe a mural?"

"What's a mural?"

Waverly explained that it was a large painting that filled an entire wall.

"Yeah, that would be cool. Like maybe with characters from some of the video games."

Waverly considered this. "That would be a lot of work."

"Yeah." Sicily pursed her lips. "And you'd need to be a real artist too."

Now Waverly smiled. "As a matter of fact, I am a real artist."

Sicily's blue eyes got big. "Really? You're a real artist?"

"Well, I haven't done much art lately, but I used to be a real artist."

"Do you want any help with the mural?" Sicily asked hopefully.

"I'd love some help."

"Really?" Sicily looked stunned.

"Are you a good painter?"

"I think so. I mean, I never painted a mural before, but it sounds like fun."

"I could pay you in game tokens," Waverly offered, "if it's all right with your parents."

"I think it's okay," Sicily assured her. "They don't really care what I do."

Waverly wanted to question this but decided not to. "I'm happy to talk to them and explain—"

"There's my dad now." Sicily pointed to the door, where an attractive man was just coming in. He almost had the look of an artist with his slightly shaggy brown hair and neatly trimmed beard. But it was his eyes that captured her. Although she couldn't detect the color, it was the expression that got her attention. They seemed to have a kind of depth to them, like perhaps his life hadn't been exactly smooth and easy.

Then, to Waverly's surprise, a familiar-looking woman walked in directly behind him. In fact, unless Waverly was mistaken, that was her cousin Janice.

"Waverly!" Janice exclaimed as she hurried up to greet her. "So nice to see you again. It's been ages."

"Janice." Waverly opened her arms to give her cousin a hug. "I'd heard you were here. So good to see you."

"You know each other?" Sicily wore a confused expression.

"Janice is my cousin," Waverly explained to the girl. "But I haven't seen her in years." She stepped back and studied Janice. "You look as beautiful as ever."

Janice lifted a brow. "You look a little stressed out, cousin. Is running a video arcade not all it's cracked up to be?"

"It's a bit of a challenge," Waverly admitted. "But Sicily here has been giving me some good advice." Waverly glanced at the man next to Janice now. "In fact, I've been offering her a job."

"A job?" He looked startled. "What do you mean?"

"This is Waverly, Dad." Sicily tugged him closer. "And this is my dad, Blake Erickson," she told Waverly. "Waverly said she'd pay me in game tokens if I helped her paint a wall."

"Paint a wall?" He frowned. "What?"

"A mural," Sicily explained. "With characters from the video games. Waverly wants me to help her."

"Oh, I don't know about that," he said cautiously.

"Why not?" Sicily demanded. "There's nothing else to do in this boring place."

"There's a lot to do," he countered.

"I'm sorry," Waverly said quickly. "It was probably out of line for me to offer your daughter a job without first consulting you." She smiled at Sicily. "You and your dad should discuss this privately. You can get back to me later on it."

"Okay." But Sicily's eyes were sad now.

"If you'll excuse me," Waverly stepped away, "I need to take care of some things." Thankfully, Rosie was back. Waverly went over to her, acting as if she had some important business to handle. But she simply told Rosie that Zach, who'd agreed to do some work at the arcade, would be coming by this afternoon to speak to her. "I'll be upstairs."

"Okay." Rosie nodded.

"I'm still trying to get the apartment set up," she explained unnecessarily. "It'll be a miracle if I can fit the furnishings in."

Then, without looking back, Waverly hurried up the stairs to her apartment. The moving van had delivered her things yesterday and, it was true, she was still trying to get the place arranged. But it wasn't as if it was urgent. Still, she felt relieved to escape her cousin and Sicily's father. Although she was curious as to their relationship, she decided she really didn't want to know.

She went into the tiny bathroom and stared at her image in the mirror. Janice had been right: Waverly did look stressed out. Frazzled, frowsy, and frumpy. She ran her fingers through her tangled auburn curls. The sea air had made her hair much wilder than usual. She even had a streak of dirt across one cheek, probably from when she'd been cleaning behind a row of machines this morning.

It figured that Rosie had never mentioned it. Dirt didn't appear to bother that girl much.

Waverly ran the cold water, splashing it on her face, which felt strangely hot and flushed. She washed off the dirty streak, dried her face, then looked again. A slight improvement, but unremarkable.

"Hello?" called a female voice in her apartment. "Waverly?"

She knew it was Janice but felt surprised she'd walked right in. "Coming," she called as she tossed the hand towel next to the sink.

"Sorry to intrude like this," Janice said. "But I told Sicily you wouldn't mind if I showed her your place."

"Is it okay?" Sicily asked carefully.

"Why not." Waverly made a stiff smile. "I'm still getting settled in but feel free to look around." She was relieved that Sicily's father hadn't come up with them.

"This is cool up here," Sicily said as she walked around the studio. "I can't believe you get to live above the arcade. You could go down and play games in the middle of the night if you wanted to."

Waverly couldn't help but laugh. "I guess so."

"Cool."

"Blake asked me to say sorry to you," Janice told Waverly. "He knows he overreacted."

"Dad's like that," Sicily explained. "He doesn't like video games very much."

"Oh." Waverly nodded.

"Anyway," Janice began, "I just called Mom and asked her why we haven't had you to dinner yet. She told me you'd been invited numerous times but had declined." She folded her arms across her front. "Don't you like us?"

Waverly smiled. "Of course I like you. But I've been busy, and I don't have a car and—"

"We can pick you up," Sicily offered.

Waverly laughed. "So do you drive, Sicily?"

Sicily smiled. "No, but Dad does. And Janice does too."

"We refuse to take no for an answer," Janice informed her. "Dinner tonight at seven."

"Only if Rosie doesn't mind working late."

"Close the place early," Janice said.

"On a Saturday night?" Waverly asked.

"Our mothers are the owners," Janice reminded her. "You can make your own hours if you like."

Even so, Waverly was unsure.

"Come on, Sicily." Janice put her hands on the girl's shoulders, guiding her toward the door. "We'll let Cousin Waverly get back to whatever it is she's doing. And I'm sure your father is tired of waiting for us."

"Do you still want me to help you?" Sicily asked Waverly with hopeful eyes.

"Of course. That is if it's all right."

"Good."

"In fact, if your dad doesn't mind, maybe you could start putting some ideas to paper. Make some sketches," Waverly suggested.

"Yeah. Good idea!" Sicily nodded eagerly. "I'll try to talk Dad into letting me help you," she said as she exited.

"And I'll tell our mothers to expect you at seven o'clock sharp," Janice called as she closed the door.

Waverly shook her head. Unless Rosie agreed to stay late tonight, which seemed unlikely, since Waverly had overheard Rosie telling her boyfriend to meet her here at six, and unless someone picked Waverly up, since she did not intend to walk, their mothers might be a little disappointed.

Waverly went over to the wide span of windows and looked out. Even in a few short days she had become addicted to this view. So peaceful and calming…and such a contrast to the chaos of the video arcade downstairs. It was here that she found serenity, here that she quietly conversed with God, and here that she found the strength to continue through another day.

Chapter Nine

....

"I don't see what the big deal is," Sicily complained from the back-seat as Blake drove them home from town.

"I don't either," Janice said. Then, lowering her voice, she turned to Blake. "You know, it's like free babysitting."

"I heard that," Sicily shot back at her, "and thank you very much, but I don't need a babysitter!"

"Yes, yes, I'm well aware of that," Janice said evenly. "But your father thinks you do."

"She's only nine," Blake reminded Janice. "You do not leave a nine-year-old unattended."

"Mom does," Sicily declared stubbornly.

"Really?" Blake glanced at her in the rearview mirror.

"Yeah. Sometimes she might *think* Alex or Vic are watching me, but usually they're not paying any attention to what I do. They treat me like I'm grown up. Well, sometimes anyway. Unless they're treating me like a baby."

"Yes, I know your mother leaves you with the older girls, but she doesn't leave you *home alone*, now does she, Sicily?"

"Sometimes she does."

Blake didn't know how to respond to that, but he intended to question Gia about it. Sicily might act like a teenager, but she was still just a little girl. And he wished everyone would start treating her like one again. As he turned toward his house, he wondered again about this Waverly person. She might be Vivian's daughter, and that was worth something since he truly did like Vivian, but why on earth would a normal adult pull up her roots and take on a job managing a video arcade? It made no sense.

"Oh, sorry," he said to Janice as he pulled up in front of his own house, "I totally forgot to drop you off at your mom's."

"That's all right." She laughed as she got out. "After all, I'm the one who bummed a ride from you today. And just think of the gas we save by doing that." She reached for her reusable shopping bag, smiling prettily at him. "Anyway, thanks for giving me a lift, Blake."

"No problem." He went around to the back of his car and opened his trunk.

"Looks like someone's going to have fun," Janice said sarcastically as he removed the large box from his trunk. "You know there are people you can hire to do those sorts of things for you."

He set the motorized grass-trimming tool down, kneeling to study the simple instructions on the outside of the box. They made it look easy enough. Still, this would be a first for him. "I plan to test this thing out on the path between our houses this afternoon."

"Then you and Sicily can use your new path when you come over for dinner tonight."

"Huh?" He looked up.

"Of course you're invited, Blake. We're having a dinner party after all. Naturally, we invite the neighbors."

"Waverly is going to be there too?" Sicily called out from where she was sitting on the porch. She sounded too interested, as if she assumed this video-arcade woman was suddenly her new best friend. That bothered Blake more than he cared to admit.

"I think she'll come," Janice told Sicily.

"Can we go, Dad?" his daughter begged him. "I really need to talk to Waverly about doing that mural with her."

He shrugged. "It appears I'm clearly outnumbered by the females in this particular neck of the woods."

Janice gave him a sly look. "Might as well give in to us then."

"Okay." He nodded at Sicily. "We'll go." Then he turned to Janice. "See you at seven."

With the kind of grin he hadn't seen in months, Sicily disappeared into the house. Blake pulled the safety goggles out of the plastic bag. The salesmen at the hardware store had convinced Blake the goggles were a necessity, telling him a story about a man who'd lost an eye thanks to a flying twig. So Blake put on the goggles and then, following the directions, plugged in the electric extension cord and fired up the new grass cutter. It was a noisy beast but effective.

Moving it back and forth through the beach grass, he created about a three-foot-wide swath, which eventually turned into a nice path between the houses. He finally reached his neighbors' property and shut down the noisy tool. Removing his splattered safety goggles, he turned to survey his work.

"I heard you met my daughter," Vivian called out as she slowly walked over to him.

He smiled at her. "That's right. I did."

"Nice little path you made for us." She nodded toward his work. "That must mean we're still friends."

"Of course we're still friends," he assured her. "Why wouldn't we be?"

"Well, I heard that you and Waverly locked horns today."

"Locked horns?" He was confused. "Not exactly."

"Janice said Waverly got in trouble for offering Sicily a job at the arcade."

"I wasn't too pleased about that, but I'm sure Waverly's intentions were good." Of course, even as he said this, he wasn't *that* sure. What sort of adult goes around offering juveniles jobs in video arcades anyway?

"She must've meant well." Vivian sighed. "But my daughter is sometimes impulsive. Rather she used to be. I think the past few years she's been stuck."

"Stuck?"

"In a job she didn't enjoy, in a city she didn't like. But she was afraid to make a change…afraid to make a move."

"That must've been hard." He wondered what kind of a job could be worse than the one she had now.

"That's one of the reasons I wanted her to come out here." Vivian plucked a piece of grass of his sleeve. "A fresh start."

"Seems like a few of us are looking for that."

"So you and Sicily are joining us for dinner then?"

"That's what I hear."

Vivian nodded. "Good. Now I better go and try to make myself useful to my sister." She leaned forward and said, with a conspiratorial tone, "Between Janice and me, poor Lou seems to be stuck with most of the cooking these days."

"If there's anything I can bring," he said, "give me a call." Then he turned and headed back to his house. As he walked, he wondered at the strangeness of this new life. Here he was, a bachelor, unexpectedly surrounded by nothing but females. Five to one was a bit staggering. And unless he liked being outnumbered like this, he should consider making a point to meet some of the other single guys in Martha's Vineyard, especially when fall came along and he needed someone to watch football with.

Blake put the grass-cutter tool in the garage, then went in the house to get something cool to drink. He was surprised to see that Sicily, instead of playing video games, was actually sitting at the kitchen room table—*drawing*. Without saying a word, because he was worried he'd break this wonderful spell, he glanced over to see that she'd helped herself to some paper from his printer, as well as a pen and pencil, and she was completely absorbed with her drawing. He pulled a soda from the fridge, popped it open, and marveled to think that perhaps they had finally turned a corner.

Shortly before seven, after he had showered and dressed for tonight's dinner date, he realized that Sicily had done likewise. He hadn't even had to nag her. For the first time, she was not complaining about being dragged over to eat with a bunch of "old ladies." He wanted to mention it but was afraid that would put her off. Instead he simply told her she looked nice. "That's a pretty sundress." Never mind that the orange stripes clashed with the purple in her hair. He was so not going there.

"Thanks." She had a cylinder of paper that she was putting some tape on.

"What's that for?" he asked.

"These are my sketches."

"Sketches of what?"

"Just some ideas for Waverly's mural." She held up the white paper tube like a sword. "I can't wait to hear what she thinks of them."

"Oh." He pressed his lips tightly together and just nodded like this was a good thing. There was no way he wanted to get into an argument with Sicily right before they went next door. So far so good and why mess with it now?

"I told Waverly that I'd find out whether or not you'll let me work for her, Dad."

"Right." He opened the front door and went out onto the porch, waiting for her to join him.

"So, is it?" she asked.

"Well, Sicily, I'm not convinced that's such a good—"

"You *never* want me to have any fun," she fired at him.

"I do want you to have fun," he tried. "In fact, I've been doing some research on the fun things there are to do on this island, and I—"

"But I want to help with the painting," she protested. "I want to work at The Gallery, Dad. What's wrong with that?"

"I…uh…I don't know." He shrugged. "Maybe nothing."

"Really?" She looked at him with wide eyes. "So I can?"

"Let's just say I'm still deciding, sweetie. How's that?"

Her mouth twisted to one side.

"And I'll be paying special attention to how mature and grown up you act tonight at dinner," he continued, thinking he might as well milk this for all it was worth, since by tomorrow she might not be speaking to him. "Maybe you'll prove to me that you're old enough to do something like work at the arcade."

She brightened. "Okay!"

Then, as they walked down the freshly cut path, Sicily began to talk to him—really talk. She told him about the drawings she'd completed this afternoon. Oh, he didn't recognize the names of the characters she described, but he could hear the excitement and enthusiasm in her voice and knew it would be difficult to disappoint her. But he also knew it would go against everything in him to give in to her on this.

Who'd ever heard of a nine-year-old working at a video-game arcade? Really, it was outrageous. As they approached the house, he remembered the bully boy who'd picked on her recently. What if something like that happened again, and no one stepped in to help her? Even leaving Sicily there for so long today had bothered him. It hadn't been his intention, since he'd only planned to get the grass cutter and go right back. But then Janice had waylaid him by dragging him with her to look at a motorized scooter of all things. For some reason she'd gotten into her head that he was in the market for a Vespa.

"Hello there," called Janice from where she was standing on the porch. As usual, she looked impeccably dressed. Tall and lithe in a sleeveless white linen dress that showed off her tan, she smiled and waved. "We're having drinks out here," she told him as he and Sicily joined her. "Strawberry lemonade for the younger set and something a little stronger for the rest of us."

"Is Waverly here yet?" Sicily asked with an expectant expression.

"Yes." Janice nodded, handing Sicily a filled glass. "My cousin is part of the younger set." She winked at Blake like this was funny. "And she is in the kitchen helping my mother at the moment."

"Can I help too?" Sicily asked her dad.

"Absolutely." Blake nodded. "That would be very nice of you."

"Trying to domesticate your daughter, are you?" One of Janice's brows arched in a way that suggested she didn't approve.

"I like Sicily to be helpful." He smiled. "And there's nothing wrong with being handy in the kitchen. I've learned to be somewhat domestic myself recently."

"You're turning into a very handy man," she teased. "Good in the yard and good in the kitchen. You might prove quite a catch for the right girl."

"The right girl." He considered that, wondering just who the right girl might be. Probably not Janice, although she was good company and knew how to have fun. Even so, he couldn't see himself with someone like her. Not really.

"I'm surprised at how much I'm enjoying my visit here." She took a sip. "I originally told my mother I'd probably only last a few days. But now I think I may spend my entire two weeks of vacation here. It really is a wonderful place to visit."

"I'm hoping it's a wonderful place to live," he admitted. "So far, I'm still enchanted."

"You've been here...what? Three months?"

"About that."

"Probably still in the honeymoon stage."

"Maybe." He looked out over the water, wondering if he'd ever tire of that view.

"Will you eventually go back to films?" she asked.

He considered this. "I don't like to say never, but I have a feeling that era of my life is over."

"So you don't think you'd get hired now?"

"I think if I really wanted to get a job, I could do it. I've still got good connections. And I still get calls about projects."

"What was your favorite film to work on?" she asked.

So he began telling her about the Tom Cruise film that they'd done in Italy. "I've always loved Tuscany," he told her. "So that made it special."

"I'm surprised you didn't want to live there. I hear a lot of the Hollywood crowd have homes there."

"It's a nice place to visit, but I'm not positive I'd want to live there. I'd hate to put that many miles between Sicily and me. Martha's Vineyard is far enough, but at least it's still on American soil."

"You could take Sicily to Sicily," she joked.

"Actually, she has been."

"Dinner is served," Sicily announced to them in a formal tone. "Chef Lou said to inform you it will be served on the portside deck tonight."

"Thank you." Blake hooked one arm with his daughter's, then offered the other one to Janice. "Can I escort you two lovely ladies to the portside deck?"

"Certainly." Janice giggled as he walked them around to the side of the house that looked directly over the water.

"This looks very festive," Blake said when they came to the table.

"I helped to set it," Sicily said happily. "Waverly drew the place cards, and I colored them for her. You get to sit by the whale, Daddy."

"Is that some kind of a hint?" he asked.

She laughed. "No, we're all sea animals. I'm a dolphin, and Janice is a shark, and—"

"A shark?" Janice looked slightly offended.

"A *pretty* shark." Sicily held up the place card to show her the sleek pale-blue shark.

"And Vivian's a stingray." Sicily continued to explain the sea animals, then showed them the centerpiece, which was made of shells and flowers. "Vivian did most of it, but she let me help."

"It's very beautiful," Blake told his daughter.

"Just wait until you see the food," Vivian said as she carried out a platter, setting it in the center of the table. "Louise really outdid herself this time."

"I wanted it to be special," Louise said quietly.

"I hope you didn't go to all this trouble for me." Waverly came out with a salad bowl, which she set on one end of the table. "You know I almost didn't make it."

"That's true," Vivian confirmed. "That silly Rosie was trying to pull a fast one on Waverly. First she said she was happy to work late—of course, we'd offered to pay her overtime to do so. But then her boyfriend showed up with tickets to some concert over in Edgartown, and Rosie changed her mind."

"Not that I can blame her," Waverly said.

"So I insisted that Waverly just close the arcade for the night."

"Hopefully we didn't lose too many customers." Louise clapped her hands. "But enough about that. It's time to eat!"

As they took their places, Blake sitting with Janice on one side and Sicily on the other, he noticed Waverly directly across from him. For the second time today, he thought what a beautiful woman she was. She hadn't dressed as carefully as her cousin. But she looked at home in her creamy silk blouse and faded jeans. With those auburn curls and blue-green eyes, combined with that fair porcelain skin...

he secretly dubbed her the Irish Fairy Queen. He knew she'd already bewitched his young daughter. What he couldn't understand was why she was content with a job as mundane as managing a video arcade. Didn't she want to have a life?

Chapter Ten

....

By the time they sat down to dinner, Waverly knew the status of Sicily's father. Divorced, semiretired (though he seemed too young), and dating Janice. "Although I wouldn't call it a serious relationship," Waverly's mother had whispered as they prepared the food in the kitchen.

"Why not?" Aunt Lou had countered.

"Well, they only just met."

"So?" Aunt Lou lifted the lid to check on the marinara sauce. "I've heard that some people fall in love within the first three minutes of meeting."

"Seriously?"

"I saw it on *Good Morning America.*"

Vivian laughed.

"Well, I *did.*"

"Yes." Vivian nodded. "I don't doubt that." She winked at Waverly. "Lou used to be addicted to that show—she's still going through withdrawal."

Then Sicily came into the kitchen to help, and she and Waverly were assigned to table-setting detail. To make it more interesting, Waverly suggested they make place cards for everyone as well as decorate the table.

"You really are an artist," Sicily said as she watched Waverly sketching the sea creatures that Sicily was assigning to each dinner guest.

"You're certain you want Janice to be a shark?" Waverly asked quietly.

"Absolutely."

"Well, we better make her a pretty shark then."

Sicily laughed. But Waverly suspected there was more to this shark business than just childish humor. It did stand to reason that a young girl would be resentful of her father's new girlfriend. Especially considering that Sicily had barely arrived when their romance began. Or at least that's what Vivian had said when she'd expressed concern.

Waverly wondered what kind of father would put his daughter in that position, to feel she was competing with someone like Janice. Waverly was a grown woman and she wouldn't care to be placed in that position herself. But then Blake appeared to be the sort of father who left his young child unattended in a video arcade, the kind who refused to let the same neglected child participate in an artistic project, like painting a mural, when it appeared obvious Sicily really wanted to.

"Dad hasn't decided if I can help you yet," Sicily confessed to Waverly as they put the finishing touches on the table. "He told me I have to prove to him that I'm mature enough." She frowned. "Like I'm supposed to know how to do that."

Waverly held up crossed fingers. "Here's to figuring it out."

"I brought some sketches," Sicily said with enthusiasm. "I left them on the front porch. Want me to get them?"

Waverly looked back into the kitchen in time to see her aunt putting the wire cage of clams into the boiling hot water. "Maybe we should look at them after dinner. We'll have more time."

"Good idea."

Waverly looked over the table. "All we need to do is light the candles, and we're set to go."

"Can I light them?"

"Why not." Waverly handed Sicily the lighter torch. Hopefully Blake wouldn't pop out here and accuse her of letting his child play with fire. But she watched as Sicily carefully lit the white votives, then stepped back and sighed.

"It's beautiful!" Sicily's smile grew big. "And we did it all by ourselves."

Waverly smiled at the girl. "We did."

Then Aunt Lou asked Sicily to inform the other guests that dinner was ready, and Waverly went into the kitchen to give some last-minute help with the serving dishes. Finally they were outside on the portside deck, where Waverly had made certain she was seated facing the ocean. Once again, she felt the strong impulse to get out her paints…to create. Maybe it was something in the air, or maybe it was desperation, but Waverly felt certain that before summer ended, she would be painting again. The idea thrilled her.

"Do you care to say grace again?" Aunt Lou asked Blake.

He looked slightly embarrassed. "Only if everyone is okay with it. I certainly don't want to push my beliefs—"

"Of course, we're perfectly fine with it," Aunt Lou assured him. "Both Vivian and I thought it was so sweet when you did that the first night we had you and Sicily over for dinner. We felt as if you not only blessed the food, but the house and everyone in it as well."

He smiled. "I have to admit this is still relatively new to me. So you'll have to forgive me if I don't do it correctly." Then he bowed his head and asked a blessing that sounded sincere and heartfelt. However, Waverly couldn't help but notice that Sicily didn't bow her head. Waverly wasn't sure of the meaning behind that, but hopefully this minor act of rebellion wouldn't rub Sicily's father the wrong way.

As usual, Janice dominated the conversation. But at least her chatter was educational as she told Waverly more about the island. How Janice had managed to pick this trivia up in such a short time was a bit of a mystery, and whether or not it was completely true would remain to be seen.

"The name Martha's Vineyard came from an early explorer in the 1600s," Janice informed them, sounding very much like a schoolteacher. "His name was Gosnold, and his wife's name was Martha. Apparently his mother-in-law was also a Martha, and she funded the expedition, so Gosnold probably wanted to keep both women happy."

"Smart man." Aunt Lou slapped her knee.

"He also had a daughter named Martha. Actually, *two* daughters named Martha."

"Two daughters with the same name?" Sicily looked skeptical.

"The first one died," Janice explained.

"Even so, that's kind of creepy," Sicily said. "To be named after your dead sister."

"I agree," Waverly said.

"You should talk," Janice told her. "You were named after a cookie."

Blake started to laugh. "A cookie?"

"Don't laugh," Sicily told him. "Waverly is a beautiful name. Even if she was named after a cookie."

"I had a lot of morning sickness," Vivian told them. "Waverly Wafers were one of the few things I could keep down."

"Good thing you weren't craving Ding-Dongs," Janice teased.

"Yes, yes." Waverly shook her head. "But back to Martha's Vineyard. I get the Martha part, but where did the 'Vineyard' come from? I heard there's only one vineyard on the island, and it's only been here for fifty years or so."

"There were wild grapes growing on the island," Janice said. "Like a vineyard." Then she began to tell them about a librarian named Lucy. "She lived in another part of the island—back in the thirties, I think. But Lucy the librarian did not approve of foul language."

"Nothing wrong with that," Aunt Lou said.

"Except that Lucy would take her scissors and cut the words out of the books."

"The librarian cut up the library books?" Sicily looked alarmed.

"She only cut the bad words out," Janice explained. "But that left holes in the books, and the townspeople weren't too happy about it. So Lucy eventually died. She had deeded a large amount of beach property to the town. Guess the townsfolk decided that if they were going to accept the beach property, they would get back at Lucy by declaring it a nude beach."

"A nude beach?" Aunt Lou looked concerned.

"Yes, Mother. Surely you know there are some nude beaches on this island." Janice smirked.

Aunt Lou blinked, then shook her head. "No, I didn't know this."

"Would that have changed your mind about moving here?" Waverly asked her aunt.

"No, of course not. But I don't think I'll be visiting any of those sorts of beaches anytime soon."

"I'm sure the sunbathers on those particular beaches will be relieved to hear that," Vivian teased.

Whether it was to intentionally change the subject or not, Blake now began to tell them about another part of the Vineyard's past. Or perhaps he wanted to one-up Janice in the history department. "Not too long after Martha's Vineyard was discovered, Thomas Mayhew purchased the whole island for forty pounds."

"Forty pounds?" Sicily repeated. "The whole island?"

"That's right. But Thomas Mayhew was more of a missionary than a businessman."

"Sounds like he was a good businessman to me," Janice injected.

"Well, maybe so. But he invested a lot of himself in educating the Native Americans about Christianity. He even sent a couple young men to Harvard. They were the first Indians to graduate from an American college. That was in the 1600s too."

"That's impressive," Waverly said.

"It is, isn't it?" Blake smiled directly at her now, and for some unexplainable reason, she felt extremely uncomfortable. But thankfully Janice, with her eternal gift of gab, something any politician should be grateful for, kept the conversation flowing by telling Sicily a Paul Bunyan sort of story about some giant who went around slinging whales by their tails. Finally everyone finished eating, and Waverly quietly got up and began to clear the table.

Waverly had never been particularly fond of groups—especially around a meal. That had been Neil's territory. Quick-witted and funny, he could keep a whole table amused with his anecdotes. But Waverly had always felt a group conversation was difficult at best and that she never contributed much. So she was relieved to escape to the kitchen, where she started a pot of coffee, got out some dessert plates, and began to load the dishwasher before anyone noticed she was missing.

"What are you doing in here?" Aunt Lou scolded.

"Just helping out," she said as she dried her hands on the towel.

"But this dinner party is supposed to be for you, Waverly."

"Then you should let me do as I please." She smiled at her aunt, then leaned over and kissed her on the cheek. "And thank you for making such a lovely meal. Best food I've had in ages."

Her aunt looked pleased. "I'm glad you liked it, dear."

"Need any help?" Sicily joined them now.

"You can be the server girl for dessert, if you like," Aunt Lou said. "It's raspberry cobbler and ice cream."

"Looks yummy." Waverly smacked her lips like she was Sicily's age.

"It's nice to see someone who appreciates good food." Aunt Lou sliced into the cobbler. "My poor Janice eats like a bird."

"Maybe she's trying to cut back on her carbs," Sicily said like a miniature adult.

"What do you know about carbs?" Aunt Lou demanded.

"I know that carbs and calories and fats are very bad for you," Sicily informed them in a serious tone.

Waverly frowned. "You seem a little young to be worrying about that."

"Don't you worry about it?" Sicily asked with wide eyes.

Waverly laughed. "Not particularly. I'd rather just eat healthy."

"What do you mean?" Sicily asked. "How do you eat healthy if you're not counting carbs and calories and stuff?"

"I simply focus on foods that are good for me, like whole grains and fruits and vegetables."

Sicily studied Waverly now. "You seem healthy."

"Well, thank you." Waverly scooped up a big serving of ice cream and put it on a piece of cobbler, handing it to Sicily. "This one is for Janice."

After coffee and dessert, which Janice barely touched but Sicily consumed most of hers, Waverly began to clear the table again. Sicily hopped up to help.

"Looks like you're trying to impress your dad," Waverly said quietly as they stacked the dishes in the sink.

"Am I overdoing it?" Sicily asked nervously.

Waverly laughed. "No. It looks just right."

"Do you want to see my sketches yet?" Sicily asked as Waverly put the last plate in the dishwasher.

"I'd love to." Waverly followed Sicily out to the screened-in front porch where, by the golden porch light, they looked over the sketches. "These are good," Waverly told her.

"Really?" Sicily put her hands over her mouth. "You're not just saying that?"

"No, they're really good. You're a good artist, Sicily."

"I like to draw."

"You should stick with it. Have you ever painted?"

"Not really. But I want to. And I want to help with your mural."

Waverly considered this. "Do you want me to talk to your dad for you?"

"Would you?"

"I'd be happy to." Waverly stood now. "Maybe we should go join the others."

But by the time they went around to the side of the house where the table was, everyone but Vivian was gone.

"Lou went inside to finish up in the kitchen," Vivian explained. "And Janice wanted to show Blake something out on the beach."

"Probably taking a little nature walk." Waverly controlled herself from rolling her eyes, since as far as she could recall, Janice had never had much interest in nature.

"Do you want to come see my room?" Sicily asked out of the blue.

Waverly didn't know what to say.

"Oh, yes, you should go see it," Vivian told her. "I even helped to fix it up."

"You did?" Sicily looked surprised.

"Yes, I hope you don't mind. Your dad was a little over-whelmed, so I offered to put it together for him...and for you."

Sicily looked impressed. "Are you an artist too?"

"In a way." Vivian smiled. "Go ahead, Waverly. I'll tell the others where you girls went to. But do take a flashlight with you. Some spares are on the front porch."

Armed with flashlights, Sicily led the way over to her house. Their house was another charming bungalow, similar to her aunt and mother's on the outside with its shingle siding and white trim and big porch. But when Sicily turned on the interior lights, Waverly could see that the inside was more sleek and modern. Definitely more masculine. But attractive.

"My room's back here," Sicily told her as she led the way, flicking a light on in the bedroom.

"This is lovely," Waverly told her as she surveyed the room. "It's like a mermaid could live here."

"I know." Sicily picked up a glass ball float. "I pretended I didn't like it when Dad first showed it to me."

"Really?" Waverly went over to look at a shell mobile. "Why?"

"Because I didn't want to come here."

"Oh." Waverly nodded like she understood. "It's hard going back and forth between parents, isn't it?"

"Were your parents divorced too?"

"Kind of." Waverly picked up a conch shell, examining its pink inside. The truth was her parents never even bothered to get married—not that she planned to go there with the young girl. "But you're lucky, Sicily. At least you get to spend time with your dad. You get to know what he's like. My father was never around. I never knew him at all."

"You didn't know your own dad?"

"Nope." She set the shell down and smiled at Sicily. "But I think he must've been a cool guy. I think I would've liked him. My mom told me he had curly red hair and freckles, and a laugh that came right up from his belly."

Sicily giggled. "He sounds nice."

Waverly nodded. "And your room is wonderful. Thanks for showing it to me."

"Want to see the rest of the house?" Sicily asked urgently, almost like she didn't want Waverly to leave yet. Or like she was lonely.

"All right." Waverly grinned. "Give me the tour."

So, acting like the lady of the house, Sicily took her on a formal tour, going through the dining area and the kitchen and back to the laundry room. Then she showed Waverly the guest bathroom, her dad's small office, and finally, her dad's bedroom. Waverly felt uncomfortable...intrusive. She was about to say it was time to go when Blake walked in behind them. "What are you doing in here?" he asked Sicily in a stern tone.

"Showing Waverly the house," Sicily said innocently.

"Yes," Waverly said as she moved past him and back out into the living room. "She gave me the whole grand tour. Your daughter is a natural hostess." She turned to Sicily now. "Thank you very much. Now I should be going."

"I heard you need a ride back into town," Blake said as she headed for the front door.

"Janice can probably take me," she told him. "She picked me up."

"Yes, but I offered to take you," he said a bit stiffly. "I thought perhaps we could discuss your job proposition."

"For me?" Sicily's eyes lit up.

"Yes. But if Waverly and I are going to discuss it, you'll have to stay with Louise and Vivian. Are you okay with that?"

"Yeah." She nodded eagerly.

They got into his car, and he drove next door to drop off Sicily, then started to leave again.

"Isn't Janice coming with us?" Waverly asked. For some reason she'd assumed her cousin would join them.

"Why?"

"Well, I figured she'd want to come...." Waverly heard the

uncertainty in her voice and realized she didn't know what she was talking about.

"I didn't invite her," Blake said as he pulled out of the driveway.

"Right." Waverly nodded.

"So, I know Sicily is determined to work for you, Waverly. I'm sure you meant no harm when you offered her a job, but as Sicily's dad, I naturally feel responsible for her, and I'm not too comfortable with the idea of her hanging out at a video arcade for hours on end."

"When you put it like that, I can understand your concern. But maybe the problem is simply your perspective."

"My perspective?"

"Your point of view, frame of reference. It's like you've predetermined that Sicily will have a negative experience, be exposed to some bad influences, perhaps even be in some kind of danger. And frankly, that's a bunch of hogwash."

"Hogwash?"

Waverly exhaled. "Yes. *Hogwash.* Another word for baloney or bull—"

"I know what the word means," he snipped. "It's a little insulting, don't you think?"

"I guess that depends on your perspective too," she fired back. "Maybe I feel insulted by you."

"What did I do to insult *you*?" he demanded.

"You're suggesting that I would knowingly and willingly put your daughter into some kind of unsafe situation. I find that insulting."

He let out a long sigh. "Fine, I get that. And I apologize."

"I can understand you feeling protective of your daughter." She paused. "Well, sort of."

"Sort of?"

"Yes." She turned to study his profile in the dimly lit car. "You did leave her unattended for quite some time in the video arcade. She seems a bit young for that."

He glowered. "Well, I hadn't meant to take that long. And she convinced me she'd be okay."

She eyed him. "So, you leave her alone like that, unattended, and I simply befriend her, spend some time with her, and suddenly I'm the bad guy?"

He shook his head. "You're right, Waverly. I guess I'm the bad guy. Rather, the bad father. My own daughter can't stand to be around me."

"You're being quite dramatic."

So then he began to pour out how hard it had been for him, how Sicily resented him for bringing her out here, how she'd been bored, how all she wanted to do was play stupid video games. "And now she seems intent on becoming a full-time employee at The Gallery. I suspect she'll want employee benefits too."

Waverly couldn't help but laugh. "Maybe you didn't give Sicily enough time to make the adjustment to moving here. I'm no expert about children, but I think your daughter is perfectly charming, and engaging, and interested in a whole lot more than stupid video games. And, just for the record, I'm fairly certain that I dislike video games as much as, possibly more, than you do."

By the time Blake dropped her off at The Gallery, they had reached an understanding. Waverly promised not to corrupt Sicily, and Blake agreed to trust Waverly to keep a careful eye on his daughter while she worked on the mural. "But if I find out that she's using this mural business as a cover-up for playing hours on end of video games, the deal is off."

"Fine," Waverly told him. "That works for me."

Now he smiled at her, and the corners of his eyes crinkled. "Thanks."

"Thank you," she said. "I will enjoy having Sicily's help as well as her companionship."

Blake frowned as if she'd said something offensive. Then he told her good night, and she got out of the car. He drove off a little too fast, especially for Main Street.

She shook her head. He was a hard one to figure out. Sometimes he was warm and charming. But then he would turn frosty and bitter. As far as Waverly was concerned—not that anyone cared— her cousin Janice was more than welcome to that contrary man!

Chapter Eleven

....

As he drove home, Blake couldn't stop thinking about Waverly. But his thoughts were disparate and disconnected...and confusing. On one hand, she honestly seemed to like Sicily—and Sicily appeared enchanted with Waverly. But at the same time, he got the feeling that Waverly had taken an instant dislike to him. For some reason, she didn't approve of him, as if he were a poor excuse for a father, and perhaps even a flawed human being. He found her attitude irksome. He disliked people who judged others without even bothering to get their facts straight first.

It wasn't until he pulled his car into the garage and went into his own house that he realized he'd totally forgotten about Sicily. Maybe he wasn't that hot as a father either. *Sometimes,* he thought as he jogged down his freshly cut path, *we don't know ourselves as well as we think.*

"How did it go?" Janice asked as he came up onto the screened porch where she appeared to be waiting for him. Her dark hair was curled around her face and the smile she wore reminded him of a cat he'd once owned. A very sweet but very independent cat who came and went as she pleased until she finally disappeared altogether.

He shrugged. "Okay...I guess."

"Sicily is inside," Janice spoke quietly, "playing gin rummy with Vivian and Mom."

"Oh." He sat down on a wicker rocker next to her chair. "No offense, but your cousin seems like a stubborn woman to me."

Janice laughed. "I used to think she was rather inflexible when we were girls. I remember trying to get her to go along with me a few times. She would dig her heels in, we would argue. I'd call her pigheaded, and she'd get mad."

He nodded. "Yes. Definitely pigheaded." But even as he said this, he felt slightly guilty. "Or maybe I've done something to make her think less of me."

"Oh, what could *you* have possibly done?" Janice turned on a little girl's voice now. For some reason, he found it grating. "You're the sweetest guy around, Blake. If silly old Waverly doesn't like you, it's because she's downright pigheaded." She laughed again.

"Well, I did agree to let Sicily work for her. But I laid down the line. I told Waverly that Sicily would only be there to help with the mural—not to play video games like a street urchin."

"See, there you go." Janice scooted her chair closer to his. "She knows what you expect. And now you have free babysitting to boot."

He frowned. "That's not why I'm letting Sicily do this."

"So I get to help with the mural?" Sicily exclaimed as she burst out the door. She'd obviously been listening. "Did I hear you right, Daddy? Do I get to work for her?"

He nodded. "Your friend wore me down."

"Good for Waverly." Now Sicily wrapped her arms around her dad from behind, giving him a tight, warm hug. "Thank you, Daddy!"

He blinked, surprised at her expression of affection. "You—you're welcome, Sicily."

"Let's go home now." She came around and grabbed his hand, pulling him to his feet. "I want to work on some more sketches."

"How about if we thank our hostesses first," he said.

So they went inside and properly thanked Louise and Vivian, who looked like they were ready to call it a night.

"Did you get everything straightened out with Waverly?" Vivian asked.

"Dad is letting me work for her," Sicily told her with bright eyes.

"That's good." Vivian nodded at Blake. "I don't think you'll be sorry."

"No, of course not," Louise assured him. "Waverly is a sweet girl and a hard worker. You can depend on her."

"*See*, Dad." Sicily grinned up at him.

"Then we shall take our leave of you ladies." He made a formal bow, which made them giggle.

"Good night," they called in unison.

But before he and Sicily made it over to the trail, he noticed that Janice was right alongside them. "I've got a flashlight," she told him. "I'll light your way home."

"I think we're fine," he told her.

"But there could be a wild boar around."

"Wild boars?" Sicily sounded a little scared.

"You never know. I heard they used to have them on the island."

Blake felt skeptical but decided not to mention it. "So here we are," he said as they were safely in his own yard. "I guess you're not afraid to get yourself back home?"

"I don't know." Janice looked uncertain. "Perhaps a cup of coffee would help."

He wanted to decline, but already Sicily had streaked off into the house, saying she wanted to work on some drawings. So he had no rock-solid excuse. Besides, why shouldn't he enjoy a late-night cup of coffee with an attractive woman? Except that he just didn't feel that interested.

"Or else I could just head on back," Janice said in a dismal tone.

"No, no," he said slowly. "A cup of Joe sounds good. I've got some good hazelnut decaf I've been wanting to try. Sound good to you?"

"Delightful." She sat down on his porch and sighed. "What a beautiful evening."

Blake went into his kitchen and began to fix some coffee. But as he went through the paces, the only thing he could think of was Waverly—and how he wished she was the one outside on the porch waiting for him. Oh, he knew it was ridiculous, since Waverly obviously despised him. And yet...

"Here you go," he said as he set the pair of coffee mugs on the little table. "I put a little cream in yours. Okay?"

"Perfect." She smiled up at him. "Already...you know me well."

"I guess." He sat down and looked out over the darkened water.

"I've been thinking about taking an extended vacation," she said in a leisurely way. "My firm was balking some, but when I explained that I had the upcoming election to contend with, they seemed to understand." She took a sip of coffee. "Besides, they know that if I make it into the state senate, it won't hurt them either."

"Meaning?" He glanced over at her.

She shrugged. "Meaning, it's a nice thing for people to take care of each other…like you scratch my back and I'll scratch yours." She snickered. "If you catch my drift."

He didn't catch it, but he did feel weary. As much as he hated to admit it (at his age), he merely wanted to grab a good book and go to bed. Really, what was wrong with that? But Janice was energized. She continued to talk about her firm and the upcoming election and where that might lead to, insinuating that nothing was too far out of her reach.

"I'm not a fool, Blake. I know I'm not part of the Kennedy family," she said wistfully. "Or the Clintons—although you know they both have connections in the Vineyard. But sometimes I get this feeling that a destiny has been handed to me. Whether it came from my father or someplace else, I can't say, but I get this feeling I'm heading into something much bigger than just the Massachusetts state senate. I know my life is heading for something much bigger. Does that make any sense?"

"Absolutely," he told her. "That makes a lot of sense. I applaud you for being willing to go for it. Not everyone has the guts to throw their hat into the ring. We need good leaders in this country."

"You think I'd be a good leader?" Her voice was soft now, like she was asking something beyond that.

"You seem like a natural-born leader to me."

She grimaced. "Meaning, I'm bossy."

"Hey, I didn't say that."

"But it's what you were thinking."

He shrugged. "I don't know what I was thinking."

The truth was, he was thinking about Janice's cousin. Not that he was going there right now.

"How do you feel about assertive women?" she asked.

"I think everyone should be assertive—male and female."

"Yes, but how would you feel if you had an assertive woman by your side? Would you be intimidated?"

He was in over his head. What was she saying? Was this a proposal? "I…uh…think I should check on Sicily," he said, standing. "She should be going to bed by now."

"Yes." She stood, stretching luxuriously. "Although it's sad to say adieu to such a glorious summer evening. Are you certain you want to call it a night?"

He stepped away from her. "Yes. I'm certain."

She made a pouty face. "Have it your way. See you for coffee then?"

He was halfway into the house already but feeling very ungentlemanly for not offering to walk her back home. "I guess so." He made an apologetic smile. "Later."

She looked clearly disappointed, but at least she kept going. He felt like he'd just escaped a bullet. A platinum bullet…with his name engraved upon it.

When he checked on Sicily, she was happily in her pajamas and sketching away.

"I came to tell you good night," he told her.

"Did Janice go home?" she asked with a hard-to-read expression.

He nodded.

"Do you really like her?"

He was stumped. "I—uh—I don't know."

"I think she's just using you, Daddy."

He paused to consider her words for a couple of reasons. The obvious one being that Sicily should make such an assumption about Janice. Where had she come up with something like that? But what really caught his attention was that she'd called him Daddy. Since getting to the Vineyard, Sicily had rarely used that old familiar term. For that reason alone, he wanted to tread cautiously with her. "Why do you think Janice is using me?" he asked gently.

"Cuz she's the kind of woman who wants a man for only one reason."

He tried not to look shocked. But he was curious—how much did his little girl know about these things? "And that reason would be…?"

"Just so *she'll* look good," Sicily said in a very grown-up way.

"Oh?" He kept a straight face as he studied his daughter.

"Uh-huh." She refocused her attention on her drawing as she continued. "Alexandra had a boyfriend like that once. She said the only reason he wanted to be with her was so she could be his *wrist candy.*"

Blake let out a snort of laughter.

She stuck out her lower lip like he'd offended her. "That's what Alex said, Daddy. *Wrist candy.*"

He nodded sagely. "Oh, I believe you, sweetie. I really do."

She looked skeptical.

"Good night, darling." He ran his hand over her silky hair, wondering how long it would take that purple streak to fade away. "Lights off by ten-thirty, okay?"

"Oh, Dad." She scowled at him.

"Hey, don't forget you're a working woman now," he reminded her. "You need to get your rest."

"Oh, yeah," she said eagerly. "Ten-thirty…lights off."

He kissed the top of her head, then left her room and wandered aimlessly through his house. Curious as to why he felt so restless, he realized he no longer had the patience to read the biography he'd picked up. And he had no interest in going online to check the latest news. Eventually he turned off the lights and went into his bedroom, where he stood for a long moment. He was still pondering what Sicily had said, implying that he might simply be Janice's wrist candy, of all things! At first it had sounded outrageous, but the more he considered it, the more he wondered. Worse than that, he wasn't positive that he wasn't guilty of the same motivations.

Chapter Twelve

....

On Sunday morning Waverly decided it was time to treat herself to a day off. After all, she'd accomplished a fair amount in only a few days. With all the cleaning she'd done and with her own furnishings in place, the studio apartment now resembled a rather pleasant place to live. Even the arcade had improved its image after her thorough cleaning. Zach was coming tomorrow to start on the basecoat of paint for their mural wall, as well as to rearrange some of the video games.

There was no denying that managing a video-game parlor had never been her dream job, but she was determined to make the best of it. And now it was time for some R & R. So, with a promise to relieve Rosie for her lunch break at 12:30, Waverly walked on over to Waterside Market to get some breakfast. There she dined on a smoked salmon and cream cheese bagel as well as a latte as she perused the local paper until she found an ad for a bike rental shop located in Tisbury. By now she knew that Tisbury was merely another name for Vineyard Haven. According to the address, this bike shop was right down the street. It was selling some of its older models for what sounded like fairly reasonable prices.

By ten o'clock she had not only purchased a retro-style bicycle in a pleasant shade of sky blue, but a helmet and several other biking accessories as well. She'd spent more than she'd planned, but compared to the expenses of running a car, she had gotten off cheaply. And, considering the summer traffic, which often moved at the pace of a weary slug, she felt certain biking was highly preferable. First she rode around Vineyard Haven, but feeling she was up for more of a challenge, she decided to head over to East Chop.

She didn't know why the pointed peninsulas were called West and East Chop, but on the map they did resemble pork chops. Not that she was going public with that theory. West Chop was where Vineyard Haven was located. And East Chop contained Oak Bluffs. She'd heard Oak Bluffs was even more touristy than Vineyard Haven, but that was hard to imagine...until she got there. Streets were clogged with cars, bikes, and pedestrians. Finally she found herself touring some of the side streets, where each house was a like a charmingly unique work of art.

So far most of the homes she'd seen had been similar with their gray Cape Cod–style shingles and white trim. But these houses were painted all the colors of the rainbow and tricked out with gingerbread, lattice, and other similar decorative touches. It was like a carnival of houses, and she couldn't get enough of them. She knew she'd have to come back with her camera next time. But for now, it was time to go and relieve Rosie for her lunch break.

She pedaled back across the bridge and into Tisbury, navigating through the traffic, hurrying to make it to The Gallery before one. She was walking her bike up to the arcade when she saw Sicily sitting on the edge of the flower planter outside. Her face looked close to tears.

"What's wrong?" Waverly asked her.

"You weren't here." Sicily stood up, folding her arms across her front with a grim expression.

"I was taking the day off," Waverly explained as she locked her bike into the bike rack.

"But I thought I was going to work for you today."

Waverly bit her lip. "But I never said that, Sicily."

"But my dad said it was okay to work for you." Sicily held up some rolls of paper. "And I made more drawings."

Waverly thought over her response. It was clear that Sicily's feelings were hurt. "I'm sorry if I gave you the impression you were going to start today," she said carefully. "I really didn't mean to." She opened the door. "Why don't you come inside, and we'll discuss what your hours will be."

"Okay."

"There you are," Rosie said in a slightly grumpy tone. "I thought you'd never get back."

Waverly glanced at the clock to see she was seven minutes late. "Sorry about that," she told Rosie. Seven minutes, and Rosie was throwing a hissy fit?

"See you later." Rosie grabbed her purse from beneath the counter and marched off.

"Guess I'm on everyone's bad list today," she told Sicily. "Hey, do you want to do some work right now?"

"Do what?"

Waverly had been about to ask Sicily to mind the counter for her while she ran upstairs but thought better of leaving a child in charge of kids who were older and bigger than her. "Could you run up to my apartment and get me a bottle of water from the fridge?"

Sicily nodded. "Yeah."

So Waverly gave her the key. "And help yourself to a soda or juice if you like. Then we can make a plan for next week."

Sicily smiled now. *"Okay!"*

Before long, Sicily was back with water for Waverly and a soda for herself. The two sat down and looked over Sicily's sketches. Then Waverly got out some more paper, and they began to lay out the way the characters could go on the wall. Finally Waverly pulled out the calendar, and they looked at the upcoming week, deciding that mornings would be best, agreeing on two to three hours a day, depending on what Sicily's dad said.

"If something comes up and you need to miss a day or two," Waverly finally said, "I'll understand." She handed Sicily her weekly schedule. "And we'll figure out the following week on next Friday. It'll be trickier because of the Fourth of July."

"I wish we could start on the mural today," Sicily said sadly.

"We kind of started." Waverly pointed to their big blueprint sketch. "At least we'll be ready to go tomorrow. I'll see that Zach paints the mural wall first thing in the morning, so it'll be dry enough for us to work on by ten."

"But what am I going to do today?" Sicily asked glumly. "Dad and Janice won't be back to get me until three-thirty or four."

Waverly couldn't help it. Her jaw dropped. "You're kidding?"

"That's what they said when they dropped me off. That's how long they needed to go to the beach."

Waverly was seriously aggravated. Why had Blake gone and done that? He knew that Waverly hadn't made any firm arrangement on having Sicily here today. What made him assume it was acceptable to dump his daughter here? Who did he think she was, anyway—the free babysitter?

"I guess I can hang out and play video games until then." Sicily stared at her backpack. "But I only have a few dollars. That won't last long."

"Do you want to call your dad and ask him to come get you?" Waverly pointed to the phone by the cash register.

Sicily pulled a cell phone with pink rhinestones from a pocket of her backpack. "I have my own, thanks."

"Right." Nine-year-olds with cell phones, being dropped off at video arcades, wearing purple hair, and carrying backpacks with skulls on them. Yes, it was a brave new world.

"But Dad can't get me for a while. He and Janice were going to Menemsha, and that's clear on the other side of the island." She looked longingly at the sketches. "I wish we could just work today."

So Waverly explained how Zach wouldn't even get the basecoat of paint on until tomorrow, and how she'd planned to take the rest of the day off. "I even bought a bicycle this morning. It's pretty much the first time I've gone around and seen things." Now she wondered about calling her mother, asking her to come pick up Sicily.

"I wish *I* had a bike," Sicily said wistfully.

So Waverly told her about the sale at the rental shop. Then she got an idea. "Maybe I could pay you in advance by getting you a bike," she suggested. "They had kids' bikes there too."

Sicily's eyes lit up. "And then we could ride around together."

"But would your dad be agreeable to that?"

"He said he was going to get me a bike anyway."

"Yes, but he might not like me stepping in like this."

"I don't see why he should care." Sicily scowled. "He's so busy with dumb old Janice." The next instant she looked worried. "Sorry. I forgot she's your cousin."

Waverly just laughed. "That's all right."

"So can we do it?" Sicily jumped from foot to foot. "Get a bike? Can we?"

"I'd feel better if you got permission first, Sicily."

"I can call Dad." She held up her phone again.

Just then Waverly spotted a couple of boys who looked like they were about to get in a scuffle over a particular machine. "Go ahead and call him," she told Sicily.

Then she hurried over to play referee, pointing up to the poster of rules that she'd repainted yesterday. "See rule number three," she told them. "No fighting. If you fight, you'll be forced to leave."

"He started it," the shaggy-haired boy said.

"He asked for it," the slightly larger boy claimed.

And now they were arguing again.

"I don't care who's to blame," she said firmly. "If you guys want to fight, you can take it outside, and I'll call the police to come deal with you."

"Really?" The shaggy-haired boy appeared slightly alarmed. "You'd call the cops on us just for fighting?"

"Really. And I'll bet they wouldn't like it any more than I do."

"My parents wouldn't like it either," the taller boy admitted.

Now she smiled at both of them. "But I'd rather not involve the police." She reached into her pocket and pulled out a pair of tokens. "And if you guys promise not to fight, and if you'll shake hands and forgive each other—and mean it—I'll give you each a free game."

Well, that seemed to settle it. Too bad world peace wasn't so simple.

"I'm back," Rosie announced as she entered the arcade. "And I'm seven minutes late too." Payback flickered in her gaze.

"That's fine," Waverly told her, ignoring the slam. Then she turned to Sicily. "Did you call your dad?"

Sicily nodded as she looped the straps of her backpack over her shoulders. "Let's go. This is going to be fun."

Soon they were on their way. Waverly wheeled her bike alongside her, as they walked to the bike rental shop. Sicily was getting enthused about the prospects of riding around the island together. Waverly hoped they had some kids' bikes left. If not, maybe they could rent one.

To her relief, there were still a couple of kids' bikes. But the only girl's bike was hot pink, and Sicily looked disappointed.

"You don't like hot pink?" Waverly asked her.

"I do like hot pink," Sicily assured her. "I just wanted to get a blue one like yours."

Waverly laughed. "Well, this way we won't get them confused. Besides, I think you look good on a pink bike, Sicily. Goes nicely with your hair."

"Really?" She smiled.

"We'll take it," Waverly told the salesman.

"And I assume you'll want a helmet for your daughter."

Sicily giggled. "She's not my mom. She's my boss."

"Oh. Right." His eyes were curious.

Before long, they were both helmeted up and on their bikes. Since Waverly felt a little concerned for Sicily's safety in this traffic, she suggested they stick to the less busy streets in Vineyard Haven. Thankfully, Sicily agreed. First they rode over to the town hall and then on up to the library, where Waverly got a library card and Sicily put an application for one in her backpack.

"Are you hungry?" Waverly asked as they were leaving. "I just realized that I am, and I have an idea."

Sicily nodded eagerly. "What is it?"

"Let's head back to The Gallery, and we'll go up to my apartment and fix a picnic lunch to take to the beach. Sound good?"

Sicily grinned. "Sounds great."

Together they made some interesting sandwiches and picked out some fruit and drinks, which Waverly wrapped up in a big beach towel. On their way to their bikes, Waverly asked Rosie to watch for Sicily's dad. "Have him call one of our cell phones," she said as they went out. "And we'll ride back here ASAP."

Then she put their picnic bundle in her bike basket, and they headed over to Owen Park Beach a couple of blocks away. Naturally, the beach was crowded. But they locked up their bikes and found a good spot where they set out their picnic and dined in style.

"I think food tastes better when eaten outside," Waverly observed.

"And these sandwiches are awesome," Sicily proclaimed.

"I must agree." Waverly grinned. "Who knew that peanut butter was better with sweet pickles?"

"This is the best day I've had since I came to Martha's Vineyard," Sicily told her after they'd finished up and were out wading ankle-deep in the cool water.

"Me too," Waverly confessed. "Thanks for sharing it with me."

They wandered up and down the beach, looking for shells and sea glass until they finally realized someone was calling their names.

"Hey, that's my dad." Sicily pointed over to where a man was standing at the edge of the sand and waving wildly toward them. "Guess we better go, huh?"

"I think so." Waverly put the last shell she'd found in her cargo pants pocket, patting to see if her cell phone was still there and wondering why he hadn't simply called.

"Hey, Dad," Sicily said cheerfully, "what's up?"

His expression grew stern. "What's up is that I've been looking all over for you."

"Why didn't you call—"

He shook his phone at her. "I did call. About a hundred times."

Sicily pointed to her backpack by their bikes. "Oops, I guess I forgot my phone in there."

"I guess so." He shook his head.

"Didn't Rosie give you my cell phone number?" Waverly asked as she bent over to unlock their bikes.

"No, Rosie did *not*."

"Sorry, I asked her—"

"Never mind," he snapped. "We have to go, Sicily. *Now*. Get your stuff and come on."

"What's the hurry?" she asked.

"Janice is driving, and she needs to get home for some big dinner shindig tonight." He reached for Sicily's backpack. "Come on, Sis."

"But it's not even five o'clock yet," Waverly pointed out.

He locked eyes with her now. "I'm well aware of what time it is, thank you very much!"

"*Dad,*" hissed Sicily, "don't be such an old grump!"

"If I'm grumpy, it's only because I've been worried about you, Sicily. For starters, you weren't at The Gallery. Rosie said you'd gone to the beach, but I had no idea which beach or where you were, and I've been looking all over the place." He pointed to the water now. "For all I knew, you could've been drowned."

"I'm not drowned." Sicily shook her head as she unlocked her bike.

"Whose bike is that?" he asked.

"Mine." She grinned at him.

"*What?*" He looked from Sicily to Waverly with a confused expression.

"I thought she told you—"

"What on earth made you think it was okay—"

"I paid her an advance," Waverly calmly explained. "So that we could—"

"If my daughter needs a bike, I will buy her a bike—"

"Dad!" Sicily scowled at him. "Be nice!"

He pressed his lips together and his face, which was already red—probably too much sun—got even redder. "We'll work out the details of this—this bike later," he growled. "But for now, you will have to deal with it, Waverly. Because, as you must know, there is not room in your little cousin's car to hold a bicycle." He grabbed Sicily by the hand now. "Come on, *let's go!*"

"Bye, Waverly," she called as her father tugged her up the beach toward the parking lot where a horn, probably Janice's, was honking loudly and obnoxiously.

Waverly struggled to walk the pair of bikes across the lumpy sand. Once she was on solid ground, it became a little easier but was still awkward. As she wobbled along, she felt increasingly irked for having to spend her day off towing two bikes through town. Her anger wasn't directed toward Sicily, since the little girl would've gladly ridden her bike back to The Gallery. But Waverly's fumes were aimed at Blake and his impatience. And she felt aggravated with Janice too. Really, what was wrong with those two? They only seemed to think of themselves.

"Looks like you could use a hand," called a man's voice.

She looked over to see a sandy-haired man crossing the street toward her. "It's a little tricky riding two bikes at once," she told him as he fell into step with her.

"Can I be of help?" he offered.

She looked into his brown eyes and wondered if he could be tricking her. What if he was really a bike thief?

"I'm Reggie Martin," he told her. "I own The Skye."

She stopped walking. "You *own* the sky?"

"It's an art gallery," he explained with a nice smile. "Not the real sky, although I do have my pilot's license. But I mean the art gallery on Main Street."

"Oh." She nodded. "The Skye. Yes, I've seen the sign, and I've been meaning to go in there. A real art gallery."

He laughed. "A real art gallery? As opposed to what?"

"It's a long story." She studied him closely. "And I'm from Chicago. I've been here less than a week, so I guess I'm still a bit wary of strangers offering help."

"Well, if you're worried I'm about to steal your bike, don't. I'm not into girls' bikes so much."

"Thanks. I'd appreciate a hand." She told him her name now, letting him have Sicily's bike to roll along. "I'm guessing you're not part of a Vineyard crime ring."

"In fact, the Vineyard has a very low crime rate," he said as they navigated past a group of pedestrians who weren't budging from where they were photographing an old building.

"So I've heard, but I'm still keeping my doors locked."

He nodded. "Probably not a bad idea during tourist season. So are you just visiting?"

"I'm not sure," she admitted as they turned onto Main Street. "I thought I was relocating." She shook her head with a rueful smile. "I also thought I was coming here to run a real art gallery."

"Oh, that's the real art gallery story?"

"Yes." She pointed to the arcade just down the street from them. "My mom and aunt bought The Gallery and brought me out here to manage it. I thought it was an art gallery—not a video-game arcade."

He threw back his head and laughed loudly. "That must've been a shock."

She briefly explained her background in art and her desire to reinvent herself, then finally paused in front of The Gallery. "So now I'm running this place."

He looked down at the small pink bike. "And who belongs to this? A daughter?"

"No. A young friend of mine."

He pointed to the art gallery a couple of blocks down. "Have you considered doing any consultations here? I could use the opinion of a real art conservationist."

"A real art conservationist?" she teased.

"Yes. A real one. Are you interested?"

"Absolutely," she told him. "Do you mind if I clean up some? I'm kind of sandy and—"

"Tell you what," he said, "you clean up. Then come over and give me your opinion on a particular painting that's been concerning me, and perhaps you'll let me pay you by taking you to dinner?" Now he looked uncertain. "Unless you're involved or married or engaged or something, although it didn't look like it." He pointed to her wedding ring finger. She'd removed her wedding rings during her cleaning spurt this past week and had totally forgotten to replace them.

"No, I'm not married. Rather, I'm widowed."

"Oh, I see. I'm so sorry for your loss."

"Thanks. It's been three—actually, almost four—years."

Hope glimmered in his eyes again. "So, how about it then? Interested in working a deal? A few minutes of work for a meal? I really do need a professional opinion on an old piece of art. Of course, I'll gladly pay you in cash if you'd prefer. I simply thought I'd give it—"

"Dinner sounds divine."

A smile lit up his face. "Great. See you in a while then? I usually close at six on Sundays."

"I'll be there before six."

Chapter Thirteen
....

Blake felt like a jerk all the way home. It didn't help that Sicily was treating him like he was about to win the title "World's Worst Father" either. As Janice drove too fast down the curvy road, he replayed the scene on the beach with Waverly and Sicily and regretted every word he'd spoken—to both of them. Why had he allowed Janice's little temper tantrum to undo him like that? Who cared if Janice was late for her big dinner date? It had been her choice to linger at the beach. Even after he'd gotten a cryptic message from Sicily and expressed the desire to head back to Vineyard Haven, had that hurried Janice?

"You will be ready to go by 6:30," Janice said as she turned down their road.

"What do you mean?" he asked.

She made a disappointed face. "I thought you agreed to go with me. To dinner tonight. Remember?"

"I didn't understand," he said. "I thought you were going alone."

"Alone?" She looked like she was on the verge of tears as she pulled into their driveway. "Why would I want to do that?"

"I don't know. I just thought—"

"Go with her, Dad," Sicily said sullenly.

"Listen to your daughter." Janice stopped the car and turned to smile at Sicily. "And my mother and aunt have invited you to spend the evening with them. I hear there's chocolate and a good movie involved."

"All right!" Sicily nodded eagerly as she reached for her backpack. "But I don't—"

"You are coming with me, Blake. You can't make me late like this and then refuse to go with me. Besides, did I tell you who's on the guest list? It's possible that James Taylor might even be there."

"You're just saying that to—"

"Six-thirty," she told him sharply. Then, turning to Sicily, her tone sweetened. "Don't let your daddy be late, okay?"

"Okay." Sicily seemed to like this arrangement. "Do you think Waverly will be there too?"

"Where?" Janice asked.

"At Vivian and Louise's," Sicily explained.

"Oh." Janice cocked her head to one side. "Maybe so. I'll try to find out."

"Cool!" Sicily threw her backpack over a shoulder and dashed into the house.

"Now you have two females who are depending on you," Janice told him. Then she smiled prettily. "Please don't be late. Okay?"

Feeling trapped, he merely nodded. "I won't be late."

"And dress is beachy casual, but that still means nice. Okay?"

Blake thought he was going to throw something if she said "okay" one more time. He nodded again. "Yeah, I think I can handle that."

"And just walk over to Mom's house. We'll take my car. Okay?"

"Fine." He gritted his teeth.

"See you soon!" Then, spitting gravel from her tires, she sped out of the driveway and on down the road.

As he went into his house, he felt like a complete wimp. How had it come down to this? Letting females bully him, having their way, with no consideration for his feelings whatsoever. What had happened to him? Or maybe he deserved what he was getting.

Trying to push negativity from his brain, Blake showered and even took the time to trim his beard before he carefully dressed in his nicest casual look. California style, of course. *Casually* pressed off-white pants, a Ralph Lauren shirt in a pale blue plaid, and wax-hide loafers, no socks. If that wasn't good enough for James Taylor, whom everyone knew was a casual sort of guy, someone could just throw Blake out. He didn't really care.

"You look nice, Dad." Sicily smiled as he emerged from his room a little past six.

"You do too, sweetie."

She frowned. "I'm wearing jeans and a T-shirt, Dad."

"Even so, you do look nice."

"Right."

He wanted to tell her that the primary reason he was going on this forced date was so she could spend the evening with Vivian and Louise (and possibly Waverly) since it appeared obvious his daughter preferred the company of old ladies (and some not so old) to him. But he controlled himself. No sense in making a bad situation worse.

"Ready to go?" she asked.

"I guess."

As they walked down the trail, she chattered to him about some of the things she'd done with Waverly that day, talking about this grown woman as if she were Sicily's new best friend. "I hope she wants to do some drawing tonight," Sicily told him as they went onto the porch. "I've got some new ideas for the mural."

"Hello there," said Vivian as she opened the screen door for them. "Come right in."

"Is Waverly here yet?" Sicily asked expectantly.

"Waverly?" Vivian looked confused.

"You know," Sicily said, "your daughter."

Vivian smiled. "Yes, I know Waverly's my daughter, but I guess I'm a little baffled as to why she would be here."

"Janice said that Waverly would—"

"Oh, there you both are," Janice exclaimed when she saw Blake and Sicily. "And right on time too."

"What did Janice say to you?" Vivian asked Sicily.

"She said Waverly might be here tonight. Didn't she come?"

"Oh, dear." Janice looked caught off guard. "I totally forgot about her."

Sicily made a disappointed face.

"But you can still call her," Janice told Sicily. "Knowing Waverly, she'll just be sitting at home doing nothing tonight anyway."

"We'll call her right now," Vivian told Sicily. "If need be, I'll drive into town and pick her up myself."

"You will?" Sicily looked relieved.

"I most certainly will." Vivian cast a glance at Janice. Blake wasn't totally sure as to the meaning, but the word *disapproval* stuck in his head.

"Come on," Janice said lightly to him. "Let's go."

"Yes, yes," Vivian told them. "Be on your way."

"Give my best to Louise," he told her.

"Certainly." Vivian nodded crisply.

With Janice gently tugging his elbow, they made their way out to her little car, which still had the top down. She ran her fingers through her short cropped hair, which never seemed to move. "I guess we can leave the top down," she said as she climbed into the passenger seat. "You don't mind driving, do you?"

"Not at all." He glanced at her as he got into the driver's seat. She looked cool and in control in her pale blue linen dress. It was quite similar to the white one she'd worn the other night. He vaguely wondered if she'd gotten some sort of bulk price on them.

"So?" She put on a pair of oversized sunglasses. "Do I look okay?"

He nodded. "You look impeccable, Janice. As always."

She smiled in appreciation. "Thank you. And we go well together too, don't you think?"

He nodded again, automatically. But as he did so, he was thinking about wrist candy. What if his nine-year-old daughter was right? What if Blake truly was Janice Grant's wrist candy? It hurt his head to even think about it.

"The dinner party is in town," she told him. "A reception really. At the old Mansion House Hotel. Do you know where that is?"

"Right in the middle of town?"

"Precisely. In fact, if you can't find a parking spot, I'll bet it would be all right to park behind The Gallery. There's a parking place back there, and Waverly doesn't even have a car yet."

"Right." He wondered why Waverly's name always seemed to come up. Or why, when it did come up, it grabbed his attention. It was as if his radar went up, or his heart skipped a beat, or something equally uncomfortable. Perhaps it was because of the influence

Waverly had over his daughter. Not for the first time, he wondered if the Irish Fairy Queen really had done a spell on his daughter. Hopefully no ill would come from having her visit at her mother's tonight.

As he pulled into the tiny lot behind The Gallery, he assured himself that he could trust Vivian and Louise to keep Waverly from doing anything overly harmful or dangerous with his daughter. Hopefully Waverly didn't like to do things like swimming by the light of the moon in the Sound. Or playing with fire. Perhaps he should've laid down the law for his daughter. Maybe it wasn't too late.

"Here we are, with time to spare," Janice said as he removed her keys from the ignition and handed them to her.

"Time to spare?" He grimaced. "You were so worked up about being late."

"I hate to be late," she said as she remained in the seat. "I always worry that people will either be talking about me…or that they won't." She laughed and opened the door. "Actually, we're just in time to get drinks before the real party begins."

Blake wanted to point out that he didn't need or want a drink but knew that comment would go right past her. So as she ordered a dirty martini, he decided to have a Coke.

"I'm sorry, ma'am," the waitress told her. "No alcohol is served in Tisbury."

"Where?" Janice scowled.

"Tisbury. Or Martha's Vineyard. It's a dry town," the waitress explained.

"How about wine?"

"It's a *dry* town," the waitress said again.

Blake concealed his amusement. "Well, I'll have a Coke."

"That we can do." The waitress grinned.

"Same here," Janice said dismally.

"So where's the big dinner party?" Blake asked as he sipped his Coke.

"In here, somewhere." Janice looked glum, like this wasn't exactly the sort of evening she'd been hoping for. Blake was inclined to agree, though he did like the idea of meeting James Taylor... unless that was merely a guise to get him to come here tonight. Just in case, he kept his eyes peeled every time someone entered the restaurant. And positioned as he was, it wasn't hard to keep a close watch on the door.

"Do you see someone famous?" Janice asked curiously a few minutes later.

"Uh, not exactly." But he knew his eyes had given him away.

"Who?" She turned to look as well. "Oh, it's just my cousin." She made a halfhearted sort of wave.

"With a guy." Blake did a quick study of the man accompanying Waverly. A nice enough looking fellow, though somewhat short and ordinary, maybe even boring, judging by his blasé expression. "Do you know who that is?"

"Who?" Janice turned to look again. This time Waverly appeared to notice them, making a small polite wave in their direction. "I have no idea," Janice whispered to Blake. "Don't look now, but they seem to be coming our way."

"It's not like they have a choice," Blake said wryly as he watched the hostess leading them across the room. "Unless they want to appear rude and walk right past us."

As they came closer, he noticed how amazing Waverly looked in a turquoise-blue dress that reminded him of the ocean in the morning and fit her shape like a well-tailored glove. Her only adornment was a simple pearl necklace, which elegantly complemented her peaches-and-cream complexion. He mentally slapped himself as he forced a smile for the couple, who was nearly at their table now.

"Hello." Waverly smiled politely as she and her mystery man paused on their way to a table. "What a surprise to see you two here tonight." The twinkle in her aqua-blue eyes suggested curiosity. Blake knew she was wondering about Janice's "big dinner event" that had seemed so all-important and pressing this afternoon. Suddenly Blake wondered about it too. Why had Janice made such a fuss? As far as he could see, no big wingding was going on here. Had he simply been duped?

"So good to see you, Cuz." Janice beamed at both of them. "And who is this?"

With a courteous smile, Waverly introduced them to her new friend Reggie Martin. "He owns The Skye," she explained.

"The whole sky?" Janice laughed. "Must be expensive."

Reggie chuckled. "You do sound related to Waverly."

Then Waverly explained what Blake already knew: that The Skye was an art gallery down the street. "I just had the grand tour, and it's truly a delightful collection. Some impressive artists. You might enjoy it too, Janice."

"If I have time." Janice examined her diamond-encrusted watch with too much interest. "Speaking of time, I wonder where that dinner is supposed to be."

"You're not talking about the fund-raiser tonight?" Reggie asked. "With the Millers hosting?"

"Yes." Janice nodded eagerly. "That's the event. I thought it would be started by now."

"We're going to a fund-raiser?" A wave of disappointment washed over Blake. Dinner with strangers was bad enough, but a fund-raiser was far worse.

"As I recall, it's being held in the hotel's library this year," Reggie explained. "The invitation said appetizers and drinks." He grinned. "We all know what that means. And, of course, there's the silent auction. I already placed some bids on a couple of things earlier today. They started the early bird bidding at five." He cocked his head toward Blake. "Easier that way, if you know what I mean."

Blake tried not to look as dismayed as he felt. "Yes. I do know."

"Well, you two have a fun evening," Reggie said lightly.

Blake nodded like he planned to do that. But *fun* was not exactly the word he would've used just now. Once they got into the hotel library, where too many people were crammed into too small of a space, he longed for an excuse—any excuse—to escape.

The appetizers were lukewarm and picked over, and the "drinks" were mock-tails of sweet-tasting sodas and fruit punch, decorated with paper umbrellas. Worst of all was the expectation that if you were there, you were expected to bid on things. By now the bidding had gotten unreasonably high. Even so, he pretended to browse the items and even considered bidding on an ATV, except that the price had gone far above the actual value of the donated item. Finally he began to wonder how believable he'd be at feigning a heart attack. He stepped out of the way of a very large woman and closer to an auction item that was garnering a lot of attention.

"Oh, I get it," he said to Janice as he read the description over someone's shoulder. "There's your James Taylor now."

"Where? Where?" Janice's head jerked anxiously from right and left. "I don't see him. *Where?*"

Blake pointed to the page of bids with James Taylor's photo pasted on the top. "Sweet Baby James is auction item number 76. And the bid is up to $5,900 already. Listen here, Janice: the winner gets James Taylor to sing them a song of their choice while he makes them a grilled cheese sandwich." He shook his head. "Wow, that's one spendy little lunch."

Janice rolled her eyes. "It's for a good cause."

"And that would be?"

She looked flustered now, and he knew she was as oblivious as he. "You could at least *act* like you're interested," she hissed at him.

He stared blankly at her. "Why?"

"Because we're *here*." She adopted a plastic-looking smile, like she thought she was a celebrity. "And someday these people might be voting for me."

Blake pressed his lips together and nodded. *Wrist candy*, he was thinking, *definitely wrist candy.* But after tonight, he was done with this charade. He would explain it gently and politely to Janice, but he was done. Perhaps he'd waited too long to end it already.

Chapter Fourteen
....

As she and Reggie were handed menus, Waverly wondered if this island might be too small for both her and her cousin. But, seriously, what were the odds of running into Janice like that tonight? And why had it bothered Waverly so much to see Blake just now? She was well aware that he and Janice were an item. Perhaps she was still irked because he'd been so rude to her earlier. That little scene at the beach had been a bit over the top. Of course, it had been thanks to Blake's bad manners that she'd met Reggie today. And that seemed to be a good thing.

She smiled at Reggie as he continued to study the menu. Really, he was a perfect date. Thoughtful, polite, good conversationalist. Plus he looked like a good match for her. Already she knew they had similar interests in art, music, and even food, she realized, when they both ordered the seafood special.

So, as their dinner was served and as they made pleasant small talk about their commonalities, why was she still thinking about Blake? Why was she obsessing over the way Blake had looked at her tonight? Like he was happy to see her, like he appreciated what he saw. Or was that her imagination? And, if so, why would she even bother?

Waverly grew even more determined not to allow Blake to ruin this evening for her and Reggie. Even if it took all of her self-control and focus, she would not let Blake win. So she asked Reggie to tell her about where and how he'd grown up, peppering him with question after question as if she planned to write his biography. But he appeared to enjoy the spotlight and amused her with a story of what sounded like the quintessential New England childhood with two well-adjusted parents, three other siblings, a number of interesting pets, summers in the Vineyard, private schools, and finally a Yale education.

By the time dessert and coffee were being served, he'd turned the table on her, asking about her own upbringing, which was much more unconventional than his. So much so she wondered at how they seemed to have so much in common now. She was just telling him about the year she'd lived in Thailand with her mother and how she'd ridden an elephant for her sixth birthday when she saw Blake and Janice exiting the building. She knew they didn't purposely stop in front of the window outside—they couldn't possibly have staged what was clearly an argument—but like watching a train wreck, she couldn't take her eyes off of them.

"Looks like your cousin and her boyfriend are having a little spat," Reggie said.

"Too bad they don't have the good sense to move it along." Waverly felt embarrassed for both of them.

"Looks like the fellow—Blake was it?—is trying to get her to take it somewhere else." Reggie chuckled as Janice held a fist in the air. "But I'm guessing that is one determined woman."

Waverly sighed. "You've got that right."

Then, to Waverly's surprise, Blake turned one way and Janice the other, and they stomped off in opposite directions.

Reggie laughed. "Well, I guess that takes care of that. Do you think it's really over between them or just a lovers' quarrel?"

"I have no idea." Waverly shook her head and looked back down at her chocolate torte. So much for trying to block Blake from her mind. Now he was all she could think about. What had happened out there? Were those two really over with? Even if that was the situation, what difference did it make to her?

She tried once again to make small talk, but she could tell it was fading. She blamed it on tiredness, which was actually true. "It's been kind of a whirlwind week for me. And I've got a painter coming early in the morning too."

As they were leaving the restaurant, she explained about the mural that she and her young artist friend were going to start on as soon as the basecoat was dry.

"So you *are* pursuing art," he said as he held the door open for her.

She rolled her eyes skyward. "I wouldn't exactly call painting video-game characters 'art.' "

He held up his forefinger. "Don't forget that art is like beauty… in the eyes of the beholder."

"Yes." She nodded. "You're absolutely right. And I'll bet my Sicily would staunchly defend her video-game characters as art too."

"Is that the owner of the bike? Sicily?"

"Yes." As he walked her to her building, she almost admitted that Sicily was Blake's daughter, but for some unexplainable reason she could not. At the steps to her apartment, she suspected that Reggie would've liked an invitation, but she was not ready for that. So she simply thanked him for dinner and told him good night.

He tipped his head politely. "And thank you for consulting with me today."

"I really do think you need to keep a closer eye on the humidity in there," she reminded him. "It's constantly changing in a climate like this, and you want to maintain a consistency."

"I'll keep that in mind. Perhaps we can discuss it further in the future."

She smiled at him. "Perhaps we can." Then she turned and hurried up the stairs. She didn't want to be rude, but she didn't want to lead him on either. In fact, as she went into the apartment, she wasn't completely sure what she wanted. This was so new to her. She had no doubts that Reggie was a good guy and possibly even boyfriend material. However, she knew she wasn't interested in him like that. She might've been out of this dating game biz for a while, but she wasn't altogether ignorant. If you were out with one man and thinking about another, something was definitely wrong.

Convinced that Reggie was gone now, Waverly went back outside and stood on the terrace, gazing out over the water and the dusky periwinkle light. Although she'd claimed to be tired—and it had been a long week—she was also restless. Too restless to go to sleep yet. She lit the big hurricane candle that she'd placed out there and sat in the deck chair beside it. What a lovely night! No wonder people fell in love with Martha's Vineyard in the summertime. However, she wondered what it would be like in winter. That might take some getting used to. If she stayed that long.

"Hello up there?"

Waverly jumped to her feet. Then, with a pounding heart, she peered down to see who was standing at the foot of her stairs. She blinked and looked again. "Blake?"

"Sorry to disturb you." He gave a feeble wave. "Mind if I come up?"

"No, of course not. Come on up." She watched as he slowly made his way up the stairs.

"These stairs are a little rickety," he said once he was on the terrace. "I wonder if you should get someone in here to sturdy them up."

"That's occurred to me." She nodded, studying his expression, which was impossible to read. "But surely that's not what brought you here."

"No, just an observation." He pointed to the pair of deck chairs. "Mind if I sit?"

"Make yourself at home." But she heard the sarcasm in her tone.

"I know I don't deserve your hospitality," he said as he lowered himself into the chair, "but it's been a long night...and a long day too."

"Reggie and I witnessed the little fight you had with Janice this evening."

He looked surprised. "You saw that?"

She suppressed the urge to chuckle. "Yeah. Are you all right?"

He nodded. "I'm fine. I'd been meaning to break things off with her for a while, but she's got a pretty persistent personality, if you catch my meaning."

"I know all about her personality."

"And she wasn't too happy when I told her where I stood."

"Janice likes to win." Waverly wondered how much to say now.

"Tell me about it."

"She also doesn't give up easily," she admitted.

"So I've already seen."

"Just so you know." Waverly sighed, enjoying the view again. "Isn't it beautiful up here?"

"Stunning."

She turned toward him, but instead of looking at the view, he was staring at her. Now she didn't know what to say.

"You're probably wondering why I'm intruding on your space like this." He sounded a little uneasy. "First of all, I wanted to apologize for being so rude this afternoon. You know, that scene at the beach."

"Oh, yeah." She nodded, remembering how upsetting that had been.

"Well, that was partly due to the pressure I was getting from Janice. But mostly I was worried about Sicily. When she wasn't at the arcade, and when Rosie said that you'd taken the day off—well, I was confused."

"So Rosie didn't give you my message?"

"Well, after I looked around town, I went back and asked Rosie again. Finally she told me she thought that you and Sicily had gone to the beach together. Of course, by then I was fairly anxious and worried about Sicily's safety. Plus it made no sense. Why was Sicily willing to go to the beach with you when she'd stated in no uncertain terms that she did not want to go to the beach today?" He ran his fingers through his beard and shook his head. "Parenting a teenage wannabe is like walking a minefield."

"Maybe you're trying too hard."

His brow creased. "I don't know about that. But I do know it's stressful. And it's not like I can simply let her go and do whatever she likes. She's only nine."

"Yes, but she's a very mature nine."

"Does that mean I should treat her like she's sixteen?"

"No, of course not. But maybe you should trust her a little more.

Show that you have some confidence in her." Then, to her surprise, she told Blake about how she was raised to be quite independent. "I know my mother was somewhat Bohemian, not to mention totally unconventional, but I turned out normal." She laughed. "Well, at least I hope I did."

"You make a good point."

She thanked him, noticing how his eyes glowed warmly in the flickering candlelight. Then, feeling uncomfortable, she turned away.

"So, as I was saying…" He cleared his throat. "I didn't mean to invade your space tonight, but I did want to apologize—and to ask you a favor."

"A favor?" She eyed him curiously.

He made a sheepish grin. "It's a little embarrassing."

"What?" She waited.

"As it turns out, I'm without transportation. I could walk home, but that will take a couple of hours, and I left Sicily with your aunt and mother, and I suspect they don't want to be kept up too late."

"But I don't have a car," she explained.

He nodded. "I know. I wondered if perhaps I could borrow your bicycle."

She laughed. "Seriously, you want my bike?"

"I do, and I promise to take good care of it and return it first thing in the morning."

"You want to ride a bike all the way out there?"

"It's only about five miles."

"Yes." She considered this. "And my bike does have a light."

"So you don't mind?"

She stifled her giggles. "No. But it's a girl's bike."

He shrugged. "Beggars can't be choosers."

"No, I suppose not."

"So, do you forgive me for the scene I made at the beach over Sicily?"

"Yes, of course."

"I felt terrible afterwards, thinking about how kind it was of you to help Sis get a bike. And then I left you stranded there with two bikes." He ran his hand through his hair, letting out a frustrated groan. "I don't usually act like such an oaf. All I can say is that trying to parent my daughter, reinvent my life, and on top of all that deal with your cousin—I think it's knocked me a little off balance."

"Totally understandable," she told him. "Maybe you'll be comforted to know that it was through that very predicament—awkwardly wheeling two bikes through town—that I met Reggie today. He came to my rescue. Now I have a new friend."

Blake's expression was impossible to read as he stood. But clearly he was ready to go.

"I put both bikes downstairs in the arcade," she explained as she stood. "If you'd like to go back down and meet me around front, I'll bring mine out."

"Great." He nodded. "Appreciate it."

She wondered why she hadn't invited him to walk through her apartment but then realized it was because the place was messy after the picnic lunch, the hurried shower, and change of clothes. If she ever did invite Blake into her apartment, she wanted it to look nice. Why she wanted it to look nice was a question she was not prepared to answer just yet.

She unlocked the front door of the gallery and wheeled her bike out to the sidewalk. "Are you positive you want to do this?" she asked. "I mean, I'll bet Janice has cooled off by now. She'd probably be glad to give you a lift home."

He looked uncertain. "I doubt it."

"You might be surprised. As hardheaded as she can be, she doesn't usually carry a grudge...once she gets past something."

"I'd rather ride a bike"—he gave a lopsided grin—"even a girl's bike, than to beg Janice for a ride right now."

Waverly nodded. "Yeah. I can understand that."

"Thanks." He bent over to roll up his pant legs. "I'm just glad you didn't make me ride Sicily's bike."

She laughed. "Now that would be fun to see."

"After my tantrum at the beach today, I wouldn't blame you."

"Be safe," she called out as he took off down Main Street, where despite the hour, the traffic was still moving rather slowly, faster than in midday perhaps, but sluggish just the same.

"Thanks," he called as he passed a car. "See you tomorrow!"

It wasn't until she was back in her apartment that she began to replay bits and pieces of their conversation. She searched for hidden meanings, wondering if she was imagining things, or if it was possible that he was experiencing the same kind of attraction she was... if she indeed *was* attracted to him, which still wasn't perfectly clear.

Besides, there was the whole Janice thing to consider. Unless she'd read Blake wrong tonight, he still seemed a little torn and unsettled by that relationship. Was it possible he was as interested in Janice as her cousin had appeared to be interested in him? Waverly remembered how Reggie had called it a lovers' quarrel earlier. Wasn't that a real possibility? Especially when it came to strong personalities like Janice…perhaps even Blake? Besides, didn't *they*—whoever they were—say that true love never ran smooth? And, if so, she wondered, why was that anyway?

Chapter Fifteen
....

Blake wasn't surprised that Janice didn't join him for coffee in the morning. However, he was rather shocked when Louise huffed onto his porch, flopped down into one of his rockers, and exclaimed, "What did you do to my daughter?"

"What?"

"As you know, I was asleep when you picked up Sicily last night." She paused to catch her breath. "But Vivian informed me that Janice was not with you."

"That's because Janice left me in town…and I, uh, had to find another way home."

"Yes, well, when Janice did get home, she was a mess."

"A mess?"

Louise nodded, reaching into her shirt sleeve to extract a rumpled tissue, which she used to daub her damp brow. "*And* she was drunk."

"Janice was drunk?" Blake was trying to wrap his head around this. Vineyard Haven was a dry town. Janice must've driven to Oak Bluffs.

"Yes." Louise looked truly miffed. "I insist that you tell me what went on between you two last night."

Blake frowned. He wasn't used to being grilled by girlfriends' mothers. Not that he'd experienced too many girlfriends or their mothers. But this was just plain weird.

"What did you do to my daughter?" she demanded for the second time.

"Nothing," he answered.

"Nothing?" She firmly shook her head. "You two left together, came home separately, and then Janice, as I said, went to pieces. Something happened, Blake."

"Yes, something did happen," he admitted. "Did you ask Janice about it?"

"I didn't get the opportunity. She cried and carried on like an adolescent last night and then, just like that, fell asleep."

"Right." He wondered if she'd passed out.

"And she's still sleeping now. Poor thing!"

He carefully considered his words. "The only thing I can tell you is that Janice and I have mutually decided to part ways."

"Mutually?" She narrowed her faded blue eyes at him.

"Yes, mutually. After the silent auction event, I was very honest with Janice. I explained that I thought she and I were too different, and it would be best—"

"Of course you're different, Blake. But everyone knows that opposites attract."

Blake wanted to tell her he felt absolutely no attraction to her daughter but knew that sounded harsh. "Not always."

"What did Janice do to change your feelings?" Louise grew meeker. "I realize she's a different sort of girl. A bit strong-willed and, Lord knows, she's useless in the kitchen. But men these days don't care so much about that sort of thing. She's an intelligent woman, a good attorney, and has a brilliant political career ahead of her. All she needs is a good man by her side."

"I agree on all accounts, but—"

"If you agree, why did you break her heart?"

"I broke her heart?" He studied Louise closely. "How so?"

"I could see she was falling for you," Louise said earnestly. "I've known Janice her whole life, and I never saw her fall so quickly or so completely for a fellow."

"Really?"

"Would I jest with you about my own flesh and blood?"

"No, I doubt you would do that." Now Blake felt guilty. He'd had no idea that Janice had been that serious. She had an odd way of showing it. She'd started that argument last night and had been equally glad to call it quits.

"At first I wondered if it was simply the romantic atmosphere here in Martha's Vineyard. That's understandable—white sails in the sunset and moonlight and all that. But then I began to realize that Janice was genuinely attracted to you." Louise clutched her hands to her chest in a dramatic gesture. "I was so moved by it, Blake. I was already adopting you into my family. You and your precious little girl. You probably think I'm a foolish old woman, but I was already planning a wedding, in my head of course. I could just imagine Sicily as a junior bridesmaid in a dress of shell pink, Janice in creamy white satin, you in a dove-gray tuxedo, a small but elegant ceremony at Gay Head lighthouse—"

"Daddy?" Sicily came out onto the deck in her pajamas, rubbing her eyes sleepily.

"Good morning, Sunshine," he said eagerly, relieved for this distraction. "Did you sleep well?"

"Uh-huh. But we need to get over to The Gallery so I can paint the mural with Waverly today."

He stood now. "That's right." He gave Louise a sympathetic smile. "I guess we'll have to finish this conversation later."

"Well, I suppose…"

"Now, if you'll excuse me, I need to see that Sicily gets some breakfast before she heads off to her first day of work."

"Of course, but I—"

"Thank you for sharing your concerns with me."

"You will keep in mind what I told you?" she questioned him. "You'll carefully consider what I said, won't you?"

"Absolutely." He gave her a stiff smile as he reached for the screen door.

"And we'll talk more later?"

He nodded briskly. "Oh, I'm sure we will." Then he turned and hurried inside, instantly wishing he'd never cut that handy little trail between their two houses. Perhaps he should consider putting up a fence now. Or maybe even a stone wall to protect him from all the things that Louise might start slinging his way if he didn't do something to smooth this thing over with Janice.

"Was Louise mad about something?" Sicily asked as she took the pitcher of orange juice from the fridge.

"Mad?" He got out the egg carton and began breaking eggs into a bowl. So far he knew five things his picky daughter would eat for breakfast, only two which did not involve cold cereal. But thankfully, and perhaps due to Waverly's influence, since Sicily had quoted her new friend, Sicily now appeared more concerned about "eating healthy" than counting carbs and calories.

"Yeah." She sipped her juice. "She sounded mad. Was she?"

"I wouldn't use the word *mad*." He dumped the egg mixture into the hot pan, listening to the sizzle as he stirred. "Upset maybe."

"Because of Janice?"

"What makes you think that?" He poured himself another cup of coffee, watching the eggs bubbling.

"Cuz you came home without her. And why did you ride Waverly's bike anyway?"

"How did you know—"

"I saw it on the porch last night, Dad. I'm not blind."

He wondered how much to say as he dished out their scrambled eggs. Then, setting their plates down, he decided to take Waverly's advice about trusting his daughter. He knew she was right. Sicily was much more mature than her nine years belied. "Truth is, Janice and I got into a little fight last night."

Sicily frowned. "You broke up with her?"

"Would that bother you much?" Now he knew he had the upper hand here. Sicily didn't really like Janice. If anything, she should be elated about this new development.

"Yes, Dad, that *would* bother me." She stared at him like he wasn't too smart. And he felt like someone had just changed the rules on him.

"Why would you care?"

"Because Janice is like family, Dad. And I really, really like Louise and Vivian and Waverly. So if you and Janice are together, it's like we're part of their family. And that is a very good thing." She smiled brightly, as if it should be perfectly clear.

"I see, and I can understand that." More than he cared to say in fact. "But what if I wasn't dating Janice, but we could still be friends with Louise and Vivian and Waverly?"

"Oh, Dad." She sounded exasperated. "Don't you get it? It's okay if I don't like Janice that much. I still like the rest of her family. And it's not like I'd be the one marrying her anyway."

"Marrying her?"

Sicily nodded. "Well, you don't plan to just *live* with her, do you? Mom wouldn't like that, Dad."

"No." He shook his head. "I suppose she wouldn't." Never mind that Gia had lived with Gregory for nearly a year when Sicily was too young to understand such things. Not that he had any intention of living with Janice—or anyone else for that matter.

"So, it's fine with me if you make up with Janice." She smiled like that settled it. "And, really, she's okay sometimes. Besides, it gives you someone to hang with, you know, like while I'm working with Waverly."

"Kind of keeps me out of your hair?" he added.

She laughed. "Yeah. Maybe so."

Sicily seemed to have it figured out. In a nine-year-old sort of way she'd decided that he could have one of the cousins and she could have the other, and everyone would be happy.

He was still pondering these things as he carefully loaded Waverly's bike in the back of his SUV. He'd even taken time to wipe the bike down with a soft rag, making certain he returned it in as good of shape as possible.

"I was thinking I should leave my new bike at Waverly's," Sicily said as she got into the car.

"Why's that?"

"Then she and I can take rides together. Like we did yesterday. It was really fun, Dad."

"What if I want to take a ride with you?" he asked.

"Well, we could just go and pick up my bike."

"Right."

She had it planned. Although he knew he should be grateful that Sicily was finally interested in life beyond video games, he felt envious. Not only was he jealous that his own daughter preferred Waverly's company to his, it miffed him nearly as much that Waverly probably preferred Sicily to him. He was definitely odd man out.

Chapter Sixteen

·····················

Waverly woke up thinking about Blake. Perhaps she'd been dreaming about him. She wasn't totally sure. But she was sure of one thing—she was determined to get control over *this thing*. Despite his surprising late-night visit, which turned out to be motivated by a necessity for transportation, there was still the Janice factor to consider. No way did Waverly intend to cross that line with her cousin. It was one thing to squabble over toys as children, but when it came to men and romance, Waverly was just not going there.

No, if Waverly was to have any future with Blake, and that was extremely uncertain, she would wait until she was convinced the coast was completely clear. Perhaps even until Janice returned to the mainland coast. From what Waverly had heard, that wasn't going to happen until *after* the Fourth. Until then, Waverly would simply keep a low profile and focus on work. Work had been her escape for years now. Why should this be any different?

She went down to the arcade and unlocked the door at seven o'clock sharp. Several hours earlier than usual, but so that Zach could get in and set up. She'd already gone over the details with him, specifying which wall to begin with, and he'd promised an early start, although according to Rosie, there was such a thing as "island time" here. Waverly checked the gallon paint cans and the notes she'd placed on top of them. For now she'd gone with a buttery yellow basecoat. In a way it was neutral. After that, whatever happened when she and Sicily applied their touches from the pint-sized cans of a rainbow's selection worth of paint was anyone's guess. To be honest, Waverly didn't really care. Anything beyond drab beige would be a vast improvement in here.

Next she dashed down the street to the coffee shop, ordered a latte and an "Egg-Witch," then hurried back to the arcade to wait for Zach. Fortunately Zach's "island time" wasn't too far off, and by 7:30 he was applying the first coat of paint. Since he appeared to know what he was doing, she took the remainder of her latte and breakfast sandwich back to the coffee shop, where she made herself comfortable at an outdoor table and took her time perusing the latest issue of *The Martha's Vineyard Times.*

"Good morning."

She looked up to see Reggie Martin, a book in one hand and a coffee in the other, smiling down at her. "Hello." She motioned to a vacant chair across from her. "Care to join me?"

"Love to." He set down his book, pulled out the chair, and sat down. "Fine morning, isn't it?"

"Gorgeous." She nodded.

"I love this time of day." He looked down the relatively quiet street.

"So do I."

"It's as if the rest of the world is still in bed, leaving the best part of the morning to us."

She took in a deep, happy breath. "And the air feels fresher too."

"I thought you'd be hard at work with your painting project."

"Mostly I just needed to get up in time to let the painter in by seven, and make certain he was set up. My young assistant shouldn't be here until nine or so. Hopefully the first coat will be dry by then."

"I'll be interested to see the fruits of your labors."

She laughed. "Me too."

"I really enjoyed getting to know you better last night," he said quietly.

"Thank you." She smiled. "I had a lovely evening too. It was the first time I'd really gone out and done something special since I arrived here."

"You need to do that more often." He took a sip of coffee. "Otherwise you might as well be living on the mainland."

"I agree."

They sat there visiting pleasantly into second cups of coffee—long enough that Waverly lost track of the time. It wasn't until she heard a child's voice calling out her name that she realized it was already past nine. Down the street she saw Sicily, dressed in overalls, coming their way with her father not far behind.

"Uh-oh." Waverly checked her watch. "Guess it's later than I thought."

"Is that Blake from last night?" Reggie asked.

"Yes. Blake is Sicily's father."

"Oh?" He lifted an eyebrow. "Kind of a family affair then?"

She was uncertain how to respond because Sicily was already within earshot. "Hey, Sicily," she called out, "I was just about to—"

"I looked in your apartment," Blake began with a furrowed brow, "and you weren't there. Sicily spotted you out here and—"

"I'm sorry for being late." Waverly stood.

"I would've just dropped Sicily off," Blake said in a slightly apologetic tone, "but the painter was the only one there and I—"

"Yes, sorry about that. I should've been there." She forced a smile. "But I got distracted."

"My fault." Reggie stood now, and Waverly introduced him to Sicily.

"This is my young artist assistant," she explained. "Ready to go to work."

Sicily turned to her dad. "See, I'm okay, Daddy. You can go now."

Blake looked at a loss for words but continued standing there.

"Thanks for dropping her off." Waverly set a tip on the table.

"Oh, that reminds me," he said with a funny grin, "I dropped your bike off at the arcade. Thanks for letting me borrow it."

She laughed. "Anytime."

"Blake's been riding your bike?" Reggie looked clearly confused.

"Long story," she told him.

"Guess I'll have to hear it later." He smiled.

She nodded, then turned to Sicily. "All right, my friend, I think we've got some work to do."

"I'll pick you up around noon," Blake told his daughter.

"Or if you want to wait until later this afternoon," Waverly said tentatively, "maybe Sicily and I could take another picnic lunch over to the beach. If that's all right, and if she wants to, that is. I know I had fun there yesterday."

"Yes!" Sicily exclaimed. "Let's do that again. Maybe this time we can stay longer."

Waverly glanced at Blake. He looked unsure. "Unless you have other plans, of course. Do you mind?"

"Oh, no, that's fine." Now it appeared a lightbulb had gone on for him. "And if *you* don't mind, maybe I'll join you girls down there. I haven't really seen much of that beach yet. And it looks like it's going to be another nice day."

"Uh, all right…," Waverly said with uncertainty.

"You don't mind, Sicily?" He looked at his daughter.

"Whatever." She made an exasperated sigh. "But will you just leave so Waverly and I can get to work?"

"That's right." Waverly turned back toward the arcade. "Time to rock and roll, girlfriend." Then she grabbed Sicily's hand and they took off, leaving Blake and Reggie behind to sort it out.

It took some time and some adaptations and compromises, but eventually Waverly, who decided she needed to take the lead in this initial project so that Sicily could see how it worked, got the cartoon-like figures sketched onto the wall.

"That looks just like I imagined it would," Sicily exclaimed when Waverly came down from the stepladder.

"Great." Waverly wiped her painted fingers onto a rag, then handed Sicily the brush. "Now you can start adding the color, and I'll go check on some things with Zach." She paused to give Sicily a few painterly tips and told her to call out if she needed anything. But she could tell the girl was eager to add her touches and, frankly, Waverly was eager to let her.

Seeing that Zach was just finishing with the opposite wall, the one they would paint another mural on, she showed him how she wanted him to mask off and paint colored stripes onto the other two walls. "It'll add some life in here," she explained, "without having murals everywhere."

"That'll be fun," he said. "Better than just painting the whole walls yellow."

"When you're finished with that, probably not until tomorrow, I want you to help me move some of these machines around. If you don't mind?"

"Sounds good."

"And when you're finished with that, I have more work for you."

"Really?" He looked pleased.

She nodded. "Yes. You do a good job, Zach. I thought maybe I'd have you paint in the apartment upstairs. It can use it."

"Cool."

"Then, if my mom and aunt approve, I think the exterior of the building could use some help too."

"Yeah, I think a lot of people will agree with you on that."

"We should easily keep you busy up until the Fourth of July," she assured him.

"Sounds good to me."

It sounded good to her too. Because, in her mind, July Fourth was turning into a sort of milestone. If she could keep herself busy until then…well, she would have to wait and see what came next after that.

It was well past noon when Waverly announced it was quitting time. "But I'm not ready to quit," Sicily protested.

"Sorry," Waverly told her. "But there are child labor laws."

Sicily came down off the ladder and looked up. "That's pretty cool, huh?"

"I'll say." Waverly smiled up at it. "Lots better than I expected."

"I'm going to go wash up," Sicily said.

"And I already packed us a lunch." Waverly held up a brown bag. "As soon as you're ready, we'll hop on our bikes and go."

They wound up in about the same place as they'd picnicked yesterday. But they had barely unpacked their lunch when Blake came walking along, carrying his own picnic basket, which was a relief since Waverly had only packed enough for Sicily and her.

"Hello, hardworking ladies," he said cheerfully.

"You made us a picnic too?" Sicily asked.

"Just in case. I brought along a few things." He set down his basket, removed a large Mexican blanket, and spread it out over the sand. "How's that?"

Waverly held up her limp beach towel. "An improvement over this."

He nodded. "Good." Then he proceeded to remove items that looked like a rather festive sort of picnic.

"Deviled eggs?" Waverly exclaimed. "Did you make those yourself?"

"I most certainly did."

"Well, your picnic is putting my picnic to shame," she admitted as she reached for one.

"Daddy," Sicily said in an exasperated tone, "don't make Waverly feel bad."

Waverly laughed. "Don't worry. I don't feel that bad."

Soon they were seated on the blanket and, once again, Blake bowed his head and asked a blessing. When he finished, Sicily gave Waverly a concerned look. "Do you mind that he does that?"

Waverly smiled. "I like it. I think it's nice to thank God."

"Really?" Sicily still seemed somewhat skeptical.

Waverly nodded. "Absolutely. I'm always trying to remind myself to thank God. I think we are better people when we remember to be grateful to God. Even if things don't go exactly the way we like them to."

Blake looked intently at her now. "Really? You believe that?"

"For the most part. To be honest, I'm still working on it. Lots of times I start to complain and forget to be thankful."

"You're not alone there," he said. "But it does feel better to be happy about something than to be whining about it."

"Kind of like that goofy movie you made me watch?" Sicily said.

He looked slightly sheepish.

"What movie?" Waverly asked.

"*Pollyanna*." Sicily rolled her eyes.

"I LOVE that movie," Waverly exclaimed.

Sicily blinked. "Seriously?"

"Yes. I haven't seen it since I was a kid on TV or VHS or something. But I loved it then, and I know I would love it now. Do you have a copy?"

"Yeah." Sicily nodded eagerly. "Dad got it on DVD. At first I thought it was kind of lame. But I guess you're right. It's pretty good."

Blake exchanged looks with Waverly.

"Do you think I can borrow it sometime?" Waverly asked.

"Do you want to watch it together?" Sicily asked eagerly. "I think if I see it again, I might like it better."

"I'd love to watch it with you."

"Any chance I can watch it too?" Blake asked.

Waverly grinned. "Well, I guess if you can ride a girl's bike, you should be able to watch a girl's movie."

"Yeah, and maybe we can dress you like a girl too," Sicily teased.

"And put a bow in your hair," Waverly added.

"And paint your fingernails and—"

"That's enough." He held up his hands. "For sweet-looking girls, you two can get kind of mean."

"Sorry," Waverly told him.

"You just need to learn to take a hint, Dad." Sicily wrinkled up her nose. "Besides, if you want to hang with girls, maybe you and Janice should go do something and leave me and Waverly to—"

"Uh, speaking of Janice." Waverly pointed to where a dark-haired woman in a red swimsuit cover and beach bag was quickly coming their way.

"What's she doing—"

"Hey, Janice," Waverly called out. "Coming to join us?"

"As a matter of fact, I am." Janice stood over them for a moment with a puzzled look. "Although I only expected to find Blake and Sicily. What are you doing here, Waverly?"

Waverly forced a smile. "Actually, Sicily and I were having a picnic and—"

"And I crashed it." Blake stood up politely, making room on the blanket for Janice to join them.

"Well, Mom said you'd borrowed her picnic basket and that you were picking up Sicily. I assumed it was the two of you."

Now Waverly stood. "As a matter of fact, I'm going to have to cut it short anyway."

"But we were going to look for—"

"I totally forgot that I need to check with Rosie about something." Waverly slipped her feet back into her sandals. "So, if you'll excuse me." She pointed to Sicily. "And I will see you bright and early tomorrow, right?"

"Right." Sicily still looked disappointed. But as much as Waverly hated to disappoint the girl, she knew by Janice's expression that it was time to go.

"Enjoy," Waverly called out as she picked up her bike and wheeled it through the sand and into the parking lot, where she got on and took off without looking back. Maybe she was a wimp. Or maybe she just knew when to make a safe getaway. But, for Sicily's sake, Waverly didn't want to be the reason for an ugly scene on a public beach. Not that she'd expected Janice to throw an actual fit. But that look in her cousin's eyes had been like a blast from the past, and Waverly hadn't been willing to risk it.

Chapter Seventeen

....

Try as he might, Blake was having a hard time getting through to Janice. He knew this had to do with Louise. For some reason she'd gotten it into her head this morning that Blake still had feelings for her daughter. Naturally, she had conveyed these sentiments to Janice. Now Janice seemed more determined than ever to show Blake how much she cared for him.

"I'm so sorry for acting like that last night," she'd told him on Monday afternoon, while Sicily was cooling her jets by wading in the water. "I don't know what came over me. I guess I was surprised at how strong my feelings for you have gotten. Can you understand?"

For lack of any other response, he'd said he *did* understand. But what he didn't explain was that he understood from an entirely different perspective. Whereas Janice seemed willing to make a fool of herself for him, he was willing to do so for her cousin. Or sort of, since he didn't particularly think it would impress Waverly if he acted like a lovesick puppy.

Throughout the afternoon, Janice continued to lavish him with her attention, even insisting on giving him a shoulder rub when he complained that he was a little sore from riding an ill-fitting bike home from town last night. Finally, he couldn't take anymore, and he started to load up the picnic basket and things. "Sicily and I need to go," he announced abruptly.

"Where are you going?"

His eyes met Sicily's. She looked as curious as Janice. "I, uh, promised to buy her a—a new video game."

Sicily's eyes lit up like she was seeing right through this. "That's right," she told him. "We better go."

"I know of a good store over in Oak Bluffs," Janice offered.

"I promised her this would be a father-daughter thing." Now he shot Sicily a warning look.

She played along. "That's right. Just Dad and me, shopping for a new video game and getting ice cream too." She stood up and started to pick up the Mexican blanket. "We better get going before the store closes, Dad."

He gave an apologetic smile to Janice. "See you around."

She sighed as if he'd just crushed her. "Okay."

"Let's get a move on." He grabbed Sicily's hand and began jogging toward the car. "I know, I know," he said quietly to his daughter, "it's wrong to lie."

Sicily laughed. "Don't feel bad. Mom does it all the time."

He tossed the picnic gear into the back of the car, then hurried to the driver's seat so that Janice wouldn't catch up with them and throw a wrench in the works. "I can't comment on your mother," he said slightly breathlessly as he started the engine. "But I don't like to lie, Sicily. I really don't."

"Why?"

"Why?" He peered at her, then backed the car out.

"Yeah. Mom says that some lies make people feel better. So then it's okay."

"Does your mom want you to lie to her?"

"No."

"Do you want me to lie to you?"

"No."

"Well, I feel badly for lying to Janice. The reason I did that was to get away from her. She can be awfully persistent, you know."

"Why didn't you just tell her you wanted to get away from her then?"

"Good question." He thought about it. "I suppose I didn't want to hurt her feelings."

"See, Dad. Like Mom says, *some lies make people feel better.*"

"Maybe it makes them feel better temporarily, Sis. But eventually the lies will only make them feel worse. Can you understand that?"

Now there was a long silence. "I guess so."

"And they also make the person who told them feel worse," he continued.

"How?"

"Like right now." He turned into the traffic heading for Oak Bluffs. "I want to make good on my lie, so I'm forced to drive you to Oak Bluffs, which feels like punishment on a hot day like this, when I'd rather be relaxing on a beach or at home. And I'm forced to buy you a video game, which you know I abhor."

"And ice cream too."

"Yeah. Ice cream too. Although that's not so bad." He turned and smiled at her.

"You're not so bad either," she told him. "For a dad anyway."

They didn't get home until after five, and he'd barely pulled into the driveway when he noticed Janice's little red car heading past their house toward town. "I'm going to return the picnic basket," he called to Sicily.

She already had her new game up on the TV screen but nodded.

"I'll be back in a few minutes." He grabbed up the basket after emptying it, and jogged over to the neighbors' house. His reason for returning the basket so promptly was twofold. One, he wanted to avoid Janice, and two, he wanted a word with Louise.

"There you are," said Louise as he came up onto the porch. "Janice said you and Sicily were having a father-daughter afternoon. How nice."

"Yes." He placed the basket on the table by the door. "Thanks for loaning me this."

"Did you have a good picnic?"

"Yes. It was fine. Although I was pretty surprised when Janice showed up."

Louise peered over the top of her glasses.

"And she seemed to think I'd told you that there'd been a misunderstanding between us."

"A misunderstanding between you and me?"

"No. I mean between Janice and me. Although perhaps between you and me too." He cleared his throat. "Somehow Janice is under the impression that I wish to continue in a relationship with her. That last night was merely a small blip between us."

"Well, wasn't it?"

"No." He leaned against the porch railing. "It was more than that, Louise. The truth is, I'm not interested in Janice for anything more than a friend."

Louise waved her hand. "Oh, that's all right. I always say the best romances start with a good friendship. My late husband and—"

"No, that's not what I'm saying," he persisted. "I'm trying to tell you that Janice and I are worlds apart, and I don't see how that can change."

"Oh, you're worried about her career in Boston. But, don't you see, she can pop over here as much as she likes. Her job is the sort that can—"

"I'm not talking about her job. I'm trying to say—"

"Excuse me." Vivian stepped out onto the porch now. "I believe Blake is trying to politely say that he sees no future for Janice and him." She looked at Blake. "Is that correct?"

"Yes." He nodded eagerly, thankful for an interpreter.

"But that's only because they hit a rough patch last night," Louise told her sister.

"Sometimes a rough patch is another term for a dead end."

"Or perhaps it's only a bump in the road." Louise stood, fanning herself with her magazine. "Now if you'll excuse me, it's getting a bit too warm out here for my metabolism."

"I'm sorry." Blake moved out of her way. "I hope I didn't upset you."

She waved her hand at him. "No, no. I'll let you and Janice sort it out for yourselves. I should know better than to get in the middle of a romance at my age."

He winced at her words.

"Don't mind her," Vivian told him. "She often gets cranky in the heat of the day. Usually she goes and takes a nap."

"I didn't mean to put Louise in the middle of anything," he explained. "But Janice thought I'd given Louise some kind of green light."

"I did hear Louise encouraging Janice not to give up on you." She tipped her head to one side and smiled. "But to be fair, I don't think Janice needed too much encouragement. She's already pretty much smitten with you, Blake."

He let out a groan. "Well, I'll do my best to set her straight. What I was trying to tell Louise is the truth. I am not interested in a relationship with Janice. Besides as a friend." He lowered his voice. "She is not my type. Not at all."

Vivian nodded. "Then you need to make that clear to her. Crystal clear."

"You're right." He smiled, wishing he could confess to her that it was her own daughter who had captured his heart. Except that seemed quite premature at this stage. In due time...hopefully. First he needed to figure out a tidy way to clean up this mess with Janice. As he walked back down the path to his house, he wondered at how, in such a short amount of time, he'd managed to get emotionally involved with two women, cousins no less, after going for years without ever connecting to anyone. Maybe there was something in this fresh ocean air.

When he got home, Sicily was talking on the phone. He assumed she was talking to her mother, since that was the only person she ever spoke to on her phone, and that was surprisingly rare. So he simply nodded to her and went on into his room, where he intended to take a shower to wash off the beach sand from their picnic. He took his time and, when he finally emerged from his room, still wearing his bathrobe, he was met by a smiling Sicily.

"Get dressed, Dad," she told him.

"Dressed for what?"

"A surprise."

"A surprise?" Now as pleased as he was to see Sicily engaging with him, making some sort of mysterious plan that didn't involve video games, he was suspicious too.

"Yeah, Dad. Go get dressed. Now."

"How do I know how to dress?" he tried. "Unless you give me some sort of clue as to what I'm doing."

"Oh." She nodded. "Just put on pants and a shirt. Nothing too fancy."

"One more question."

She crossed her arms across her chest in exasperation. "Just one. And make it quick."

"Who were you talking to on the phone?"

She put one finger to her chin like Mini Me. "Okay. I guess I can answer that. It was Waverly."

"Waverly?"

"Yes, Dad. That's all I'm saying. Now go get dressed and hurry!"

"All right." He remembered again how Waverly had told him to trust his daughter. So he would. Besides, if she'd been talking to Waverly, how bad could it be? He hurried but picked his clothes carefully. A clean pale-blue oxford shirt and his favorite khaki pants. He combed his hair and even put on a light splash of cologne. He was just coming out when he heard Waverly's voice.

"So, are we all ready?" she asked.

"Yeah. Dad's just getting dressed," Sicily said.

"Here I am," he announced pleasantly as he entered the room. "What's up?"

"Don't *you* look nice?" someone else said.

He turned to see Janice standing by the door. "Wh—what?"

"Just on time too." Janice smiled as she held up her hand with a glittering wristwatch. "Let's go."

"Waverly is babysitting," Sicily announced.

"Not babysitting," Waverly corrected. "Just hanging with you and watching movies until Janice and your dad get back."

"And you guys are going on a mystery date," Sicily told him.

Blake felt sick. Literally sick.

"Come on," Janice urged him. "We better hurry before the boat leaves."

"Boat?"

"Oops." She held her hand over her lips. "Loose lips sink ships." Now she giggled, grabbed him by the hand, and quite literally dragged him out of the house.

* * * * *

A sunset dinner cruise aboard a fifty-foot sailboat through Nantucket Sound should be romantic. It should be delightful and memorable and amazing. But all Blake could do was count the minutes until this mystery date would end. He had attempted to gently put the brakes on the whole thing as Janice sped to the dock. But when he learned that the tickets, which she'd purchased online, were nonrefundable, and how she'd been looking forward to a sailboat trip forever, he didn't have the heart to ruin it for her. And there was no way he could break up with her on the boat. Not without a trustworthy life preserver in hand and a lifeboat nearby. Instead, he was coolly congenial to Janice and everyone as he silently hummed the words of "Fifty Ways to Leave Your Lover."

Fortunately, Janice made friends easily. Amongst the ten or so other couples aboard the cruise, she managed to find some individuals with business or political connections. So, all in all, or so he hoped, the evening wasn't a complete wash. But the drive home was silent. Blake had opted to drive, since Janice had been drinking, and he considered trying to gently let her down, but he was worried that in her slightly inebriated state, she might fly off the handle. And driving with an emotional woman, he knew from experience with his ex-wife, could prove dangerous. Therefore, he said nothing. But words like "slip out the back, Jack…make a little plan, Stan…" continued rumbling through his mind.

"Thank you for a very interesting evening," he said stiffly as he parked her car. He'd driven her back to her mother's house and was about to hand her the car keys but thought better of it.

"Yes, I suppose it was *interesting*," she said sarcastically. Then, as she got out of the car, he slipped the keys under the driver's seat. Hopefully she'd figure it out tomorrow.

"If you're not busy, I'd like to talk to you tomorrow, Janice."

She brightened. "Really?"

He nodded with a somber expression. "See you tomorrow then." Now he turned and hurried down the trail. He felt a mix of emotions. On one hand, he was extremely relieved to be home—and still in one piece. On the other hand, he was slightly enraged at whoever had set up the ridiculous mystery date, and he meant to get to the bottom of it.

He tiptoed up the steps to his porch, peering through the screen door to see that Sicily and Waverly were in the kitchen, working on something together. It was one of those kinds of scenes, so sweet and homespun and quaint, that he wished he had a camera handy. Instead, he decided to simply linger awhile as he filmed it in his head. Of course, he felt somewhat guilty for overhearing the soundtrack of this particular movie. But nothing and no one was going to budge him now.

"My mom doesn't know how to make brownies," Sicily was saying.

"Oh, she probably does. All you do is read the directions on the box. In fact, you could probably do it yourself, Sicily. You know how to read and mix things. You did most of it yourself tonight."

"Yeah, but you put in applesauce instead of oil," Sicily pointed out.

"To make the brownies healthier." Waverly took the bowl over to the sink. "I think healthy is always better when it's yummy, don't you?"

"Uh-huh." Sicily was licking a wooden spoon like it was a lollypop. "How come you don't have kids of your own, Waverly?"

Waverly paused from rinsing the bowl. Turning off the water, she just stood there, like she was trying to think of something.

"I'm sorry," Sicily said quickly. "I shouldn't be so nosey, huh?"

"No, it's fine. But remember I told you how my husband died about four years ago? So unexpected. And, well, we'd been planning on having kids but never had the chance."

Now Sicily dropped the wooden spoon in the sink and wrapped her arms around Waverly's waist from behind. "I'm sorry."

"It's all right, sweetie." Waverly turned around, and Blake thought he saw tears in her eyes as she hugged his daughter back. "Knowing someone like you is about as good as having my own kid."

Blake couldn't believe he was actually tearing up right now. But he was. And no way did he want Waverly or Sicily to see him like this. How would he begin to explain himself? So he soundlessly backed away from the screen door, crept down the porch steps and away from the house, and sat on an old log bench on the edge of the beach.

As he gazed out toward the Sound, which shimmered in the light of a half moon, he wasn't even sure why their simple yet heart-felt conversation had cut him to the core like that. But it had. Maybe he was overreacting due to the fact he'd been about to go in there and let them have it for aiding and abetting in tonight's *misery* date. But the weird thing was that he no longer felt angry at them. Mostly he felt as if his eyes had just been opened. Oh, he'd already suspected that Waverly was the real deal. He'd been hoping to get better acquainted with her, but he'd been trying to straighten this thing out with Janice first. More than ever he was determined to cut Janice loose. Then he planned to do whatever it took to win over her cousin.

But first he planned to pray about it. He'd had enough of trying to do things his own way. Part of moving his life all the way across the country had been to help him on his new mission of doing things God's way. And he wasn't about to forget that now!

Chapter Eighteen

....

"Dad's out there," Sicily said as Waverly removed the brownies from the oven.

"Out where?"

Sicily pointed out the dining room window. "Out on the bench by the beach."

"Oh, is Janice with him?" Waverly set the brownies on the stovetop, then went into the dimly lit dining room. She placed a hand on Sicily's shoulder, ready to move her from the window in order to give the couple their privacy.

"No, Dad's alone. And he looks sad."

Now Waverly leaned forward and peered outside. It was like Sicily had said: there sat Blake, hunched over with his head in his hands—looking as if he'd truly lost his best friend. "Oh."

"I wonder what's wrong."

Waverly glanced at the clock. "Well, it's getting late, and Janice was supposed to take me home. How about if you go out and talk to your dad, and I'll run over and see if Janice can run me back into town?"

Sicily nodded, still staring out the window with a concerned expression.

"Thanks for the fun evening," Waverly told her, "and for sharing your *Pollyanna* movie. I still love it."

"Me too."

"And maybe right now your dad needs you to be his little Pollyanna," Waverly said as she got her bag, "and to give him a big hug too. You think?"

"Yeah, I think you're right."

Waverly leaned over and kissed the top of Sicily's head. "You are a pure delight." Then she went out through the laundry-room back door, so she wouldn't disturb Blake and Sicily, cutting around the front of the house, then down the path to her aunt and mother's house. She had no idea what was troubling Blake, but she suspected it had to do with Janice. That in itself was a mystery. Talk about an on-again, off-again relationship. Waverly didn't even want to figure it out.

She'd been completely taken aback when Sicily had called this afternoon to invite Waverly to come stay with her (and watch *Pollyanna*) so that her dad could go on a sailboat trip with Janice. Janice had explained it in a bit more detail when she picked Waverly up. "The whole thing is going to be a surprise for Blake," she'd bubbled. "He said that he wanted to do a trip like this, and I found this incredible deal online today. Really, the timing couldn't be better. When I told Sicily about it, she came up with the idea to have you come babysit."

Naturally, Waverly hadn't questioned any of this. She'd promised to come visit (not babysit), and that had been all she planned to do. Still, she had wondered. Perhaps, if truth be told, she'd been a little disappointed. Maybe a lot disappointed. But what could she do?

To her surprise, most of the lights in the house were off, but she saw Janice's car in the driveway, so she knew she was here. She went onto the porch and peered inside. Not seeing anyone about, she decided to try the door and, since it was unlocked, silently let herself in. "Hello?" she called quietly. "Janice?"

"Waverly!" It was her aunt, emerging from the bathroom. She had on her robe and, judging by her odd-shaped mouth, had already taken out her false teeth. "What are you doing here at thith hour of the night?" she lisped.

"Janice was going to give me a ride home."

Aunt Lou shook her head. "Not tonight, sheeth not. She came home inebriated *again*. You know, for a dry town, there thertainly theems to be a lot of drinking going on."

Waverly suppressed the urge to burst into laughter, then remembered her predicament. "But I need to get back into town."

"Take Janice'th car." Aunt Lou pointed to a large basket on a table by the front door. "There'th key-th."

"You're certain that's all right?"

Aunt Lou waved her hand in a disgusted sort of way. "I'm going to bed."

"Thanks." Waverly looked through the basket until she found a set of car keys with a rhinestone-encrusted *J* dangling from the key ring. That had to be it. Feeling a little like a crook, but excited at the prospect of driving her cousin's hot little sports car, she quietly went back outside. Of course, once she was inside the car, she wondered at the sensibility of this. Oh, she knew how to drive and even had a license, but it had been years, literally years, since she'd been behind the wheel. Still, she assured herself as she turned the key in the ignition, it had to be like riding a bike. And she'd certainly mastered that easily.

She studied the fancy panel and controls as well as the shifting stick, which she thought wasn't an actual stick shift, although she had learned to drive one of those once in Mexico. She fastened her seat belt, put the car in drive, gently touched the accelerator with her toe, then nearly jumped out of her skin when the car shot forward in the circular drive, shooting gravel from the tires. "Whoa, girl," she said as she tried the brakes. "Remember, slow and easy wins the race."

Feeling a bit like a grandma, she slowly, very slowly began to drive toward town. Thankfully the traffic was fairly light now and, about a mile from town, she thought she could get used to a sweet little car like this. Not that she ever expected her cousin to let her borrow it again. In fact, she didn't care to think of how Janice would react once she found out about tonight.

Very carefully she turned the car into the tight parking lot behind The Gallery, easing it into the one and only parking spot back there. Feeling satisfied that she'd accomplished her mission, and feeling surprisingly sleepy, she went up to her apartment and began getting ready for bed.

Chapter Nineteen

....

While sitting outside in the moonlight, contemplating his life and God and gazing out over the water, Blake was struck literally speechless when his daughter came up from behind, quietly wrapped her arms around him, and whispered, "I love you, Daddy."

He couldn't believe it. Almost afraid to move or breathe, and definitely hating to ruin or end this amazing moment, he simply sat there, silent as a stone. Finally he reached up and gently patted her small hands, which continued to rest on his chest. His little girl was back. The sweet, happy child he remembered had been returned to him. Or so he hoped. Now he wished for time to stand still...or to slow down some. Because, more than anything, he wanted to savor this moment.

"I love you too," he told her in a slightly choked voice. "More than anyone in this world, Sicily, I love you. I hope you always know that."

"More than *anyone*?" she asked, as if not fully convinced.

"Yes," he said eagerly. "Absolutely."

"Even more than Janice?"

"Definitely more than Janice. Way more than Janice. A million zillion times more than Janice."

"Oh." Now her hands slipped away, and he feared he had lost this moment after all. "So did something go wrong with Janice?" she asked in a concerned tone. "Did you guys have another fight? Is that why you're so sad?"

He turned around to face her now. "Sad?"

"Yeah." Her big eyes grew larger in the moonlight. "Waverly and I thought you looked really sad tonight, sitting out here all by yourself."

He considered this. "No, Sicily, I'm not sad. The truth is, I was just thinking…and praying too."

She blinked. "Praying?"

"Yeah." He tried to decide how much to say. "It probably sounds corny, but I was asking God to help me figure out my life."

She giggled. "Did God tell you what to do?"

He chuckled too. "Not exactly, but I think half of the solution lies in the asking."

"Huh?"

"I guess I'm trying to say that when we take time to be with God, when we remember to ask Him to guide us, well, it's like we're finally in a place where we're ready to listen. It's like we're trying to tune in to Him. Because, if you think about it, why would you ask for something if you weren't willing to listen? Does that make sense?"

"Sort of." She had a thoughtful look now. "Is it like when you want to talk to me, and you keep saying all this stuff I'm not interested in, stuff that's pretty boring? And then finally you say something that gets my attention and makes me want to listen? Kind of like that?"

He nodded. "Yeah, I think it's similar to that. Like, what's the point of having a conversation with someone who isn't even listening to you? Why not save your breath? Right?"

"Right." She smiled. "And you should remember that next time you want to talk to me."

He laughed. "I'll try to remember that. But don't forget, I'm not God. I'm just a regular dude who needs some help being a dad sometimes—to be honest, most of the time."

"Yeah, but at least you're getting better at it."

"Really? Am I?" He could hardly believe his ears.

"But don't worry, you still have a long ways to go."

"Oh, good, I didn't want to be accused of being too perfect."

"I was worried I was the one who made you sad," she said quietly. "I know I haven't been very nice to you lately. I'm sorry."

"I understand, Sicily. It was probably selfish of me to drag you out here to Martha's Vineyard."

"But I like it now."

"I'm glad to hear that."

"And I'm glad you're not sad." She laughed. "It's like we're playing the glad game, huh?"

"It is." He stood now and, taking her hand in his, began walking her back toward the house. "And I'm glad not to be sad too. In fact, I was feeling pretty happy this evening."

"What about?"

He didn't want to say too much yet. So much of this felt new to him. But he did want to be honest with her. "I was happy knowing that you're my daughter, Sicily, and that you haven't given up on me yet. And I was also happy to know that you've made a good friend in Waverly." They were in the house now, and it smelled delicious. "Speaking of Waverly," he continued, "where is she? We need to give her a ride home before it gets too late." He looked around expectantly.

"No, that's okay, Dad. We don't have to give her a ride."

He was puzzled. "Huh?"

"Janice will take her home."

"Janice?" He studied Sicily closely.

"Yeah. Waverly went next door to get a ride with her."

He slapped his forehead now. "Oh, no!"

"Oh, no, what?" she demanded.

"How long ago did Waverly leave?" he asked.

"I...uh...I don't know. Before I went—"

"Come on, Sis." He grabbed the flashlight by the door. "Let's go stop her."

"Stop who from what?" Sicily ran to catch up with him.

"Stop Waverly from letting Janice drive her anywhere."

"Why, Dad?" She was right on his heels as they both ran fast, with the flashlight beam bobbing up and down on the trail in front of them.

He stopped and turned toward her. "Because Janice is drunk."

"Oh, no!" Now Sicily took off running, passing him and racing toward the house.

But when he saw the driveway, he knew they were too late. Janice's car was already gone.

"Maybe Waverly's not with Janice," Sicily said breathlessly. "Maybe Janice drove somewhere by herself, and Waverly is still—"

"You could be right." Now Blake approached the porch.

"Hello?" called a woman's voice.

"Vivian!" Sicily exclaimed as she ran up the steps. "Is Waverly with you?"

"No." Vivian shook her head.

"Sorry to disturb you," Blake said.

"I'm not disturbed." She held up a mug. "Just having some herbal tea to help me sleep better."

"So I assume Janice did drive Waverly home then?"

Vivian shrugged. "Janice's car isn't here. Was that the plan?"

Sicily let out a gasp. "We have to go save her, Dad!"

"Save who?" Vivian set down her mug with a clunk. "From what?"

"Janice is drunk," Sicily told her. "And she's driving Waverly home."

"Is that true?" Vivian stood with a creased brow.

"I'm afraid so." Blake turned. "I'd meant to drive Waverly myself. Anyway, I'll run and get my car and try to catch—"

"No." Vivian stopped him. "We'll drive the car from here. It'll be quicker." She was already heading in the house now.

"I think you should stay here with Louise," Blake told Sicily.

She frowned. "Why?"

"Because we might need to have some adult conversations," he explained. "I know I'll want to give Janice a piece of my mind, and it will be easier if no one else is around to hear."

She nodded reluctantly. "Okay."

"Ready to go?" Vivian held out her car keys.

He nodded. "If you don't mind, I'll let Sicily stay here with Louise."

"That's fine. But Lou already went to bed." She turned to Sicily now. "Just wake her if you need something. And lock the door when we go."

"I will. Just hurry and make sure Waverly is okay," Sicily said.

Vivian handed Blake the keys, insisting he should drive, and he didn't argue. "Do you mind if I go a little fast?" he asked as he started the car. "I haven't been drinking."

"Go as fast as you like."

"I'll be careful." He didn't mention the spun-out tracks of tires in the driveway, because he didn't want to worry her too much.

"I did hear Janice come home earlier," Vivian said as he drove. "She sounded nearly as bad as the other night. But I must've been in the shower when Waverly came by. I didn't even see her. And Louise had already gone to bed by then."

"Well, Janice had no business driving Waverly in that condition."

"Perhaps she let Waverly drive."

He thought about that. "But then Waverly would've known she was drunk. And how could Waverly allow Janice to drive back home in that condition?"

"Good point." Vivian held onto the dash as he went a bit fast around a curve.

He slowed down some. "And now Janice won't be driving herself home tonight. We'll see to that."

"Good thing I came along."

"Yes. Thanks."

"You know, I was rather surprised that you and Janice went out again tonight," she said quietly.

"So was I." Now he explained the mystery date and how he felt tricked by all three women.

Vivian laughed. "Oh, dear. What a night you've had."

"Can I be honest with you, Vivian?"

"I would hope so."

"And can I trust you with a secret?"

"Certainly. Ask any close friends, and you'll hear that I am quite trustworthy."

"Well, tonight, even more than before, I realized how extremely interested I am in your daughter."

"What happened tonight?"

So he filled her in on seeing Waverly and Sicily together and how it had deeply touched him. "It's like something in me just clicked. Almost audibly. And I thought to myself, that's the girl for me."

She simply nodded, but there was a smile in her eyes.

"But I realize I need to clear this mess up with Janice—once and for all, and hopefully tonight. Then I won't let Janice or anyone else trick me again. Looking back, I can see how manipulative Janice has been."

"She's always been a girl to go after what she wants."

"Well, I plan to make it totally clear that she can't have me." His fingers tightened on the wheel. "Frankly, I can't even see why she's been so determined. Janice is an attractive and intelligent woman. I can't imagine she has trouble finding men."

Vivian laughed. "No, she's had numerous boyfriends. But for some reason she seemed to be set on you. Maybe it's merely a case of wanting what you can't have. Also, I've heard her speaking to her mother about how you have all these celebrity friends. Janice has always been into that sort of thing."

"Celebrity friends?" He grimaced. "It's true I've worked with some big names, but it's not like we socialize together much. And I told her that."

"Apparently she sees it a little differently."

"So I've noticed. But back to my secret confession, Vivian. Once I've completely cut Janice loose, hopefully tonight, I'm curious as to what you think my chances would be—I mean, with Waverly. Or did I already ruin any hopes, due to my reluctant involvement with Janice?"

Vivian smiled. "I'd like to think my daughter is not that small-minded."

"No, I didn't think she was."

"Unfortunately, I haven't been able to spend much time with Waverly yet." She sighed. "She's been so busy renovating The Gallery. I had no idea she would jump in like that, especially after her initial disappointment."

"She's pretty enthused about giving the place a facelift," he agreed. "She's certainly gotten Sicily on her bandwagon. Not that I'm complaining…"

"Okay, now that you shared a secret with me, Blake, may I share one with you?"

"Absolutely."

She paused for a long moment, and he got worried she might change her mind. After all, town was only a couple of minutes away. But at last she said, "Louise is the only one who knows this so far. I do plan to tell Waverly, but—well, the timing hasn't been quite right."

"Uh-huh?" He waited.

"I'm in the final stages of cancer, Blake. I don't care to go into the medical details. Suffice it to say that I have opted for no more treatments. I would rather live out my final days on my own terms, and not under the influence of chemo or radiation or endless doctor's appointments, none of which have worked anyway. I came to this conclusion while spending time in Nepal. I don't want anyone, most of all Waverly, to argue with me about it."

He nodded somberly. "I can respect that. But I am sorry to hear—"

"So, you see, I had multiple reasons for wanting Waverly to move to Martha's Vineyard."

"I can understand that." They were just coming into town now. He was extremely relieved that they hadn't spotted any smashed-up red convertibles or emergency vehicles along the way. At the same time he was saddened by Vivian's news. "Do you know how long you have?" he asked quietly.

"No, they never really know those things for certain. The last doctor said it could be weeks…months…perhaps even a year."

"How long ago was that?"

"A couple of months now."

"And you still haven't told Waverly?" He turned onto Main Street.

"First, I wanted to get my affairs in order. Then, as you know, I did what I could to get her to come out here."

He pointed to the arcade as he turned down the alley that ran alongside it. "So I've heard, but you didn't actually tell her this place was an art gallery, did you?"

She smiled weakly. "No, I honestly did not do that. Not consciously anyway. I call it a gift of fate. Or perhaps God's hand was in it. Because if she'd known what it really was, she never would've come."

"Yes, she mentioned that."

"Janice's car!" Vivian pointed to the red convertible. "There it is."

Relief washed over him. "So, at least we know Waverly made it safely home."

"Now you can drive my wayward niece home too." She shook her head. "Good luck with that."

He put the car in park, then reached over, placing his hand on Vivian's shoulder. "It means a lot that you told me what you did tonight, Vivian. I promise your secret is safe with me, but I do hope you'll tell Waverly *soon*."

"In due time. First, I want to just be with her, get to know her again—without all the focus being on…well, you know."

"I guess that makes sense." He looked curiously at her now. "And you're okay to drive back by yourself?"

"Yes, yes," she snapped at him. "I'm perfectly safe behind the wheel, thank you very much! Now, please, don't you start acting like I'm a sorry old invalid. Do you understand me, Blake Erickson?"

"Absolutely." He nodded.

They both got out of the car, and despite her short lecture, he waited for her to get into the driver's seat, then closed her door. He was only being a gentleman. Then, feeling slightly protective of her, he watched from beneath the shadows of the stairs as she maneuvered the car out of the tight alley, back onto the street, and on her way.

Bracing himself for whatever came next, he went up the stairs. He wondered if Waverly might've figured out Janice's condition and talked her into staying the night. Perhaps that would be for the best. Except that, knowing Janice, she could become fairly irrational under the influence. Because of that, he wanted to make certain all was well. And, he realized, he'd need her keys to drive her car home. She obviously must've found where he'd hidden them. Really, he could've been a bit more creative.

Midway up the stairs, he felt them shaking and was reminded how these steps needed some serious structural attention. Then he was nearly to the top step when he heard a loud cracking below him. Suddenly the whole works swayed dangerously beneath him—almost like an earthquake. Fearing he was about to go down with the entire staircase, he made a flying leap to the top deck where he grabbed onto the doorknob in fear that the whole structure was about to tumble.

Just then there was a loud crash—it sounded like an explosion—and a light went on. Standing before him, dressed in a tank top and shorts, with a toothbrush hanging from her lips, Waverly stared out the glass door with a horrified expression.

"What on earth is going on?" she asked as she flung open the door.

"The stairs!" He pointed down to where the stairs were now missing. "Let me in before the whole deck gives way."

She grabbed him by the arm and jerked him into the room with surprising strength.

"Thank you," he gasped.

"What happened" she demanded, "to make the stairs fall?"

"Well, you knew they were in bad shape."

"Yes, yes. But what are you doing here, knocking down my stairs, at this hour in the first place?"

"I was—uh, just coming up to see that everything was okay—"

"Of course everything's okay. Why wouldn't it be okay?" With a drip of white toothpaste on the side of her mouth, she shook her toothbrush at him. "Just for the record, Blake Erickson, this is a pretty lame way to get yourself invited into a girl's apartment late at night."

At that instant she looked down at herself, as if she'd just realized her state of dress, which he had to admit was rather attractive, then turned to make a dash to the bathroom. After a couple of minutes, she emerged with a white terry robe tied securely around her waist and a foamless mouth.

"Seriously, Blake, what is going on with you?" she asked in a slightly gentler tone.

He glanced around the studio. "Is Janice here?"

"*Janice?*" Waverly shook her head like she couldn't believe him. "You came all the way here, knocked down my stairs, to see Janice, who lives right next door to you? Have you utterly lost your mind?"

"Then she didn't drive you home?"

"No, of course not. She was drunk. As if you didn't know." She frowned at him.

"Yes, you're right. I did know."

"So, you knew she was drunk, yet you thought it was okay for her to drive me home—"

"No, no. That's just the point."

"What *is* the point?" She pushed an auburn curl away from her face.

"The point is, I was worried that Janice had driven you here, and that she was drunk, and something might've happened to, uh, both of you."

"Oh." Her expression softened. "I guess I can understand that. Thank you."

He was disappointed now. He'd already prepared his final farewell speech for Janice, and now it would have to wait until tomorrow. "So she really isn't here?"

"I already told you Janice is *not* here, Blake. So sorry to disappoint you. Maybe if you go home, you'll find her waiting on your front porch."

"No, no, that's not it. It's not like that at all, Waverly." He ran his fingers through his hair and moaned. "You don't understand."

"Look, Blake, I'm sorry if your date wasn't so great. Sicily and I saw you on the beach, and you looked a little sad."

"I'm not sad," he said for the second time tonight.

"Oh?" She blinked. "Okay, then. You're not sad. And Janice is not here. I suggest that perhaps it's time for you to go home."

"Yes." He nodded. "But I, uh, I need the keys to Janice's car, so I can get home…unless you'd like to loan me your bike again." He smiled weakly.

She smiled back. "No, no, I think I'll keep my bike right here. And I'm sure that your girlfriend will be most pleased to have you return her car. Although I did enjoy driving—"

"She is NOT my girlfriend!"

Waverly jumped. "You don't need to shout."

"I think maybe I do." He was starting to pace now, rubbing his beard, and about to begin rambling. This was something he only did when he felt backed into a corner, and normally only when he was alone. "It's like no one is listening to me, Waverly. Certainly not Janice. I think that woman is blind, deaf, and plain dumb. And Louise? She doesn't listen either. Louise has it all figured out; she's already planning weddings."

"Weddings?"

He turned and shook his head. "No. Definitely no. *No weddings!*"

"Fine." She held up her hands like she was slightly afraid of him. "I'll get the keys."

"Even my own daughter won't listen to me," he continued loudly. "I told her I was finished with Janice, and what does she do? She goes out and helps to arrange tonight's stupid misery date."

"Did you say *misery* date?" Her eyes twinkled as she returned with the keys.

"Yes. It was perfectly *miserable.* I was trapped and trying to figure a way out of it, and the next thing I knew I was on a sailboat. I nearly broke up with your stubborn cousin right there on the boat, but then I realized she'd probably tie the anchor around my neck and feed me to the fishes."

Waverly laughed now. "Yes, probably so. And could you blame her? The way you've been leading her on?"

"I have NOT been leading her on."

"You went out with her tonight, didn't you?"

"I was shanghaied by her tonight. I was shanghaied by the three of you, for that matter. Sicily, Janice, and you—you females all ganged up on me. It wouldn't surprise me if Louise was involved too. In fact, I think the only one of you five women that I can fully trust is your mother."

"My mother?" She narrowed her eyes.

Now he knew he had to be careful. "Yes. Vivian, bless her heart, gave me a ride to town tonight so I could rescue her daughter."

She put her hands on her hips now. "Is that so? Well, you both should know that her daughter does *not* need rescuing."

"Says *who*?" He stepped closer to her now, glaring straight into her eyes like he meant to challenge her to a duel.

"Says *me*." She leaned closer too, staring defiantly.

He didn't even know what came over him (although he would

think of plenty of excuses later), or maybe he was simply confusing himself with Rhett Butler, but the next thing he knew he grabbed Waverly and kissed her. Solidly kissed her right on the lips. Even more surprising was that she kissed him back. Minty, sweet, and perfectly delightful.

Now they both stood there, staring at each other and saying nothing. In shock.

"What was that?" she demanded.

"I'm so sorry," he said abruptly. "I honestly don't know what came over me. I don't usually act like this. It's just been a very bizarre evening."

"I'll say." She stepped back and, holding the car keys at arm's length, pointed to the door. "I think you should go now."

He gingerly took the keys, apologized again, then headed to the same door he'd blasted through earlier. It wasn't until he was all the way outside on the deck that he remembered the stairs were gone. Concerned over the stability of the remaining deck, he held onto the railing and peered down.

"You're still here," Waverly announced as she opened the door. "Oh, yeah, the stairs. I totally forgot. Come back in, Blake. I'll let you out through The Gallery."

He turned and stared at her.

"What's wrong with you?" She peered curiously at him. "Honestly, you look like you just saw a ghost."

"I *did* see a ghost."

"Seriously?" She started to come out now.

"No!" He held up his hands to stop her. "Stop right there. It's very dangerous out here. The whole thing could go any minute."

He hurried to the door, pushing her back into the apartment, then closed the door and locked it.

With hands on hips, she stood peering out the window now, as if she expected to see a real ghost. "But, really, what did you see?"

"I saw a ghost...the ghost of your cousin's car," he said in a serious tone.

"Huh?" She frowned at him. "What?"

"The fallen stairs—they fell on Janice's BMW."

"No way!"

"It's true. The whole structure fell smack on top of her car. Crushed it."

Waverly's eyes got incredibly big. "Seriously? Crushed it as in totaled?"

"I'm no expert, but that's my guess."

"Oh no." Her hands flew to her mouth. "What do we do?"

He shook his head. "Nothing for now. But...uh...can I use your bike?"

Chapter Twenty

It wasn't until Waverly was on her way to get coffee that she remembered about Janice's car. But even as she replayed last night's strange visit and conversation, she felt like it had to be a dream. Blake looking for Janice, the stairs falling, that kiss—it seemed surreal in the morning sunshine. So, just to be certain, she went around back, and there, even worse than she'd envisioned it would look by the light of day, was a dusty heap of wooden rubble piled over the crumpled remains of a little red car. So sad. Waverly shook her head and turned away.

Walking to the coffee shop, she wondered how she would break the news to Janice. Or maybe Blake had already done so. Whatever the case, she was in no hurry to experience her cousin's reaction. As she sat down outside with a latte and a blueberry muffin, Waverly recalled the summer when she was about Sicily's age and spending a couple of weeks at Aunt Lou's while her mom went on a buying trip somewhere in Asia. As a joke, Waverly had tattooed Janice's favorite Barbie doll with a peace sign right on Barbie's well-endowed chest area. Unfortunately, what Waverly assumed were washable markers turned out to be permanent, and Janice had thrown a fit that lasted for days. Even when Waverly bought Janice a new Barbie, the complaints continued because the new Barbie was not "exactly the same."

223

"You look like you're deep in thought."

She glanced up to see Reggie standing with a cup of coffee and small bag. "Feel free to join me, although my company might be less than sunshiny today."

"Something wrong?" He pulled out a chair and sat down. And she spilled out last night's story, leaving out certain details.

"You're kidding!"

"I wish I were. This morning I actually thought I'd dreamt the whole thing, but I went to look—and it was no dream. Now it feels like a nightmare."

"Does Janice know yet?"

She shrugged. "I haven't told her. Blake may have, although I'm certain she would've called me by now." She glanced at her watch. "But it's early, and I suspect she'll have a hangover."

"Maybe you can convince Janice that she crashed the car while driving drunk. Might teach her to be more careful."

She gave him a rueful smile. "Tempting, but I think not."

"Well, hopefully she'll take it easy on you. After all, you're cousins, right?"

She rolled her eyes. "Blood might be thicker than water, but if Janice has her way, she might be spilling some of mine before the day is over."

"It's not fair to blame you. Don't your mothers own The Gallery? Why not blame them for the faulty stairs?"

"I wonder if they have insurance." Waverly was trying to remember what she'd seen while going over the books for the arcade. Surely there'd been insurance.

"I'd think Janice's car would be covered. Wasn't it practically new?"

"Ugh. Don't remind me. And it was such a sweet little car too. I really enjoyed driving it last night."

"Maybe we should change the subject," he suggested. "I'm glad I found you here. I was hoping to run into you this morning." He smiled at her fondly.

"Really?" She tried to look interested, but seeing his expression reminded her of Blake...and last night. All she could think about was the way Blake had kissed her so impulsively—and how she'd returned the unexpected kiss. What had that meant? And why had she reacted like such a prim little old lady? And why had he apologized?

But Reggie was talking now, telling her about his friend who was giving a big party and how much fun it always was...and would she be interested in going?

"Who is it?" she asked, bringing herself back to the present.

"Belinda Vale."

She blinked. "The actress?"

He nodded.

"I love her films!"

"And you should see Belinda's guest list. Not just Hollywood types either. She has a lot of connections in the art world as well."

"Really?"

"Yes. Her father is Vince Vale of Boston—"

"The *artist* Vince Vale? That's her father?"

Now he listed off some more impressive names. "Want to go with me?"

"Well, of course. I mean, I don't know. When is it? And where is it? And are you sure she'd be okay if I came?"

He laughed. "Of course she's okay with it. Belinda and I go way back, and she loves it when I bring friends. The party is always on the Friday night before the Fourth. So it's this week. Belinda calls it Pre-Fourth Friday. She even has fireworks set off out over the water behind her mansion. Anyway, it's always a wonderful—"

He stopped talking now. With a serious expression he looked beyond Waverly, tipping his head. "Don't look now, but your cousin Janice this way comes," he said quietly.

"Oh, no."

"I could be wrong, but she looks rather angry."

Waverly didn't know what to do, so she did nothing. And she continued to do nothing as Janice began ranting and raving at her, saying crazy things like Waverly had stolen her car, then intentionally wrecked it.

"I didn't steal it," Waverly said. "Your mom told me to—"

"It is NOT my mom's car. Therefore you stole it, Waverly Brennen, and then you totaled it. I am holding you totally 100 percent responsible for—"

"Excuse me," Reggie attempted to interrupt. "Waverly didn't total your car, Janice, it was the result—"

"If Waverly hadn't *taken* my car, it would not be totaled now. Therefore Waverly is responsible."

"Well, certainly the building has insurance for things like this." Waverly looked at Reggie for help. "Don't you think?"

"Oh, I'm sure of it." He pointed to Janice. "And your auto insurance will cover the rest of—"

"No!" Janice held up her hand to stop him midsentence. "Waverly is 100 percent liable for this. And she will see that I'm recompensed for the full cash value—and I don't mean the depreciated value either. I mean the price of the BMW when I custom-ordered it from the BMW dealership over a year ago. Not only that, but I expect Waverly to cover the cost of an equal-caliber rental car until another identical BMW is delivered to my doorstep, spotlessly shining, with a big box of Lady Godiva chocolates and a heartfelt apology sitting on the fine leather seats. Furthermore—"

"You sound like you should hire an attorney," Reggie wryly told Janice, and Waverly winced.

"I AM an attorney." Janice tossed him a withering look.

Reggie glanced at Waverly with sympathy.

"Look, Janice, I'm really, really sorry about what happened to your car. And I hope you can find it in your heart to forgive—"

"You can talk to me about forgiveness after the replacement car is in my driveway with a big box of—"

"Yes, yes. I get it," Waverly told her. "I just wish you could cool off a little, Janice. It's probably not good for your health to be so angry."

Janice's face flushed a deeper red. "You steal and total my car, yet you sit there acting like I have no right to feel angry?"

Waverly held up her hands. "Fine. If you want to be angry, have at it. But if you give yourself a stroke or heart attack, don't try to sue me for that too." She pointed at Reggie. "You're my witness. I told her to calm down."

He smiled. "I'm sure she'll cool off eventually."

"Don't be too sure," Janice tossed at him. Now she pointed to Waverly's coffee. "I'd like one of those too, please, only make mine a skinny."

Waverly was tempted to tell Janice to get her own stupid latte, then decided that would not only be juvenile but would exacerbate the situation. "Coming right up." She forced a smile. "Anything else?"

"No." Janice glared at her.

Grateful for this little escape, Waverly ordered Janice's latte. Then, seeing a dark chocolate raspberry bar, she ordered that too. Janice might turn her nose up at the peace offering, but it was worth a try.

Waverly was just exiting the pay line when Sicily came into the coffee shop. "Waverly?" she said quietly, motioning to her with a curled forefinger. "Come here for a sec."

Carrying the latte and chocolate bar, she followed Sicily into a dim corner. "What's up?"

"Dad's out there with her now."

"So you heard about it?"

Sicily nodded with eyes wide. "I think everyone in our neighborhood heard about it. I know it woke me up when she started yelling."

"How did she find out?"

"Dad told her. I guess she stopped by for coffee, and he thought he'd break the news to her gently. But, man, she totally flipped out."

"Oh."

"He told her it wasn't your fault, Waverly, but she wouldn't believe him. It's like she thinks you intentionally wrecked her car. How wacko is that?"

"I know." Waverly held up the coffee. "I better get this to her."

"I hope she doesn't throw it at you." Sicily looked seriously concerned.

"Oh, I don't really think..."

Sicily grimly shook her head. "I wouldn't put it past her."

"Right." Waverly made a stiff smile. "Just keep a safe distance from me, in case."

As they went back outside, Waverly was surprised to see Blake sitting with Janice and Reggie. Of course, he'd probably brought Sicily to town. But why had he stayed?

"Here you go, Princess," Waverly said as she set the latte and chocolate bar down.

"What's this?" Janice poked the plate that held the treat.

"Something to sweeten your, uh, disposition." Waverly watched as Blake stood and went over to another table, getting a couple more chairs.

"Oh?" Janice broke off a piece and tasted it primly.

"Actually, I was trying to sweeten her disposition too," Reggie told Waverly. "In fact, I hope you don't mind that I invited Janice to Belinda's party. When I heard about her political aspirations, I had a feeling she'd enjoy meeting some of those people."

"It sounds like a fun evening," Janice said to Waverly. "And I felt fairly certain you wouldn't mind if I went." Janice narrowed her eyes at her cousin.

"You don't mind, do you?" Reggie asked.

Waverly felt disappointment mixed with appreciation as she sat on one of the chairs that Blake brought over. She shrugged. "Not at all. Janice can go in my place."

"Not in your place," Reggie assured her. "But with us."

"Oh." Waverly sighed. "Although I'm surprised Janice is willing to go anywhere with me."

"But only if Blake can come too." Janice switched to a childish tone now. "I refuse to go along as the fifth wheel."

"Wouldn't that be a *third* wheel?" Sicily asked.

"Whatever." Janice turned to Reggie. "Otherwise the deal is off."

"What deal?" Waverly asked.

"I told Janice the condition for going to the party with us was that she had to stop terrorizing you over the loss of her car. And she agreed," Reggie said quietly.

"Although that doesn't mean you're not still 100 percent responsible." She shook her finger at Waverly. "I expect you to make good on it too, *Cousin.*"

Reggie looked sternly at Janice. "So if Blake comes, will you be on your best behavior toward Waverly, starting right now?"

"Wait a minute." Blake held up his hands. "What if I don't want to come?"

Waverly looked at Blake now. "Why wouldn't you come with us?"

He appeared torn. "Well, I just—"

"I refuse to go stag to this party," Janice said sullenly.

"Maybe you could go with Reggie," Waverly offered.

Reggie cleared his throat. "Does Reggie have a vote here?"

"Look, I appreciate your diplomacy." Waverly stood. "But maybe we should forget it. If Janice wants to be mad at me for a while, why not just let her?" She turned to Sicily. "And we have work to do, right?"

"Right." Sicily stood.

Leaving Janice with Reggie and Blake, Waverly linked arms with Sicily and began singing, "We're off to see the wizard…," and barely missing a beat, Sicily joined in.

They'd just laid out the drop cloths, gotten the paints opened and arranged with brushes, and were beginning on the mural when

Blake knocked on the front door. Since it wasn't officially business hours until ten, Waverly had kept the doors locked.

"Yes?" she said as she opened the door, glancing down the sidewalk to see that Janice wasn't with him.

"I'm alone and unarmed," he said with a twinkle in his eye. "May I come in?"

So she let him in, relocking the door even though it was only a quarter until ten now. She waved her hand toward the machines. "Did you want to play video games this morning?"

Sicily laughed from her ladder perch. She was painting a bright yellow button on a purple vest that was worn by one of her game characters.

"No thanks." Blake followed Waverly over to the counter.

She went on one side, keeping him safely on the other. "What can we do for you then?"

"Well, this was more about what I can do for you."

"What?"

"I agreed to go with the three of you to that party," he told her. "But I want you to know that I am only doing this for you. Not for Janice. Is that clear?"

She shrugged. "It's clear to me. I can't vouch for my cousin."

"No, I didn't think so. But I need to make a disclaimer."

"A disclaimer?"

"After I tell Janice what I must tell her, she might not want me along at all."

"What are you going to tell her, Dad?" Sicily peered down at him with interest.

"The same thing I've been telling her or trying to tell her

practically since we met. That I'm not interested in a serious relationship with her."

"What kind of relationship are you interested in?" Waverly questioned.

"No relationship to be honest." He paused. "Or, at the very least, a friendship, but I have my doubts that she's capable of that."

"Why don't you wait and tell her *after* the party?" suggested Sicily.

"Because I don't want to," he said back. "I want her to get this, Sicily. To know where I stand."

"Oh." She nodded. "Okay." She turned back to her painting.

He ran his fingers through his hair. "So I have your blessing then, Sicily?"

"Yeah. I never liked Janice in the first place."

"Really?"

"Yeah. I just thought you did, Dad."

"There's a lot of that going around lately."

"A lot of what?"

"General confusion."

"So, is that it then?" Sicily squinted at the clock.

"Uh, no, there was something else." He glanced over at Waverly. "And I think I might as well say this in front of both of you."

With brush in midair, Sicily turned to stare at him again. "What, Dad?"

"I might be about to make a fool of myself, Sis, but I figured you'd enjoy it."

"Huh?" She looked thoroughly confused.

"Well, I wanted to tell Waverly that one reason I've been trying very hard to break things off with her cousin was so that I'd be free to pursue someone else."

Waverly took in a quick breath, bracing herself. What was he doing?

"Who?" Sicily came down the ladder with a curious expression.

"I've been hoping to ask Waverly out. But everything—mostly Janice—has been getting in the way."

"You *like* Waverly?" Sicily was down the ladder now. She came over and stared at her dad with a hard-to-read expression.

"Yes." He nodded. "Is that okay with you?"

She looked perplexed. "I don't know."

Waverly wondered if she should say something, but for the life of her, she couldn't think of a single word.

"But you like Waverly," Blake tried.

"Yeah, Dad, but she's *my* friend."

"Oh?" He glanced uncomfortably at Waverly now. "Is my face getting red yet?"

She nodded. "A little."

"Maybe I should leave." He started toward the door.

Sicily looked at Waverly now, holding up her hands in a helpless gesture.

"I have an idea," Waverly said.

Blake turned with a slightly desperate look in his eyes. "Yes?"

"Why don't we all try to be friends?"

"All?" He appeared confused. "As in all who?"

"The three of us. You and Sicily and me."

He broke into a smile. "Yeah. That sounds good." He turned to Sicily. "How about you? Does that sound good?"

She grinned. "Okay. But don't forget, Dad, she was my friend *first*."

"Don't worry. I won't forget."

Waverly went over to unlock the door for him. As their eyes locked, she felt an unexpected warmth rush through her. What had she just agreed to?

Chapter Twenty-one
....

Blake wasn't eager to go home, so he ran some errands in town, taking his time to get the mail and gather a good selection of groceries and a few other things. He knew his leisurely morning was simply his guise for delaying the inevitable—breaking it off with Janice. And he did plan to do it today. It's just that he was in no hurry. The more time he put between Janice's fit at his house this morning and now was a good thing. But finally he had no more excuses to linger in town, yet he still had more than an hour until it would be time to pick Sicily up. Also, he was well aware that the heat of midday would wreak havoc on his groceries, plus there was ice cream involved.

So he drove slowly home, enjoying the sights of beach properties, the Sound, and boats as he went. He still couldn't get over the serene beauty of this place. At home he unloaded his car and put things away. At last, saying a little prayer along the way, he walked the path between the houses. As he knocked on their front door, he stood straight. Determined to permanently end this thing with Janice—no loopholes, no backdoors, no clauses—he braced himself.

"Janice caught the ferry this morning," Vivian informed him after he'd asked for her.

"She's gone?"

"Yes. She wanted to return to Boston for a few days. Louise

offered to drive, and they both left here around ten. They took a chance of getting on a ferry without a reservation, but Louise called awhile ago to say they were safely loaded on the boat and on their way. Janice plans to find a rental car, as well as order a replacement for her wrecked car. Plus it sounded like she needs to attend to some other business. They expect to be there a few days."

"Oh, I see." His sigh was partly relief, partly frustration.

"You didn't get a chance to talk to her, did you, Blake?"

"No, not really. The drama with her car sort of took over."

Vivian shook her head with a look of wonder. "Wasn't that the strangest thing?"

"You're telling me." Then he filled her in about speaking to Waverly this morning, and how they had agreed to be friends. "All three of us." He grinned. "Sicily gave us her children's stamp of approval."

Merriment twinkled in Vivian's eyes. "Maybe you'll consider including me in your new pact of friendship."

"Of course!" he said eagerly.

"With Janice and Louise gone, maybe we could do something together this week, just the four of us."

"Absolutely. In fact, why don't we have you and Waverly over for dinner at our place tonight? I just got groceries, and I have no idea why I bought so much." Well, except that he was avoiding something. "How does that sound?"

"Lovely."

"Great." He nodded, pleased with this plan. "My culinary skills aren't as good as your sister's, but I'll do my best."

"I've heard it said that dandelion weeds, eaten with friends, taste better than top sirloin steak that's eaten with enemies." She smiled. "Something easier to commit to back when I was still a vegetarian."

"Hopefully I can do better than dandelion weeds. Is seven okay?"

"Perfect."

And it was perfect. Or almost. The chicken he'd grilled was a little on the dry side, but no one complained. Thanks to Waverly, the salad was delicious. Mostly it was the company that was perfect. What a difference it made, knowing that Janice was back in America for a while. He'd just heard that was what *real* Vineyarders called the mainland—*America*. Like it was a different country, and in a way it was. And right now, as they sat eating fresh strawberries and ice cream with their toes in the sand, it felt like they were a world away.

* * * * *

The next few days passed blissfully, wonderfully, magically. With Janice and Louise still gone, Waverly had decided to stay with her mother and enjoy the benefits of beach living. Blake gave Waverly rides into town and even let her use his car for the whole day sometimes, leaving him happily homebound. While Sicily was off helping with the mural and other things, he puttered on a screenplay he'd started several years ago. And sometimes he sat and visited with Vivian, sharing iced tea or lemonade on the screened porch. Also he took photos, lots of photos. Not just of the gorgeous seascape or wildlife either. He was getting lots of great candid shots of the three different generations of "women" in his life.

It was interesting watching the four of them interfacing together. Not only did they get along extremely well, they functioned like a real family—a small, happy, healthy family. In the evenings, after dinner, he and Sicily and Waverly would take bike rides, exploring different parts of the shore. But Blake continued to take it slow and careful with Waverly. He could tell she was keeping him at a polite, safe distance, and he thought that was probably best…for now. Plus, it reassured Sicily that they truly were friends—all of them.

On Thursday night he decided to take Sicily out—just the two of them. "Why don't we invite Waverly and Vivian along too?" she asked. But he explained that mothers and daughters sometimes needed time to themselves. What he didn't mention was that Janice and Louise were expected to return tomorrow.

In a way, this week had almost seemed too good to be true. Sometimes Blake had wanted to pinch himself to check if he was dreaming. But tonight he was reminded that it had merely been a brief interlude. Like an island waiting for the hurricane to hit, he knew that Janice and Louise would get back tomorrow afternoon. According to Vivian, Janice had secured a rental car, ordered a new BMW, and was anxious to come back for the Pre-Fourth Friday party.

On Friday morning Waverly came over just like she had the previous mornings during this blissful week. She showed up to either get a ride or borrow his car, but then he lured her to visit with a cup of coffee by reminding her she was saving money that way. But he was pleased to see that this morning, she'd come even earlier than usual.

"You know that Janice and Louise get home today," she said as they sat on his porch sipping their coffee.

"I know, although I've been trying not to think about it."

"Mom told me that you haven't completely broken things off with her."

"Not for a lack of trying," he said. "Although I'd meant to make my intentions—rather my lack of them—a lot more clear by now."

"Mom said that Janice is in good spirits. She got a good rental car, which Louise is footing the bill for, and she ordered a new Beamer that's even better than her other one. Between her insurance and The Gallery's, it's pretty much covered."

"Well, that should be a relief to you."

"It definitely is." Waverly cleared her throat. "She also said that Janice shopped for a new outfit for tonight's party, and she's really looking forward to it."

"Uh-huh." He gazed out over the calm blue water.

"And you."

He turned and stared at Waverly. "What?"

"And she's looking forward to you too, Blake. I just thought you should know that."

He groaned. "Thanks. And I was having such a nice morning too."

"Forewarned is forearmed."

"So should I be expecting some kind of battle?" He studied her profile, which was perfect. Even with her lips pressed tightly together like that, she was still beautiful.

She shrugged. "I guess that remains to be seen."

Now he realized that, although he'd made his attraction fairly clear to her, not to mention her mother, Waverly had never said or done anything to state exactly where she stood with him. Oh, he still had that kiss to remember, but what if he was imagining that she'd enjoyed it as much as he did? What if Waverly was thinking along the same line as Sicily—that they were all just very good friends? Like the Three Musketeers. Not that Waverly wasn't a delightful friend. But was he willing to settle for only that?

"Shouldn't we be heading into town by now?" Sicily asked as she emerged from the house fully dressed.

"What about breakfast?" he asked.

"Already ate."

"Oh." He looked helplessly at Waverly now. "So do you want a ride?"

"Why don't you just let Waverly take the car," Sicily suggested, "since you told me I could spend the whole day there since we're trying to get the painting finished today. Okay?"

"Okay."

"Are you certain?" Waverly asked.

"Yeah." He nodded. "I can work on my screenplay. It's actually starting to gel, and a full day at it would probably be good."

Sicily leaned over and pecked him on the cheek. "Thanks, Dad."

"Yeah, thanks, Dad," Waverly echoed with a twinkle in her eye.

"Hey, I might be older than you, but I'm not old enough to be your dad."

She looked slightly hurt now, like maybe she wanted a dad.

"Not that I wouldn't be willing to try," he said congenially.

"How old are you anyway?" Waverly asked.

"He's forty-three," Sicily informed her. "How old are you, Waverly? Like twenty-something?"

Waverly laughed. "See why I love this girl? You bet, Sicily, I'm like twenty-something—just add at least ten years, and you'll be closer."

Sicily looked genuinely shocked. "Really, you're *that* old? Like as old as my mom?"

"I don't know about that," Waverly confessed. "But I'll be thirty-six on my next birthday."

Sicily cocked her head to one side as if seeing her with new eyes. "Wow, I had no idea you were *that* old."

"Yes, dearie, I am." Waverly inserted a shaky old-lady tremor into her voice and stood up and walked with a hunched back. "Now, if you can help me find my cane and my hearing aid and my—"

"You're not *that* old!" Sicily laughed.

Then they were off, and Blake was home alone to think about how he was going to get Waverly to let him know whether or not he even had a chance with her. He was determined to find out. But first there was Janice and tonight's party. The only reason he'd agreed to that in the first place had been to placate Janice and take some pressure off Waverly. But if Janice had gotten over everything, and the car situation was smoothed out, maybe it wouldn't rock Waverly's boat too much for Blake to change his mind about being Janice's escort to the party tonight.

Really, who needed an escort to a beach party anyway? As enamored as Janice was with celebrity types, she'd probably be willing to go as a single. Plus, she'd have Reggie and Waverly to hang with. But therein was the problem: *Reggie and Waverly*. On a date together. Perhaps it was immature or selfish, or maybe it was plain old love, but Blake decided he was going to the party with Janice after all. After the party was history, he would calmly and maturely explain the facts to Janice.

He worked on his screenplay until past one. Then, feeling hungry and a little lonely, he decided to call Vivian, inviting her to join him for a late lunch.

"That sounds lovely," she told him. "I haven't eaten yet either."

"Are tuna-fish sandwiches okay?"

"Perfect. How about if we take our lunch out on the beach—have a picnic?"

"You are my kind of woman."

She laughed heartily.

"I'll be over in about half an hour," he promised.

"I'll be here with bells on."

He took care making the sandwiches, chopping celery and using some fresh crisp lettuce. Then he added in some chips, a couple pieces of fruit, and some other goodies, and loaded it all into a grocery sack. Realizing it might be difficult for Vivian to get up and down to sit on a blanket on the sand, he decided to grab a couple of folding chairs. He'd noticed she was moving slower and with a bit more difficulty, although it could be his imagination, spurred on by knowing about her "condition." Slinging the straps of the folding chair bags over one shoulder, he grabbed his grocery bag with the other.

He happily went down the trail to her house, whistling along the way and thinking how handy this trail had been this past week. He set his picnic things by the porch, then went to the door and knocked. And waited. Then he knocked again, louder this time. And waited some more.

"Vivian?" he called out, going around the house to see if she might be puttering with the flower pots or something.

But no one was there. So he went back around and knocked

again. Then he opened the door. "Vivian?" he called again, walking through the quiet room.

He could hear water running somewhere and, following his ears, realized it was in the kitchen. "Vivian?" he said as he went around the cabinets, thinking he'd turn off the faucet.

But then he saw her, laid out lifelessly on the floor with shattered glass nearby and a spilled bottle of aspirin beside her. "Vivian!" He fell to his knees, leaned over, and checked for a pulse in her neck. Seeing it was there, but faintly, he wondered what to do first. Realizing she'd probably been about to take an aspirin, which he knew could be lifesaving, he quickly crushed one and slipped the white powder into her mouth. In the next instant, he called 911 on the kitchen phone.

Before the ambulance arrived, Vivian regained consciousness and tried to sit up.

"Wait," he told her as he slipped a folded towel beneath her head. "Paramedics are on their way. Don't move."

"No hospital," she whispered.

"But Vivian," he pleaded.

"I just fainted," she said in a hoarse voice. "Lightheaded... blacked out."

"Maybe so, but what can it hurt for a doctor to look at you?"

She closed her eyes and sighed.

He felt like her betrayer as the paramedics checked her vital signs, hooked up some oxygen and IV tube, then loaded her into the ambulance. Her face was pale, her eyes frightened.

"I'll follow and meet you there," he assured her. Then, realizing he was car-less, he asked one of the medics for a ride. They let him sit in the back, telling him to stay out of the way of the two medics who continued to help her. As the ambulance rushed through town with sirens on, Blake bowed his head and prayed.

Holding her hand, he started to go with them into the ER but was instructed to remain in the waiting room. "Promise you won't call Waverly," Vivian told him in a firm tone, still holding his hand. "Not yet. Not like this. Promise?"

"Okay, I promise."

She released his hand and was wheeled away. But now he was torn in two. How could he not call Waverly? What if her mother was dying? And at the same time, how could he break his promise to a possibly dying woman? Finally he realized that all he could do at the moment was to pray. And that's what he did.

It was past four by the time he was allowed to see her again. She'd been moved to a private room and, to his surprise, looked rather well. The color had returned to her face, and she was even smiling. "Did you keep my promise?" she asked as soon as he was by her bedside.

"It wasn't easy, but I did."

She patted his hand. "Good boy."

"I'm not convinced your daughter would agree."

She sighed. "I know. You're probably right about that. But I didn't want Waverly to find out about—well, you know—like this."

"Would you rather she'd found out about it if you'd died?"

She seemed to consider this. "Well, she couldn't very well be mad at me if I was gone, now, could she?"

He shook his head. "Don't be so sure of that."

"Anyway, I'm not gone. Not yet. I knew it wasn't my time to go."

"What made you so certain?"

"I could feel it inside me. Like God wasn't finished with me yet."

He made a small smile. "I hope you're right."

"Of course, now they want to put me on hospice."

"Hospice?" He tried to remember what that meant exactly.

"You know," she told him, "when you're going to die within a year or so."

"Right."

"They say their program is one of the best. And I have to admit I was impressed with the woman I met. Maybe it's not such a bad idea." She handed him a brochure. "What do you think?"

He glanced through the highlights. "It sounds like a good organization, Vivian. It allows you to remain in your own home with some help and some control…and dignity. What's wrong with that?"

"Nothing, I suppose." A tear slipped out, and he reached for a box of tissue, handing it to her. "It's just that…" She wiped the tear away. "I've always been so healthy and independent. It's hard to admit I might need some help."

"But what if your need of some extra help is a way for you to connect more tightly with others?"

Her thoughtful expression deepened.

"And keeping your secret from Waverly seems cruel to me."

"Cruel?"

"Yes. If she knew what was going on, she'd probably spend less time working and more time with you. I personally think that would be good for both of you."

She nodded. "Perhaps you're right."

"I know I'm right, Vivian. Trust me on this."

"But what are you going to tell her? I mean, on the phone?"

"What do you want me to tell her?"

Vivian looked worried. "Can you tell her I fainted?"

He shrugged. "As long as you tell her the rest of the story. After all, you did sort of faint, right?"

"In a manner of speaking."

"So, please, let me call her," he urged. "Especially before she goes home and finds us both gone and wonders what's happened."

"Yes, yes," she agreed. "You're right. Besides, Lou and Janice will be getting there now. Naturally, they'll wonder too."

So, realizing that he didn't even have his cell phone on him, he went to the nurses' station and borrowed a phone. When Waverly answered, he kept his voice was calm and even. "I don't want you to be alarmed, Waverly, but I'm here with your mother at the hospital and—"

"What happened? Are you guys okay?"

"I'm fine. Your mother had a little fainting spell."

"Oh, good. Not good that she fainted. I'm just relieved it's not too serious—"

"Actually, it's a little more serious than that. But she needs to be the one to tell you."

"Oh, okay. Well, Rosie gets here in a few minutes. But I could lock up and leave if—"

"No, it's fine to wait for Rosie. Your mother is resting nicely now. And she looks fine. But she still needs to talk to you. I don't know if they'll release her today or what the plan is. But, even so, I'll need a ride."

"Oh, that's right. I have your car."

"So don't hurry. Just come."

"We'll get this stuff put away," she said, "and I'll be there by five."

He returned to Vivian's room, quietly chatting with her. Then, seeing she was drowsy, he focused his attention on reading more of the hospice material. She drifted off to sleep just before five, so Blake went out to the parking lot for some fresh air and to watch for Waverly and Sicily. When he spotted his car parking near the entrance, he walked over to meet them.

"Is she okay?" Waverly asked as she handed him the car keys. Her worried expression seemed to contrast with the splotch of green paint still smeared across her cheek. He resisted the urge to reach up and wipe it off.

"Yes. Vivian's fine. Just sleeping, which is probably a good thing. She's had quite a day."

"What's wrong with her?" Sicily asked.

"That's for Vivian to explain." He said this more to Waverly than Sicily.

"So you do know what's wrong with her then?" Waverly pressed.

"Well…" He glanced uncomfortably away.

"So you do know," she continued. "How long have you known, Blake?"

"Look, Waverly, I've been encouraging Vivian to speak to you for some time. I actually thought this week, with Janice and Louise gone, she'd get the chance."

"Speak to me about what?" she persisted.

"Like I said, Vivian wants to tell you herself." He ran his hand over Sicily's hair, twisting the purple streak in his fingers. "But for some reason, it's hard for her. She sees herself as this fiercely independent and totally healthy sort of person. I don't think she likes appearing to be weak."

"That's true enough," Waverly admitted. "She's always been a health nut, and no one's more independent than Vivian. Good grief, she's traveled the world—lives out of the country for months at a time."

He put a hand gently on her shoulder now. "That's all changing, and you're going to have to change the way you perceive her as well. But if you give her the chance, I know she wants to tell you what's going on with her."

"I still can't believe she told you and not me." Waverly pressed her lips tightly together.

"Yeah, Dad," Sicily chimed in, "that doesn't seem fair."

"Can't you give me a hint about what's going on?" Waverly searched his eyes.

"I want to, Waverly, but your mother made me promise. All I can say is this: go easy with her, okay? I think she might be in some kind of denial about some things. Today was probably a good wake-up call. But, most importantly, she needs to feel like she's in control of this, uh, her situation. She doesn't need anyone telling her what to do. Okay?"

"Okay…" Waverly frowned. "I called Aunt Lou. They just got home, and she was pretty worried because it looked like something was wrong at the house. Anyway, she's on her way over here to pick me up. And Vivian too, if she gets released. So you and Sicily can go home."

"I don't mind staying."

"It's not necessary. And Sicily probably can't go see her anyway. You guys should just head on home."

Blake felt unneeded and dismissed. Yet he knew that Vivian was Waverly's mother, not his. "Okay, tell Vivian good-bye for me then."

"I will. And thanks for helping her today." Waverly started to go inside, then stopped. "Oh, yeah, I almost forgot. Aunt Lou offered to keep Sicily while you and Janice go to the party tonight."

He slapped his forehead. "The *party*? I totally forgot. Under the circumstances, I think I'll bow out. I never really wanted to go anyway."

Waverly shrugged. "I guess that's up to you." She opened her arms to Sicily now, giving her a big hug and swaying her back and forth from side to side. "Thank you so much for your help this week, Sicily. I don't know what I would've done without you."

"Thanks. I had fun. And tell Vivian I love her," Sicily said sweetly.

Waverly nodded. "Will do. See you guys later."

As they got into the car, Sicily asked if Waverly was mad at him.

"What makes you think she was mad?" he asked her back.

"Because you wouldn't tell her what's wrong with Vivian."

"Oh."

"But I understand, Dad. If you made a promise to Vivian, it was right to keep it."

"Thanks, sweetie. That's how I felt too."

Of course, as he drove back home, he felt a whole slew of other things as well.

Chapter Twenty-two

....

By the time Vivian finished explaining to Waverly about her stage IV ovarian cancer, they were both in tears. "But can't you do something?" Waverly demanded. "Medicine advances every time you turn around and—"

"No." Vivian stubbornly shook her head. "This was the main reason I didn't want to tell you at first. I was afraid you'd react like this." Then she explained how she'd already gone through chemo and radiation the previous time. "That was about four years ago," she said sadly. "I had a bad feeling then, but I'd hoped that was the end of it. Unfortunately it wasn't."

"You never told me."

"No. Why should I have?"

"Because I'm your daughter." Waverly blew her nose.

"Yes, my daughter who had just lost her husband. Why would I want to tell you that I...that I was ill?"

Waverly had no answer for this.

"I appreciate your concern, Waverly, but I refuse to spend my last days in and out of medical facilities, undergoing painful treatments that steal what quality of life there is left to me. The reason Louise and I came to Martha's Vineyard was to enjoy what's left... to spend time with you."

"So Aunt Lou knows too?"

Vivian nodded. "Although Louise and I have had our differences over the years, she went out of her way to connect with me after Vance died. After my last diagnosis, I had to talk to someone. She was a good support system. And she reminded me of how some of our sweetest summers as children were spent at the Vineyard with our parents and suggested we come here." She sighed. "I must admit she was right. The natural beauty of this place, the serenity, the smell of the air—it's like a form of healing in itself. Perhaps not physically...but so good for the soul."

"That's why you wanted me to come here, to spend time with you before it was too late?"

"Yes, but I want you to understand that I did NOT mean to trick you about The Gallery, Waverly. That was a legitimate mistake."

"So why did you and Aunt Lou buy The Gallery?"

Vivian held up her hands. "Oh, I don't know. It appeared to be a good investment. I wanted something that could provide a livelihood for you...while you were here. I suppose I hoped I might still have a few years left. I've always been an optimist."

"You're positive that you don't?"

"According to the doctor...probably not." Now she smiled. "But who knows?"

"What about today? What happened anyway?"

"I think maybe my electrolytes were out of whack. At first I thought I was having a heart attack, but apparently I simply fainted." She made a sheepish smile. "It's a bit embarrassing—all the fuss I've caused everyone."

"Well, at least it got me on the same page with you." Waverly hesitated. "But I'm a little offended."

Vivian appeared perplexed. "Offended? Why?"

"I can't believe you would tell Blake and not me."

She sighed. "Blake is a good boy, Waverly. Rather, a good man. He really is quite special."

Waverly turned to look out the window.

Now Vivian reached for her hand. "Are you saying that you're not attracted to Blake? Is that why you keep pushing him away?"

"Pushing him away?"

"Yes. You look like you're trying to keep a distance between him and you. I think you're afraid there might be something real there, and you're not ready for it. Or else you just don't like him—you know, in a romantic sort of way." Her eyes twinkled. "He's awfully good-looking, don't you think?"

"I suppose."

"And he's a gentleman. Something you don't see all the time in the younger generation. I personally find it rather refreshing."

"Oh." Waverly picked at some yellow paint under her thumbnail.

"So what is it then?"

"What is what?" Waverly looked up.

Vivian narrowed her eyes ever so slightly. "Good grief, Waverly Lynn, what if I were truly on my deathbed now? Would you still clam up like this?"

Waverly blinked. "Sorry."

"So tell me the truth." Vivian's eyes searched hers. "Do you think there might be a future for you and Blake and his dear little Sicily? Or am I only daydreaming? We had such a lovely few days together this past week. There were moments when I felt truly hopeful for you three. But are you saying you don't feel that way?"

"I don't know how I feel."

"So you have no feelings whatsoever for Blake?"

Waverly studied her mother now. Vivian looked so frail and vulnerable in the pale-blue hospital gown with the IV tube stuck into her arm. "You really want the truth, Vivian?"

"Of course I do." She got a slightly coy look now. "If you tell me the truth, maybe I'll share a little secret with you too."

"I can trust you with what I say?"

"I'm your mother, dear. If you can't trust me, who can you trust?"

Waverly nodded. "Okay, yes, I am attracted to Blake. Very much so. I was from the start. But that whole business with Janice has been kind of a bummer. It's so on and off again. He'll say he's breaking it off, and then it doesn't happen."

"But there have been some obstacles," Vivian pointed out. "Surely you've seen that."

"Maybe. But even tonight, Blake is supposed to take Janice to the party and—"

"Blake mentioned that. But wasn't that to appease Janice over her smashed car? It almost sounded as if you'd offered poor Blake up as the sacrificial lamb."

Waverly laughed. "Did he say that?"

"Not exactly. But I could tell he felt somewhat used and abused by you two women."

"Yes, and he's a grown man who should be able to make up his own mind and deal with things in his own way."

"But don't forget, he's also a gentleman. And he's trying to make you happy, Waverly. I know that he is."

"By continuing a relationship with Janice?"

"Oh, Waverly, sometimes you can be very stubborn."

Waverly laughed. "Yes, and I wonder who I get that particular trait from."

"So, you plan to keep holding Blake at arm's length until he makes a clean break from Janice? Is that what you're saying?"

"I'm saying that until Blake and Janice resolve whatever it is that's going on between them, I'm staying out of it." Waverly pulled out her phone now. "Fortunately I won't be going to the party tonight so I—"

"Why on earth not?" Vivian sat up in bed with wide eyes. "From what I've heard, this is going to be quite the party. You really should go."

"No way. Not with you here in the hospital and—"

"The doctor is releasing me soon." She gestured toward the clock. "In fact, he should've been here by now."

"Even so, I don't want to go to the party, Vivian. I want to stay with you and—"

"I have Louise to stay with me, Waverly. If you think I invited you to Martha's Vineyard so you could play my nursemaid, you better think again. I only invited you here so that you and I could spend some quality time together. Like we did last week."

"Even so, I don't want to go to the party anyway. It'll just be awkward. Whether he likes it or not, Blake will be stuck with Janice, and I'll be with Reggie and—"

"Do you *want* to be with Reggie?"

"He's a nice guy, Vivian. A good friend."

"And you prefer him to Blake?"

"No, of course not!"

"Then this is what I want you to do, Waverly." She took in a deep breath. "Now if you must, simply consider this a dying mother's last request."

"Are you dying?" Waverly stared at her mother.

Vivian shrugged. "Eventually, yes. We are all dying, if you stop to think about it."

"Yes, but are you really dying, I mean right now?"

"Just humor me, Waverly. I don't know how long I have in this world. And I don't know how many dying requests I'll be making." She made a weary smile. "But I am making this one today. It's up to you whether you respect it or not."

"Fine." Waverly nodded. "What is it?"

"I want you to go to the party with Reggie tonight."

"Okay, I'll go."

"And…"

"And what?"

"And I want you to *come home* with Blake." Vivian grinned deviously. "Do you think you can do that?"

Waverly shook her head. "I don't know."

"Will you at least try?"

"That's your dying mother's request?"

"It is…for today anyway."

"Meaning I can expect more?"

Vivian gave her a sly wink. "I suppose I could milk this illness for all it's worth. But, really, that's not my style. I doubt there'll be more."

"Hello, hello!" Aunt Lou came bursting into the room. "Now whatever did you do to get yourself in here, Viv?"

So Vivian filled her in on the fainting story. "So very silly, if you think about it. But poor Blake thought I was having a heart attack, so you can't really blame him for calling for help. The next thing I knew I was having a ride in an ambulance. That was a first."

"Oh, my." Aunt Lou shook her head. "What a day you've had."

Vivian handed her a brochure. "But perhaps fortuitous too."

"What's this?" Aunt Lou studied the pamphlet. "Hospice?" She looked surprised, but without saying anything, she perused it. "Well, I suppose hospice might be helpful." With a doubtful look, she peered over her glasses at Vivian. "You'd be okay with that? People coming to the house to check on you and all that?"

"I met one of their people today. She seemed nice. She told me they've got some new options for pain control that I might want to look into."

Just then a doctor, followed by a nurse, came into the room, announcing his plan to release her. "But first we'll check some things," he told Vivian. "If all is well, you can be on your way."

Waverly and Louise stepped out to make more room. Waverly led her aunt to the nearby waiting area, where they both sat down.

"Goodness, Waverly, what is on your face?" Aunt Lou demanded.

"What?"

Aunt Lou pointed to her cheek. "It's lime green."

"Oh." Waverly held up her splotchy hands. "Just paint. Sicily and I finished up at The Gallery today. You'll have to come by and see it."

Aunt Lou checked her watch. "Aren't you attending that big shindig tonight? No offense, dear, but you really need to get home and fix yourself up some."

"I don't really want to go tonight," Waverly admitted. "Vivian insisted that I should go, but I think I'll—"

"You'll do as your mother says." Aunt Lou shook her finger at her. "Vivian won't tell you this, Waverly, but she could literally go at any moment."

"That's exactly what I'm worried about," she confessed. "In that case, I don't want to leave her alone at all—not even tonight."

"No. No. *No.*" With a grim expression, Aunt Lou shook her head so hard that her double chin shook. "You do not understand, Waverly. If you start treating Vivian like that, you will ruin everything."

"What do—"

"Listen to me, young lady, because I only plan to say this once. Do you understand?"

Waverly nodded.

"For starters, the only reason Vivian agreed to live with me at all was because I promised to act as if nothing is wrong with her. The reason she's been hesitant to tell you is because she's worried that you'll start to fuss over her. She does *not* want that. In fact, she warned me that if I begin to fret or worry over her, if I do as much as tell her to put on a sweater or take a nap—even once—she might pick up and leave. With no forwarding address. Certainly you know your mother well enough to know she would do that. Do you not?"

"You're right. I do."

"If we make Vivian feel like an invalid or a dying woman, she would hop the next flight to Timbuktu, go find herself a grass hut, and die alone. Do you understand?"

"Yes."

"Good." She nodded. "Janice knows this too. She has the good sense not to mollycoddle Vivian either."

Waverly bit her tongue from declaring that Janice Grant would never mollycoddle *anyone*.

Aunt Lou waved over to the doctor who had just exited Vivian's room. "Excuse me," she called out. "Does Vivian get to go home now?"

He nodded. "Yes. But I highly recommend that she sign up for our hospice program."

"Yes. I believe she's interested."

"I also gave her the name of an associate, a brilliant oncologist who—"

"Save your breath," she told him. "My sister has no interest in pursuing additional medical services."

"So I heard." He slipped a pen in his jacket pocket. "Now, if you'll excuse me."

Waverly returned to the room, where the nurse was just removing the IV tube and placing a bandage on Vivian's arm. "Do you want me to help you get dressed?" the nurse offered as she tossed some things in the garbage.

"No, thank you." Vivian gave her a tired smile. "I've been dressing myself for more than six decades now. I think I can remember how to do it."

"Okay. I'll be back in a few minutes with a wheelchair."

"I do not need a wheelchair."

"Hospital policy," the nurse said crisply, then gathered her things and left.

Waverly was torn now. Everything in her wanted to offer to help her mother too, but she also wanted to respect what Aunt Lou had said. "Anything I can do for you?" she asked timidly.

"No. You and Aunt Lou go wait for me in the lobby, please. I'll be down shortly."

Aunt Lou tossed Waverly an I-told-you-so glance, and together they left Vivian to fend for herself. As they waited in the main lobby, Waverly knew this wasn't going to be easy. But she also knew she didn't want to be the reason Vivian ran off to the ends of the earth for her final days.

"There you are," Aunt Lou said happily as Vivian was wheeled toward the entrance.

"You look good," Waverly told her. And it was true. Dressed in her normal clothes, Vivian seemed like her old self again.

"Thank you." Vivian slowly stood, straightening her spine and smiling. "Now let's get out of here."

As Aunt Lou slowly maneuvered her car through the island traffic, making her way across the bridge and back into Vineyard Haven, she and Vivian chatted amiably in the front seat, discussing the weather and shopping in Boston, and acting as if nothing whatsoever was wrong. Meanwhile, in the backseat, Waverly felt like she was watching a movie where two actors were giving a somewhat believable performance.

"So, Waverly, what are *you* wearing to the party tonight?" Vivian asked as she turned onto Main Street.

"I have no idea at the moment."

"Well, Janice found this scrumptious little coral red dress," Aunt Lou said. "I can't understand how that girl can wear those vibrant colors. Must be her dark hair and dramatic features. But the dress looks magnificent on her. Of course, it was some fancy-schmancy designer name and costly, *oh, my word*! It's a good thing that girl is an attorney. She has such expensive taste."

"Well, here you are." Aunt Lou pulled the car in front of The Gallery.

"I hope you have an enjoyable evening," Vivian said. "And please, don't forget your promise to me, Waverly."

Waverly had tried to forget her mother's command that she go to the party with Reggie and come home with Blake. Like that was an easy achievement, even if someone like Janice was not involved. "I can't guarantee anything, Vivian, but I promise to do my best." Waverly leaned over the seat, kissing her mother on the cheek. "I'll let you know how it goes, okay?"

"Perfect."

"Love you," Waverly called as she got out. "Both of you."

They waved and Waverly went into the arcade, which was surprisingly busy for this time of day, though it was a Friday. She studied the freshly painted walls and the mural, which looked even better than she remembered.

"How's it going?" Waverly asked Rosie and Zach. After Zach had finished with the painting, he'd complained about a lack of summer work on the island this year. So Waverly had offered him a job working in the arcade. To her delight, he'd happily accepted, and tonight Rosie was training him.

"It's going great," Zach assured her. "So far so good."

Rosie rolled her eyes. "Yeah, well, the night is young."

Then Waverly went on up to her apartment and headed straight for the shower and a scrub brush to clean out the paint from her fingernails. Reggie was supposed to pick her up at seven, and that meant she had only thirty minutes to pull off a Cinderella act. As she scrubbed, she tried to make a decision on what to wear. It had been a fairly warm day and didn't seem to be cooling off much. Before she'd heard that Janice was dressing to the nines, she'd considered wearing something a little more casual. Now she didn't know. Parties like this were way out of her league.

Finally she decided on a summery dress she'd purchased in Chicago, something she'd imagined wearing on a warm summer night when the art gallery was having some special showing. The bodice was fitted with spaghetti straps that crossed in back, and the flowing skirt with an asymmetrical hemline was constructed of layers of hand-dyed gauze in shades of blues and greens. The dress had reminded her of the ocean when she'd first spotted it in the exclusive shop window. The salesgirl had commented on how the colors were similar to Waverly's eyes, then shown her a pair of pale aqua espadrille sandals that went perfectly with it. The dress had been a splurge for Waverly then, but she was thankful to have it now.

As she checked her image in the mirror, she realized she'd probably look beachy compared to what Janice would be wearing tonight. This was only a sundress, but it felt feminine and fun, and by the time she had her still damp hair pinned in a loose updo and had added the pearls her grandmother had given her for a wedding present, she did feel a bit like Cinderella! Though when she went down to wait for Reggie, she noticed she still had some paint under her fingernails.

Chapter Twenty-three
....

Sicily scowled at Blake. "Your outfit does not go with Janice's, Dad. Not even close."

"Huh?" He studied his daughter—from her purple-streaked hair, orange T-shirt with some unidentifiable cartoon character, faded jeans cutoffs, down to her fluorescent green flip-flops—and she was giving him fashion advice? "What makes you think that?"

"Cuz I went over there while you were in the shower."

"Why?"

"I went to see Vivian."

"Oh, you should probably let her rest and get—"

"No, Dad. She was happy to see me. And I took her a seashell bouquet."

"A seashell bouquet?" He combed his wet hair, attempting to smooth the natural waves and reminding himself he was overdue for a haircut.

"Yeah, it was an idea Waverly and I got on the beach one day— you take seashells and glue them on top of sticks, then arrange them in a vase and you have a seashell bouquet."

"And you made one for Vivian?"

"I'd already started on one, but I decided to give it to Vivian today. You know, for a get-well present." She smiled. "Vivian thought it was beautiful."

"You're a very thoughtful girl, Sicily." He ran his hand over the top of her head. "You make me proud to be your dad."

"Anyway, when I was over there Janice showed me what she was going to wear tonight. It was really sparkly and swanky. You know, pretty uptown."

"Oh." Once again he questioned the whole idea of escorting Janice to this party tonight. What had they all been thinking?

"I mean, what you're wearing—it's nice and everything, but it won't go with what Janice is gonna wear."

He looked down at his clean white crew shirt and neatly pressed khakis. "Don't forget I'll put my navy sports jacket over this. That'll spiff me up, don't you think?"

She shook her head. "That won't cut it, Dad."

"Really?" Now he went over to the mirror on his closet door and studied himself closely. "You know, when I asked Reggie what the dress was for the party, this is pretty much what he told me." He turned and smiled expectantly at her.

"Does Reggie even like you?"

"Huh?"

"Well, there's this thing that girls sometimes do—you know, like if they don't like someone."

"What are you saying?"

"It's usually mean girls who do stuff like this. They'll tell a girl to wear something that's totally wrong—like they know it's a formal party but they tell the girl they don't like that it's a pool party, so she'll show up in a bikini, when everyone else is dressed to the nines. Just to embarrass her."

"Wow, that is mean. Did that ever happen to you?"

"No, Dad. But maybe that's what Reggie did to you."

Blake laughed. "Oh, I don't think so. I'm guessing Reggie is more grown up than that by now."

"I don't know." She shook her head in a dismal way, like she was seriously concerned her father would be the laughingstock of tonight's gala event, perhaps even be written up in Martha's Vineyard Worst Dressed column, if there was such a thing.

All the same, he now felt unsure. After all, Reggie obviously liked Waverly. What if he suspected that Blake liked her too? Would he try to sabotage Blake? No, that was ridiculous—not to mention juvenile. Yet he didn't want to offend Sicily by not taking her advice seriously.

"You could be right about that, Sicily," he said slowly. "Unfortunately, this is as good as it gets with me, sweetie. I don't get dressed up much anymore. In fact, my city clothes are still packed and stored in the attic above the garage. After all, this is Martha's Vineyard, not LA or New York." He held up his hands. "I guess this'll have to do."

She shrugged. "And you do look nice, Dad. I'm just saying…."

He checked his watch. "And I'm saying we better get over there to pick up Janice." He tried not to grimace at the sound of her name on his lips.

"You really don't like her much, do you?" Sicily got her backpack. "I mean, even though Janice is pretty, she's really not girlfriend material, right?"

"Janice is okay, but definitely not girlfriend material. Not for me anyway." He closed and locked the door.

Sicily looked relieved. "Yeah, that's what I thought."

"You know I only agreed to take her tonight to help Waverly."

He shook his head as he got into the car. "Although that seems a moot point now."

"What's a moot point?"

"It's *moot* when something doesn't really matter anymore. Now that Janice has her wrecked car business figured out because insurance is covering everything, she shouldn't still be mad at Waverly. For that reason, it shouldn't really matter whether I take her to the party or not."

"Oh, I don't know, Dad, I think it matters to Janice."

"Maybe so." He drove the short distance to their house, parking in the driveway right next to a small red convertible that, despite being produced by a cheaper manufacturer, looked strikingly similar to her Beamer, before the staircase flattened it.

"Are you still going to break up with her then?"

With a warning look, he nodded with his fingers to his lips. "But we'll keep that under wraps for now, okay?"

Inside the house, they were warmly greeted by Vivian. She looked much healthier in her colorful caftan than she had in the drab hospital gown. "Hello, my lovelies." She hugged each of them.

"So you really are feeling okay?" Blake asked.

"Never felt better." She smiled. "But thank you again for your help today, Blake."

"Something smells delicious in here." He glanced over to the kitchen, where Louise was stirring something on the stove.

"I'd invite you to stay for seafood pasta," Louise called out, "but I think you have bigger fish to fry tonight." She laughed at her joke.

"I don't know," he called back. "If I had my choice, I'd rather stay here."

"I think Janice is almost ready," Vivian told Blake. "But if you'd like to sit out on the porch and wait, Louise has made us some delightful raspberry lemonade."

"I told Dad he wasn't dressed up enough," Sicily told Vivian in a conspiratorial tone.

Vivian laughed. "I think he looks perfect. After all, this is Martha's Vineyard. No one dresses up too much here."

Sicily looked surprised. "That's exactly what Dad said."

Louise joined them now. "So what are you two planning to do for the Fourth?" She set a tray of crackers and cheeses on the low table. "If you haven't made other plans, I'd love if you joined us for a little barbecue here."

"I thought it would be fun to take Sicily to Edgartown for the parade and fireworks show," Blake said. The truth was, he hadn't made any real plans yet, but the idea of spending the Fourth with Janice—after what he planned to tell her before the evening was over—was quite unsettling.

"But you'd still have time to come to our barbecue in between those events," Louise urged him. "Unless you plan to spend the entire day at Edgartown. But it'll be crawling with tourists over there. Surely you'd like to come back here for a reprieve and some delicious food."

"Why don't you let Blake think about it, dear?" Vivian said quietly. "Let him get back to you later."

"Yes, of course. Just know that you're welcome. It'll be a small affair, only a dozen or so people." Louise smiled as she refilled his glass. "I love to entertain. Vance and I used to throw the grandest Fourth of July parties back in Boston. I've missed that. Anyway, we've made a few friends here in Vineyard Haven, and I thought it would be fun to have a beach party."

Blake refrained from checking his watch again but was about to ask whether or not Janice really intended to go to the party tonight, when she suddenly made her appearance. "Here I am," she announced breezily. "Sorry to keep you waiting, Blake."

"Don't you look gorgeous," Vivian gushed.

"Thanks, Aunt Viv." Janice did a little swirl turn for them.

"Isn't she glamorous?" Louise said. "That color is so dramatic, Janice. You'll be the belle of the ball, with all eyes on you!"

Blake stood. "You look very pretty, Janice."

She smiled at him. "Really? You think so? Not too much, is it?"

No way was Blake going to answer that honestly. "You're mother is absolutely right," he assured her. "That color is stunning, and everyone will probably be looking at you."

Now Janice pouted. "But you certainly didn't dress up much, did you?"

"Sorry about that, but my formal wear is still packed." He shrugged. "I guess you'll have to take me or leave me."

She rolled her eyes slightly. "Guess I better take you. Speaking of that, shall we take my rental tonight? It's not as nice as the Beamer, but it makes more of an entrance than your SUV."

He jingled his keys. "I think I'd rather drive my car, if you don't mind." He nodded to Louise, Vivian, and Sicily. "Have a nice evening, ladies."

As they walked out to the car, Blake noticed that she was struggling to keep her stiletto heels from sinking into the gravel. But he waited for her, opening the door like he always did—the way his dad had trained him to do when he was still a boy. As she got in, he had to admit that she did look rather stunning—in an Oscar's night, glitzy sort of way. Not his favorite look, but a lot of fashion-minded women seemed to enjoy it. Hopefully everyone wouldn't look like that tonight. If someone at the door handed him a tie, he might have to excuse himself and go home. After all, he'd agreed to take Janice to the party...not to bring her back home.

"Do you know where you're going?" she asked as he started the engine.

"I already programmed Martha."

"Martha?"

He laughed. "Right before I came out here, I got my GPS installed, and the first destination I put into it was for Martha's Vineyard. So I named it Martha."

She laughed too. "Okay, Martha, lead us on."

Janice made pleasant small talk about her recent trip to Boston, car shopping, her most interesting legal case, as well as some political name dropping, which mostly went right past him. But he nodded and made the appropriate small talk responses back to her.

"I'm afraid we're going to be a little late," he said. Although that was an exaggeration, since according to Martha, they were running ninety minutes late. And he remembered how Janice liked to be prompt and on time, or so she'd said before.

"Fashionably late," she assured him.

Surprised at her nonchalance, he just nodded. Although he knew it wasn't good manners to be early or even on time to most parties, he also knew that an hour and a half was a little beyond fashionable too. Still, it wasn't like he'd wanted to come tonight anyway. For all he cared, they could be three hours late. Except that he wanted to see Waverly. If only briefly. Although he'd do whatever he could, within the confines of good manners, to be sure it was more than that.

"Looks like this is it," he said as he turned into the long drive-way of what looked like a very impressive estate.

"Valet parking," she pointed out. "Too bad we didn't bring my car."

He didn't respond to that as he pulled up under the portico, got out, handed the valet his keys, then went around to open the door for Janice. "Here we are," he said in a stiff voice. As he walked her toward the stately house, he felt certain that both Sicily and Janice were right—he was underdressed. He gave their names to the security guard in front, saying they were friends of Reggie Martin, and for a moment, as the guy searched his list, Blake wondered if they were even going to get in. He actually hoped they wouldn't.

"Have a nice evening," the security guy told them as he nodded to the doorman to let them in.

"I hope we're not too late," he muttered as he and Janice went into the elegant home. Marble floors, oriental carpets, sculptures, art—everything suggested money, old money. He couldn't help but notice that Janice, in her formal cocktail dress, appeared to fit in perfectly with the décor.

Then, to his relief, he observed a few other guests milling about inside the house, and they were dressed very similar to him. Blake continued on through the foyer and into a large room, where he pointed to a wall of enormous glass doors that completely opened to the outdoor living area beyond. Out there some happy calypso music was playing. Colorful outdoor lights reflected over the satin surface of a sapphire-blue pool, and white-clothed tables were filled with food. Guests dressed a lot like Blake mingled and talked.

"Looks like we found it," he said as he led her outside to where the party was in full swing.

"Am I overdressed?" she hissed in his ear.

He shrugged. "Not for the red carpet."

She shot a dark look his way.

He was about to make his way to the food, since he was quite hungry, when an attractive brunette walked toward him. He could tell by her expression she recognized him, and although she was familiar, he couldn't quite place her.

"Blake Erickson!" She came close and air-kissed him. "Fancy meeting you here in my old stomping grounds."

Suddenly he remembered she was a fairly new but up-and-coming actress in one of the films he worked on last year. A supporting role with Scarlett Johansson in the lead. Stella Something.

"Stella," he said, still trying to recall her last name, "so great to see you. You look lovelier than ever." He introduced her to Janice.

"What are you working on?" Stella asked him. "Anything exciting?"

So he explained his early retirement plan.

"You're kidding?" she said. "You *live* here full-time?"

He nodded. "I'm still a Vineyard newbie, but so far so good. In fact, I'm enjoying it immensely."

She turned to Janice. "And you live here too?"

Janice laughed. "No. I wouldn't survive long here. More than a couple of weeks in this place and I might go into a coma. Really, I'm a city girl at heart."

Stella glanced at Janice's dress. "Yes, I can see that." She turned back to Blake now, telling him about a new project she would be starting in the fall. "I wish you were working on it. You're the best."

"Thanks, but for now I'm enjoying this slower pace."

"How do you know Belinda?" Stella asked. "Did you do a film with her?"

"I haven't met Belinda. A friend of hers invited us here tonight. Do you know Reggie Martin?"

"Oh, I've known Reggie for years." Stella lowered her voice. "Isn't this house spectacular? It's been in Belinda's family for years. We used to spend summers here as kids. I still love coming out here with her for a few weeks." She pointed to a pretty blond coming their way. "Speak of the devil." Then Stella introduced them to their hostess, Belinda Vale.

"Sorry to be so late," Blake told Belinda. "Looks like a great party."

Belinda waved her hand. "Oh, that's okay. Although I think the lobster's pretty picked over now. But there are plenty of other goodies." She peered curiously at them, particularly at Janice, who stood out like a sore thumb in her bright red sparkly dress. Blake suspected that Belinda, too polite to say it, was trying to place who they were and why they were here.

"Reggie invited Blake," Stella explained.

"Oh, that's great. Reggie's friends are my friends." Belinda grinned at Blake. "I meet more new Vineyard people through dear old Reggie."

"Blake has another connection to you too," Stella told her. "He's a retired filmographer." She even listed some of Blake's projects. "But can you believe he left Hollywood for Martha's Vineyard?"

Belinda nodded in a way that suggested she understood. "Someday I'll be here permanently too."

"Not me," Janice said curtly. "This little island is far too claustrophobic for my taste."

"And what do you do?" Belinda politely asked her.

Janice explained she was a Boston attorney. "But I'm also in the senate race this year. You may have heard of my father, the late Vance Grant?"

Belinda looked slightly surprised. "That was your father?"

"Yes." Janice nodded with pride. "I hope to follow in his political footsteps. As my campaign says, it's time for a change."

"Oh, well, good luck to you with that. Personally, I try to avoid political discussions, but I'll warn you that some of my guests are... uh, let's just say *not so neutral*."

"Yes, I'm well aware that many of my opponents think of Martha's Vineyard as their haven." Janice laughed. "Is that why they call it Vineyard Haven?"

"I don't know about that. I think it has more to do with the harbor and boats—you know, a safe haven." Belinda made a polite smile. "Now if you'll excuse me." But before she left, she glanced curiously at Blake, as if she wondered about his connections with Janice Grant. As if he didn't question them himself.

Stella was introducing them to various acquaintances when Blake spotted Reggie and Waverly. But it was Waverly who caught his eye. Although he made congenial small talk with the middle-aged couple whom Stella said, among other things, "were close friends of the Clintons," most of his attention was on Waverly. She looked amazing, like a sea goddess, in a breezy sort of sundress in aquamarine colors. He wished he could photograph her.

"You're Vance Grant's daughter?" the woman was saying to Janice. "Really?"

Janice laughed lightly. "Yes, I'm sure it seems incongruous for me to be here, but I like to think of myself as politically tolerant."

"Am I correct to assume you are your father's daughter when it comes to politics as well?" the man asked with a concerned expression.

And so Janice, acting as if she were making a campaign speech, began to espouse some of her opinions, which it was plain to see this couple did not share. Though he was impressed by her commitment to her political convictions, Blake winced inwardly. This just didn't feel like the right atmosphere for this discussion.

Before her captive audience had a chance to respond, Blake stepped in. "It's a pleasure to meet you," he said to the slightly startled looking couple. "But if you'll excuse me, I see a friend." Then, without even glancing at Janice, he made his getaway. If she wanted to get embroiled in some political brouhaha, let her. Just because he brought her here tonight didn't mean he had to endure her idea of "socializing."

"Hello, friends," he said to Waverly and Reggie. "I've just made a run for my life."

"What's going on?" Waverly asked.

"Your cousin, my date, thinks she's on the campaign trail. Or maybe it's the warpath."

"She's talking politics here?" Waverly looked over to where several people were conversing in a rather animated way with Janice.

"Unfortunately." He gave Reggie a sympathetic look. "I hope Belinda doesn't hold this against your friendship, although it sounded as if you and she are fairly tight."

"Belinda's a peach." Reggie shook his head. "But that Janice... she's a real piece of work, isn't she?"

"I have to give her credit," Blake admitted. "She is courageous."

"That's true." Waverly nodded. "I still remember when we were kids, and she tried to eat a bee."

"She ate a bee?" Reggie made a face.

"First she dared me to eat one," Waverly explained. "I said *no way*. But Janice kept bragging that she'd done it before—lots of times. Naturally, I didn't believe her, and I told her so. So, to prove me wrong, she caught a honeybee in a Dixie cup and actually put the poor bee in her mouth." She started laughing now. "It stung her on the bottom lip, and she let out this bloodcurdling scream that most of Boston must've heard."

"So Janice Grant was like the pioneer of lip injections?" Reggie said, making them all laugh even harder.

Waverly's eyes sparkled as she continued. "You should've seen her bottom lip swell up. Honestly, it got as big as a hotdog."

"Did you get photos?" Blake asked,

Waverly was laughing hard now. "I called her Hotdog Lips until she told her dad, and he made me stop."

"Hotdog Lips!" Reggie let out a howl of laughter. "I might need to remember that one if she keeps harassing Belinda's guests."

Blake glanced over to where Janice still appeared to be holding court with an irritated audience. "Do you think I should go over there and rescue her?" he asked Waverly.

"Rescue Janice?" Waverly grimly shook her head. "You obviously do not know my cousin as well as I thought you did."

He didn't admit that was not only true but fortunate as well.

Chapter Twenty-four

....

Waverly knew she shouldn't feel responsible for Janice's bad manners at Belinda's party, but she couldn't help but feel guilty as the political discussion, aided by the influence of intoxicants, grew louder.

"Should I do something?" Waverly asked Reggie. "Since we are sort of your guests here tonight?"

"Hey, if your cuz wants to hang herself, politically speaking, why not let her?" Reggie laughed, then finished the last of his drink. Waverly was trying not to count, but she felt certain this was his third one—and it worried her.

"Not that any of these people are her constituents anyway," Blake pointed out.

"No, I wouldn't think so," Waverly agreed. "Even if they lived in Janice's region, they're clearly not in her party. I just hope Belinda isn't too offended by her."

"Anybody else want a drink?" Reggie held up his empty glass.

"No thanks," Waverly told him. "Are you certain you want to—"

"Don't worry about me, pretty lady." He gave her a goofy grin.

"But you're driving and—"

"I can hold my liquor," he assured her. "Ask anyone."

After he left, Waverly turned to Blake. "I may need to beg a ride home from you," she said quietly.

"Not a problem."

"Hopefully I can get Reggie to see the wisdom in that."

Blake glanced around at the partiers. "But I think I might like to make an earlier night of it. That is, if I can drag your cousin away from her forum."

"I'd love to call it a night," she said eagerly. "I've met some nice people, and I was actually having fun earlier in the evening." She lowered her voice. "Until Reggie started drinking like a fish, and Janice started picking fights with Democrats."

Blake elbowed her gently. "Looks like you and I are a couple of old party poopers."

She smiled at him. "Hey, call it what you like, but I can think of better ways to have a good time."

"So can I." When his eyes met hers, she felt like he was looking a lot deeper than just the surface; for that matter, so was she.

"I'm sorry I twisted your arm to bring Janice tonight. Although, for my sake, I'm glad," she admitted.

"Not as glad as I am," he told her. "Do you mind if I tell you how stunning you look?"

Feeling uncomfortable, she waved her hand. "Oh, go on with you."

"Okay." He nodded. "I will go on. You look like a sea goddess in that dress, Waverly. The way it brings out the color in your eyes, your creamy skin. You're the most beautiful creature here tonight. If you weren't here with Reggie, I would…well, I'm not sure what I'd do. But I might ask the sea goddess to take a midnight swim with me."

She laughed. "I haven't seen you drinking, Blake, but you sound slightly—"

"If I'm intoxicated, it's simply with your beauty, Waverly."

"You know, Blake, my grandparents were Irish. Hence the name Brennen. But I wouldn't take you for Irish, except for all your blarney just now."

"It's not blarney," he insisted. "It's the truth."

At that minute Reggie returned, sitting down at the table with not one but two drinks. "I got a spare." He winked at Blake now. "Just in case someone changes her mind."

"Waverly and I were both thinking we'd like to make it an early evening," Blake told him.

Reggie looked surprised. "You would?"

"It's been a long day," Waverly said quickly. "Remember I told you about my mom going to the hospital? That was pretty stressful. Blake was the one who was with her when it happened, and that was pretty stressful. Plus Sicily and I have been slaving to finish the mural, which is finally done." She held up her still-stained fingernails. "I haven't even had a chance to get the paint out of my nails."

Reggie leaned over to peer at her hands. "Well, now that you mention it, I see you haven't." He shook his head. "No shame in that, Waverly. You look like a real artist now." He took a sip of his drink. "Remember when you asked if I had a *real* gallery?"

"I do remember." She patted his arm, resisting the temptation to remove one of those drinks and pour it into the potted plant behind him. "So, anyway, if you don't mind too much, I think I'll catch a ride home with Blake. I'd like it if you came with us too."

"Came with you?" He looked at her like she was nuts. "But the party's barely begun, sweetness. I can't leave yet."

"So you don't mind if I do?"

He looked dismayed. "Well, I do mind. But, hey, it's a free country."

"Thanks for inviting me tonight."

He nodded. "It was a pleasure arriving with the prettiest girl."

She thanked him, then told him to take care. "Please, when it's time to go, call a taxi, won't you?"

"You bet," he told her. "Probably a bunch of us will get a ride back to town together. You know, with a *designated driver*." He snickered like that was a joke.

Waverly exchanged glances with Blake, but he looked as much at a loss as she was. "Do you think Janice will be ready to go?" she asked him.

"Guess we'll find out."

So the two of them went over to where it almost seemed that the political "discussion" was quieting down some. Only three of Janice's audience still remained, all men who appeared to be in their forties or thereabouts. Waverly supposed, based on their expressions, that these men were more interested in Janice as a woman than as a politician, but she could be wrong.

"Excuse me," Blake said as he stepped up to Janice. "But Waverly and I are ready to head for home and I—"

"Why is Waverly going *with you*?" Janice demanded.

"Is your date dumping you?" a balding guy asked, interest flaming in his eyes.

Janice narrowed her eyes. "Are you, Blake?"

"I'm not exactly her date," Blake explained to the man. "More like an escort."

"An escort?" the tall thin guy echoed. "You're telling us that a gorgeous girl like Janice Grant, successful attorney and candidate for state senate race, has to hire an escort to—"

"I did *not* hire an escort!" Janice shook her martini glass at him, and Waverly had to jump to miss the contents splashing over the edge.

"She's right, I'm not exactly an escort," Blake said casually, "since I'm not charging her anything for my services. You see, I agreed to escort her for free. Guess that makes me more like a cheap date. A forced cheap date."

Some of the onlookers guffawed.

"Actually, I'm the one who forced him into it." Waverly decided to go with the lighthearted banter now. It seemed preferable to Janice throwing an ugly fit. "But I'm letting him off the hook now."

"Letting him off the hook," the balding guy asked, "or hooking him good?"

Blake smiled. "Hey, if Waverly wants me on her hook, I'm glad to oblige."

"Wait a minute!" Janice held up her hands. "Just a cotton-pickin' minute. What's going on here anyway?"

"Nothing," Waverly calmly said. "We're simply trying to get you to come home with us, Janice. Are you coming or not?"

"So, is this how it is?" Janice put her face close to Waverly's now. "While my back is turned, you put a move on my man?"

"I'm not your man," Blake said evenly. "I was simply your driver tonight. And your driver is going home now. Are you ready?"

Janice was still glaring at Waverly. "I know what you're doing, Waverly. I can read you like a very short book." She reached over and took Waverly's pearl strand in her fingers. "The same way you stole these, now you're stealing my man." Waverly could smell the alcohol on Janice's breath, a reminder that she needed to go carefully.

"No one is stealing anything, Janice." Waverly gently but firmly moved Janice's hand from her necklace. "Blake and I are just tired and want to go home and—"

"Going home *together*, I'll bet!"

"No, we're not. And we'd like you to come with us. I'm pretty tired. It was a long day with my mom going into the hospital and everything." Waverly felt close to tears now.

"Your mom's in the hospital?" the tall thin guy asked her.

"She was. But they released her. And then she told me she's got cancer and—" Her voice broke.

"Hey, that's rough. My mom had cancer too." The balding guy looked at her with real empathy. "But Mom's been almost five years without—"

"*Shut up!*" Janice shouted so loud that Waverly jumped.

"Anyway, I want to go home," Waverly told her irate cousin. "Are you coming or not?"

"Don't worry. I'll give the illustrious Janice Grant a ride if she needs one," the balding guy offered. "Don't know where I'll drop her after hearing all her political views tonight. But I promise not to throw her into the ocean."

"You could always call a cab for her," Waverly suggested.

"Look, Cousin, I'm not worried about how I'll get home," Janice shot at her. "I'm worried that you not only wrecked my car." She pointed to the pearls again. "And stole my grandma's pearls." Her face flamed more red. "But now you're stealing my man too!"

"Woo-hoo," one of the guys said, "this is getting even more interesting."

"You girls are cousins?" the balding guy asked, curiously looking at one and then the other. "You don't look much alike."

"And you wrecked Janice's car?" Another guy shook his finger at Waverly. "Not nice, Cousin."

Waverly forced a laugh. "To be fair, it was a staircase that wrecked her car."

They started to kick that one around when Blake interrupted. "The deal is, we're leaving," he told Janice. "I assume you can find a ride home." Now he linked his arm in Waverly's. "We'll say our adieu."

"Good night, everyone." Waverly started to go but was stopped by someone's fingers digging into her forearm. Turning, she saw Janice now glaring at her with dark, angry eyes.

"You're not going *anywhere* until you explain yourself!" Janice spat.

"Hey, lighten up, lady," one of the guys told her.

"Stay out of this," Janice shot back. Then she turned to Waverly. "What is going on between you and Blake? I have a right to know."

Waverly didn't know what to say.

"If you really want to talk about this," Blake said quietly to Janice, "maybe we should take it someplace more private."

"*Private?*" Janice laughed, but it was a mean laugh. "My whole life is lived in the public forum. You bring me here tonight, then leave with my cousin? You think that's private? If you're breaking up with me, do it now! Unless you're afraid to...not man enough?"

"Janice," he said gently. "I can't very well break up what's never been an authentic relationship. But if you're asking if whatever we had is over, I'd have to say absolutely. It's over and done. Finished. I've been trying to tell you that since the very beginning. But you don't listen."

"Now that's true enough," one of the guys agreed. "Ms. Grant might be easy on the eyes, but her ears don't work too well. We keep trying to talk some sense into her, but she just won't—"

"Shut *up*!" She shook her finger at him.

"See." The guy nodded like she'd proved his point.

"Good night, Janice." Blake's arm was still linked in Waverly's. But Janice hadn't released her viselike grip on Waverly's arm. Waverly was literally being pulled between the two of them now. With several more onlookers joining to witness this little display, Waverly hoped she wasn't about to play the rope in a tug-of-war game.

"Janice," Waverly said firmly, "let go of me."

"Not until you tell me what's going on between you two, Waverly. *I mean it.*"

Waverly glanced nervously at Blake.

"Fine. If this is what it takes, I'll tell you exactly what's going on." He focused his gaze directly at Janice. "I have fallen hopelessly in love with your cousin. I am totally smitten, over the moon, cupids and arrows, head over heels in love with her. Is that clear enough for you?"

Now everyone within about a ten-foot radius made little oohing-cooing sounds.

"Well!" Janice released Waverly's arm.

"Thank you." Waverly rubbed the sore spot where bright red finger marks showed.

"Why didn't you say so in the first place?" Janice shot indignantly at Blake. "You didn't have to be such a chicken—"

"Aw, give 'em a break, Hotdog Lips," Reggie called out from behind Janice.

Now everyone was laughing.

"Hotdog Lips?" the balding guy echoed. "Did you just call Janice Grant 'Hotdog Lips'?"

While the others laughed and cracked a few more jokes, Blake gently eased Waverly away from the crowd. They were just going into the house when they ran into Belinda coming out.

"Hey, where are you two heading off to?" she asked with a suspicious grin.

Blake politely thanked Belinda for her hospitality and told her they needed to get home.

Waverly nodded. "Yes, blame it on me," she explained. "It's been a very long day, and I'm tired."

"But you won't see the fireworks," Belinda said.

"Actually, we already saw some fireworks." Waverly smiled weakly. "Maybe you missed that show."

"Oh, you mean Janice Grant." Belinda laughed. "I saw some of that."

"I hope she won't be a problem," Blake said quickly. "We offered her a ride home, but she declined."

Belinda shook her head. "Oh, don't worry about her. I absolutely love controversial guests. Gives everyone something to talk about the next day."

They continued making their exit, hurrying toward the front door as if they expected to be accosted by Janice.

They were barely outside, waiting in the shadows for the valet to come around with his car, when Waverly realized she was already replaying Blake's public proclamation of love. "Did you really mean *that*?" she asked without even thinking.

"What?" He looked confused.

Now she felt embarrassed. "Uh, nothing."

But he was staring at her now, obviously trying to figure out what she'd meant. "Oh," he said finally. "You mean what I said to Janice about my feelings for you…in front of everyone?"

"Yes." She nervously fingered her strand of pearls. "Did you mean it?"

He barely nodded, but he looked worried.

She bit her lip, unsure as to how to respond and wondering why she'd blurted that out like that. Did she really want to deal with this right now?

"Did I come on too strong?" he asked with sincerity. "You looked a little freaked, but then again, it was a pretty weird situation. Who knew Janice would be so in your face with all that?"

"She'd been drinking."

"Even so, I assumed she'd be more concerned about her public image."

"Janice has always been something of an exhibitionist."

"So I'm gathering."

Waverly was grateful that his SUV was being delivered just now. It gave her a moment to attempt to get her bearings. Things were moving way too fast. And her mind was not keeping up.

"I'm sorry," he said as he drove them away from the estate. "I probably overstepped my bounds by speaking out like that. But, seriously, your cousin was making me crazy. Maybe crazy begets crazy. You think?"

"So, you said that because of Janice? You wanted to get the message to her once and for all?"

"Well, yeah, sort of." By the dim light of his dashboard, she could see his perplexed expression. Maybe he was as overwhelmed as she felt.

"Oh, Blake." She let out a long sigh. "I'm sorry, but I am truly exhausted. Emotionally exhausted."

"You've had a long day, Waverly."

"And you were right. I'm still in shock, hearing that my mom is dying. It's like I can't even process it yet."

"That's a heavy load."

"So, please, forgive me if I just sit here in stumped silence."

"You are absolutely forgiven." He nodded with his eyes fixed on the road. "And you'll forgive me if I acted like a fool tonight?"

"Of course."

Then, to her relief, he turned on some music. Some quiet instrumental jazz. But it sounded blessedly soothing after the noise and chaos of the party. Trusting that he would get her safely home, she leaned back into the comfortable seat, closed her eyes, and finally relaxed. Although it made no sense, this was the first time she'd relaxed in days, weeks…perhaps even years.

Chapter Twenty-five

....

The next morning, Blake wanted to lay low. Mostly to avoid Janice, but he told himself he was focusing on his daughter and that there was a lot to see and experience on the island, and he planned to use Sicily as his excuse to go see it. To start with, he got her up early, and they drove to see the sun rise over at the East Chop lighthouse, where he got some pretty sweet photos. Then they came back home for a late breakfast. Blake would've liked to have spent the day just hanging at home but worried that Janice might drop in and make a big ugly scene. So he began to hatch a plan to keep them out and about for the duration of the day.

"Do you think Vivian and Louise are fighting?" Sicily asked him as they sat on a dock at Lake Tashmoo. With their bare feet hanging in the water, and sipping on drinks, they were recovering from their bike ride in the hot sun.

"What makes you think that?" he prodded gently.

"Because, when you were cleaning up the breakfast stuff, I went next door to take Vivian the shell I found on the beach this morning— you know, to add to her seashell bouquet. But Vivian wasn't even there. And Louise seemed kinda upset about something."

"Oh?" He wondered if this had anything to do with Janice.

"Louise said that Vivian went to stay with Waverly for a few days."

"Really? She's staying in Waverly's apartment?"

"Yeah. But Louise wasn't too happy about it. Do you think Vivian and Louise had a fight or something? Gregory sometimes runs off after he and Mommy have a fight."

"Oh." He searched for an appropriate response. He was curious to hear more about how often Gia and Gregory fought like that, but he'd find out about that some other time. Right now Sicily sounded more concerned about Louise and Vivian. "Maybe Vivian went to stay with Waverly so they could have some private time together."

"You mean because Vivian is dying?"

"Who told you that?"

"I heard Louise talking about it to Janice this morning."

"Oh." Blake was curious about the context of this statement, but he didn't really want to go there just now. "So how does that make you feel?" he asked her. "You know...to hear that Vivian is, uh, well...dying."

"Sad." She took in a jagged little breath. "I don't want her to die, Daddy."

"No, neither do I." He slipped his arm around her shoulder and pulled her close. "It makes me sad too."

"When is it going to happen?" Sicily asked quietly. "I mean, when is she going to die?"

"No one knows exactly when, sweetie." He was struggling for the right words to explain this to her—but what if there were no right words? Then he remembered something Vivian had said not long ago. "But you do understand, don't you, that dying is just a natural part of living?"

She didn't answer. Instead she folded her arms across her front, intently picking at the edge of a Band-Aid on her elbow.

"You do realize everything that's alive has to die someday. You get that, don't you?"

"I guess so."

"Good. But beyond that, I believe God has something far better for us when we die."

"You mean heaven?"

He looked overhead to where a couple of gulls were squawking. "Yeah, heaven."

"What's heaven supposed to be like, Dad?"

"Good question."

"Meaning you don't really know?"

He considered his answer. "I don't think anyone knows for absolute certain, honey. But do you want to hear what I believe it could be like?"

"Yeah." She nodded.

"Well, I look at the most beautiful things in this world. You know, like some of my favorite kinds of things." He pointed out toward the clear blue lake. "Like this spot right here. Or like the beach and the ocean, boats and lighthouses, and I imagine those things in heaven—only I imagine them being a lot better."

"Like the boats might be able to sail over the water as well as over the clouds and everything?" she asked with growing enthusiasm.

"Yes," he said eagerly. "Like that. Now tell me something you really love or enjoy doing." He hoped she wouldn't say video games.

"Horses," she declared.

"Horses?" He was surprised he'd never heard of this before.

"Yeah, I keep asking Mom to let me take riding lessons, but she says I have to be bigger to do it. But I know girls my age who get to ride horses."

"Right." He thought hard. "So maybe there will horses in heaven, and maybe some will be like Pegasus—you know, with wings and able to fly. And maybe they can do even more than fly."

"Like swim underwater," she suggested.

"Sure, why not?"

"And I can have my own horse in heaven?"

"Who knows?" He shrugged. "But since it's heaven and because God is an incredible creator and He made an amazing earth, doesn't it make sense that heaven will be a whole lot better than earth? Really, don't you think *anything* would be possible in heaven?"

"Yeah. That makes sense."

"In fact, I'll bet we can't begin to imagine how fantastic heaven will be, Sicily. Even if we have really good imaginations. It won't just be about horses and boats and things—people we love will be there too."

"People like Vivian?"

"Yeah. Some people just get there sooner than others. Maybe it's to avoid a traffic jam." He exhaled. "Like it was on Main Street this morning. Although I'm positive there will be no such thing as a traffic jam in heaven."

"Mom will be relieved to hear that." Sicily laughed as she kicked her feet in the water, splashing it up on his legs. "Especially since she says traffic jams are hell."

"Right." Now he kicked his feet, splashing her back. Before long they were both thoroughly dampened and standing on the dock, looking out over the lake.

"So if Vivian dies…" Sicily paused, then let out a long sigh. "I mean, *when* she dies, she'll be in a really good place. Right, Daddy?"

"That's what I believe. And that's what Vivian believes too."

"But we'll still miss her."

"Yeah. We will." He slipped his arm back around her shoulders again.

"But she'll be happy."

"I think so, honey." He gave her another squeeze. "I really do."

Nicely cooled from their impromptu splash fest, they rode their bikes over to the Island Alpaca Farm. After that, they stopped by the Black Dog for a very late lunch, followed by two rounds of mini golf at Island Cove. Finally they biked over to Mad Martha's for ice cream, which they took to the beach to eat.

"Maybe we could stop by The Gallery on our way home," Sicily suggested in a tentative tone as they were finishing up their cones. "Not just to play video games," she said quickly, "but so you can see the mural, Daddy."

"Sounds good."

She seemed surprised that he agreed so easily. As if she didn't know what would make him so eager to go hang out in a video arcade. Naturally, that made him want to explain some things to her. So, as they walked back across the sand, toward where their bikes were locked together on a pole, he made his attempt.

"Remember when you thought Janice was my girlfriend?" he began cautiously.

"Yeah. But then you said you didn't like her, Dad. Did you change your mind again already?"

"No, of course not. I never changed my mind in the first place,

Sicily. To me Janice was only a friend. That was all. You do understand that, don't you?"

"I guess so. But last night, after you and Janice left for the party, Louise was talking about your wedding and how great it would be—"

"My wedding?" He groaned.

"Louise thinks you're going to marry Janice," she declared.

"Well, that's totally ridiculous."

"Vivian tried to tell her that. But Louise wouldn't listen."

"Is that why you thought Vivian and Louise had had a fight?"

"Uh-huh."

"Do you know why Vivian doesn't agree with Louise? I mean, about me getting married to Janice?"

"Because she knows you don't like Janice that much?"

"Yes. And also because she knows I like someone else much better."

"You mean Waverly?"

He tried not to look surprised. "As a matter of fact, I do mean Waverly."

"Do you like Waverly enough to marry her, Daddy?"

"What would you think if I did?"

He shot a glance her way. Seeing her perplexed expression, as if she were deep in thought, he waited.

"I don't know," she finally said.

"Oh." He was stumped now. "But I thought you really liked Waverly. I thought we all agreed we could all three be friends. Remember?"

"Yeah. Being friends is not the problem, Daddy."

"So, tell me, what is the problem?"

She stopped walking and turned to look at him. "Do you promise not to laugh?"

"Absolutely." He held up his hand like a pledge. "I give you my word."

"Well, I always hope that you and Mommy will get married again."

"Oh." He felt blindsided by that one. "Really?"

"Yeah. But every time I say that to Mommy, she laughs."

"That's probably because your mom is already married, Sicily." He noticed a bench near the sidewalk and, taking Sicily's hand, led her over to sit down.

"I know." She sat down and focused on her lap.

"As far as I know, your mom and Gregory don't have any plans to get unmarried." He sat down beside her, turning toward her and studying her sweet pixie-like face. Her eyelashes brushed over her flushed cheeks ,and there was a smudge of chunky-monkey ice cream on her upper lip. The Band-Aid on her elbow was hanging halfway off. Suddenly she looked so small and young and slightly helpless. Even the purple streak in her hair suggested neglect or insecurity or something else he couldn't quite peg. He felt a lump in his throat, wondering why he hadn't seen her like this before.

"But what if they *did*, Dad? What if Mommy and Gregory got divorced? I've heard Mommy say she's going to divorce him—you know, when they're in the middle of a really bad fight, and they don't know I'm listening." She stared up at him with defiant blue eyes.

"People say things they don't mean when they're fighting, Sicily. You know that, don't you?"

"Yeah, I guess so. But what if they really did get divorced, Daddy?

It could happen. Olivia Martin's parents did that. They got divorced, and then they got married again. It really does happen sometimes. Would you marry Mommy again?"

"I don't…I, uh, I don't…" He didn't know what to say. He didn't want to hurt her any more than she'd already been hurt, and he wished he could undo all that had been done—make her life perfect somehow. Sicily deserved perfect. But how was that even possible?

Her eyes brightened now. "And then you and me and Mommy could all live together in the same house."

He thought hard about this. He knew this was simply a child's perspective, trying to put back together what had been broken so she could have what she wanted—her two parents living happily together under one roof. But he also knew that Sicily didn't know all that had transpired, back when she was too little to understand such things. Sicily had no idea of everything her mother had done to destroy their marriage. Not that Blake didn't blame himself too. He did. For years he'd gone over it again and again, wishing he'd done it differently. If only he'd been less focused on work and more attentive to his wife. Then maybe Gia wouldn't have gone looking for attention from others. But even as he took that blame, he knew that their marriage had probably been doomed from the start. But what do you tell a nine-year-old?

He took in a deep breath. "You know, Sicily, if this were a perfect world, and I wish it were a perfect world—kind of like heaven will be someday—but if it was, I'd say, *sure*, your mom and I could get back together. To be honest, there's a part of me that still wishes that could happen, in a perfect world."

As his voice trailed off, her countenance fell, but he knew he had to continue. He had to help her understand this. "You see, this isn't a perfect world, sweetie. Like we wish Vivian wasn't sick, that she could live for a long time. I know you wish your parents could be happily married to each other. We all wish we lived in a perfect world. But we don't. Not until we get to heaven anyway."

"So you're saying you and Mommy won't get married again?"

"I honestly don't think it's possible. Mommy chose to marry Gregory. That's just the way it is."

"Yeah, I figured you'd say something like that."

"Really?"

She let out a deep, sad sigh and stood up. "We should go, Dad."

He stood too, but he wasn't ready to end this conversation. "So do Gregory and your mom fight a lot?"

She shrugged but started to walk toward where the bikes were parked. "Sometimes they do. But they both were a lot happier when Mommy got that part in the new series. Gregory helped her to get it too."

"I'll bet your mom appreciated that a lot too." Blake knew that had been one of the main reasons Gia had been attracted to Gregory in the first place. "Your mom's been trying to get on a show for a while now. She sounded pretty thrilled."

"Yeah, she was." Sicily's voice still sounded sad. Sad and a bit lost.

He stopped by the bikes, bent down to unlock them. But before they got on them, he put a hand on her shoulder. "Can I ask you a question now?"

"I guess so."

"I know this world isn't heaven," he began slowly, "and nothing will ever be perfectly perfect down here. But if you could have it your way—I mean, except for your mom and me being remarried—what would you want, Sicily? In regard to things like where you live, or who you live with…like would you want me to move back to California so we could spend more time together there?"

"No, I like it here, Dad. I like your house, and it's fun doing stuff with you. Like today. And I like Martha's Vineyard a lot."

"Really?" He felt relieved. "I thought you hated it at first."

"I know. But that was just an act." She held her bike by the handlebars now, slowly walking it along the sidewalk.

Encouraged, he walked alongside her. "So you wouldn't mind coming out here from time to time to visit your old man then?"

She seemed to be thoughtfully considering this as they paused to wait for traffic.

Then it was safe to cross, but still she didn't answer him. They continued to walk their bikes down a side street. Soon they would be at The Gallery, where he knew this conversation would end. To his dismay, Sicily seemed to want it to end right now, because she was not talking. He considered pressing her for her answer, but it was too late. Sicily, two steps ahead of him, was already parking her bike in the bike stand outside of The Gallery.

He followed her lead and, although she said it was unnecessary, he locked their bikes together. Then she ran eagerly to the door of the arcade, opening it, then waiting for him, holding it for him like a miniature doorman.

"Hey, I'm supposed to be the one to open the doors for you," he reminded her.

"Sorry, but hurry up," she commanded. "I can't wait for you to see it."

Before she let him go inside, she insisted he close his eyes and let her lead him to the perfect viewing spot. Feeling a little silly and somewhat conspicuous, he agreed, closing his eyes and holding her hand as she led him like a blind man past several noisy video games.

"Okay," she said. "Open your eyes now."

He opened his eyes and was quite impressed. "Hey, that's really good, Sicily." He nodded with approval. "You're a very talented artist."

"Well, you know, Waverly helped too."

"But you were the one who came up with the idea," he reminded her. "You put a lot of hard work into it, Sicily. Don't sell yourself short."

"Yeah. That's true." She nodded. "I learned a lot about painting too."

Now she began pointing things out to him. As he saw the sparkle returning to her eyes and heard the enthusiasm in her voice, he knew this experience had been about a lot more than just painting a mural. Thanks to Waverly, Sicily's confidence and self-esteem had blossomed during the past couple weeks.

"Can we go upstairs and say hi to Waverly?" she asked. "And Vivian too?"

"I...uh...I don't know." He glanced over to the doorway that led to the upstairs.

"*Please*, Dad."

"How about if you go up and say hi, sweetie. I'll wait down here."

"All right." And *zip*, she was gone. He was a little disappointed that she hadn't pressed him harder since he really wanted to see Waverly. Instead he walked around and scrutinized the arcade more closely, noticing how the freshly painted walls brightened the place up nicely. It was thinned out in there too. Some of the machines had been removed or rearranged, clearing an open space over by the counter. All in all, it was much more pleasant.

"Hey, you." Waverly came up from behind him. "What are you doing here? Want to buy some tokens?"

"Sicily insisted we stop by." He smiled as he took her in, those auburn curls pinned loosely up from her neck, her ocean eyes, sweet smile—he hoped he wasn't staring. "Uh, she wanted me to see the completed mural."

"So what do you think?"

"I think The Gallery is starting to look more like a real gallery."

She laughed. "I wouldn't go that far, but it is an improvement." She glanced around. "Where's Sicily?"

"She went upstairs to see you."

"Oh. Well, Vivian's up there. Maybe they're visiting." She held up a brown bag. "Dinner."

"Don't let us keep you from it."

"It's all right. We're just having soup tonight. I think Vivian's still recuperating from that whole hospital thing."

"Yes, I can imagine." He looked directly into her eyes—then had to control himself for saying what he really wanted to say. *Not here. Not now. Give her time and space. Don't overwhelm her again.* "So are you and Vivian having some good visits?"

"Actually, we are. It's been a great day."

"Sicily was worried that Louise and Vivian had been in a fight."

"A fight?" Waverly laughed. "No, not at all. I just wanted to spend some time with Vivian...alone. So I offered to bring her over here for some peace and quiet—you know, some mother-daughter time. Plus, I guess Janice was in a bit of a huff today. Anyway, Vivian was perfectly happy to get away."

"I can imagine." He grinned wryly. "Truth is, I've been avoiding being home too."

"Worried that Hurricane Janice will come breezing by?"

"A little. Mostly for Sicily's sake." He sighed. "I assume Janice still plans to stick around until after the Fourth?"

"Oh, yeah."

"Well, that's understandable. But I thought Sicily and I might run over to Edgartown tomorrow to see the parade and maybe the fireworks later in the evening." He smiled at her. "Do you think you'd want to come with us?"

Her eyes lit up. "That sounds really fun!" Then, a second later, her expression changed. "Well, except I hate leaving Vivian like that—even for a day. I can't tell her, of course. She'd read me the riot act and tell me to live my life or even threaten to go live her last days somewhere else."

He nodded. "I understand."

"Besides that, she and Louise are having their barbecue tomorrow. And they expect you and Sicily to be there too."

He nodded in a halfhearted way. "Yeah, I know."

"You'll come, won't you?"

"I seriously doubt that Janice would appreciate my company too much."

"Oh, don't worry about her. She knows how to mind her manners."

"But what if she drank too much and lost it? We'd have an unexpected fireworks show on our hands. I hate to expose Sicily, or any of the other guests, to that." Although by now he suspected that Sicily had seen some rather fiery displays between her mom and Gregory.

"I see your point." Waverly tried to think of another option. "But it's too bad. I know both Aunt Lou and Vivian wanted you and Sicily to be there."

"Maybe there's more I can do to defuse the volatile situation," he said. "Do you suppose I could have a civilized conversation with Janice? Or do you think that would help?"

Waverly bit her lip. "It's hard to say. With Janice, you never know. She might totally ignore you, like nothing ever happened. Or, like you said, she could blow up in your face. But that's Janice."

Just then Sicily came bounding down the stairs. "Oh, there you are," she said as she ran up to hug Waverly. "Vivian said you went out to get soup."

"That's right."

Sicily looked dubious. "That's what you're having for dinner? Just plain old soup?"

Waverly laughed. "Not just plain old soup. It happens to be lobster bisque. It's Zephrus's soup of the day, and it's really scrumptious. Plus, we have homemade bread."

"Oh." Sicily nodded like that was fine. "Anyway, Vivian said we'll see you guys tomorrow at the barbecue." She looked at Blake. "Right, Dad? Because we are going, aren't we?"

"Well, we were just discussing it, sweetie, and I'm not convinced it's a good idea."

"*Dad.*" She was using that preadolescent tone again. "Why *not*?"

Waverly grinned. "Yeah, *Dad*, why not?"

"Fine." He held up his hands, knowing he was outnumbered. "You girls win. Sicily and I will come to the barbecue. But be prepared in case we have our own special fireworks show."

"Really, our own fireworks show?" Sicily looked innocently hopeful. "That would be so cool, Dad."

Blake winked at Waverly and, to his pleased surprise, she even winked back. As far as fireworks, well, he planned to do his best to keep it to the sparkler and sky rocket varieties, if at all possible.

Chapter Twenty-six

....

After the contractor bolstered up the apartment's back deck with some hefty-looking posts beneath it, and enclosed it with sturdy railings, he proclaimed it "safe for occupancy." Although the structure was stairless, Waverly began using and enjoying her outdoor space again. So it was that Independence Day morning found Waverly and her mother comfortably reclined in the Adirondack chairs, enjoying the morning sun and a cool marine breeze, along with their coffee and cinnamon rolls.

"I could get used to this little spot." Vivian took in a deep breath, slowly letting it out. She pointed to a corner of the deck. "But you really could use a big pot of red geraniums right there. Perhaps some kitchen herbs over here. And then it would be absolutely perfect."

"Good ideas." Waverly nodded. "You know you're welcome to stay here as long as you like. It's been fun having you."

Vivian smiled. "Thanks, sweetie. But I sort of miss the beach house too. In fact, I'm looking forward to Louise's barbecue today."

Waverly gazed out over the harbor, where a ferry was coming in, probably loaded with yet more tourists. How the Vineyard managed to house and feed all these summer people was still a mystery to her, but it seemed to work out. Perhaps some of the vacation people brought along their own food.

"But you're not?"

Waverly looked at her mother. "Not what?"

"Looking forward to Aunt Lou's barbecue?"

Waverly didn't know if that was a question or a statement. "I, uh, I guess I'm looking forward to it...."

"Just not looking forward to seeing your cousin?"

Waverly nodded. "But knowing Janice, she could be completely over the whole thing by now." She exhaled loudly. "Or not." Then she told Vivian what Blake had said about having a special fireworks show today. "Of course, Sicily took him literally. She probably thinks her dad's going to do some fabulous pyrotechnics today. I hope she's not too disappointed."

Vivian laughed.

"But I do think it's sweet that Blake wants to protect her from an ugly fight."

"From what I hear, Sicily is used to that sort of thing."

"Really?" Waverly stared at her mother with interest. "What have you heard? And who did you hear it from?"

"Oh, this and that. Between Sicily and Blake I've managed to patch some things together."

"Such as...?" Waverly wanted to appear nonchalant, but she was extremely curious.

"Well, for starters, it sounds as if Sicily's mother, Gia, is something of a firecracker. In fact, Sicily actually compared her to Janice—except, as she pointed out, they don't look anything alike."

"What does Gia look like?"

"It sounds like she looks like Sicily, only in a grown-up package."

Waverly nodded. "Then Gia must be quite pretty."

"Yes."

"I haven't gotten the feeling that Sicily and Gia are very close," Waverly said carefully. "Sicily doesn't appear to miss her mother much."

Vivian slowly shook her head. "I've noticed that too. Although I'm sure Sicily loves her mother."

"Of course. What child doesn't love her mother unconditionally?"

Of course, even as Waverly said this, she felt uneasy since, until lately, she and her mother had never been overly close—never had a traditional mother-daughter relationship.

"I suppose mothers are lucky that way." Vivian's expression grew somber. "When we're young and inexperienced and find ourselves the parent of a child, we think we're doing a decent job. Then we get older and wiser, and we realize how much we've blown it. Yet, if we're lucky, our offspring will forgive us and continue to love us—hopefully unconditionally."

Waverly didn't say anything. Was this Vivian's way of apologizing to her? And, if so, did Waverly need to acknowledge it? They'd never really been like that in the past.

"I'm curious, Waverly," Vivian continued. "You've never said much. But sometimes I wonder how *you* perceive your childhood. As a grown-up, what do you think when you look back over the way you were raised?"

Waverly shrugged. "Oh, I think I had a very unique and interesting childhood."

"In other words, your mother was a weirdo. But you were always all right with that?"

"I suppose there were times, like when you'd be on a trip and

I'd be staying at Aunt Lou's, that I'd start to feel a little envious of their traditional home."

Vivian looked slightly crushed. "You really wanted a traditional home?"

Waverly snickered. "Well, my jealousy was usually short-lived. I'd get a sneak peek at the underside of their so-called traditional home, and then I'd be thankful I wasn't a full-time resident. And, of course, there was Janice. As a child I thought she was totally spoiled. I called her PB."

"PB?"

"Short for *Princess Brat*. I gave her that nickname. Of course, I told her that PB stood for Pretty Baby or else she would've killed me." Waverly laughed. "But she called me names too. Not just with initials either."

"Like what?"

Waverly thought. "Let's see…she called me Earth Worm and Art Freak and, of course, there was always Waverly Wafer. But it was Dippy Hippie that I really hated. I don't even know why now. It's not really that bad."

"She probably called you that because I used to dress you somewhat unconventionally when you were little. Tie-dye and overalls and moccasins and things. I thought you looked adorable, and you fit right into San Francisco and the other places we lived, but it was rather unconventional for the likes of Boston." Vivian peered at her. "Anything else I did that you've had to have therapy for?"

Waverly shook her head. "No, but I do recall how much I hated it when we'd move," she admitted. "Not so much when I was little, more as I got older. I'd make a couple of friends, and then it was time to go. It was especially hard as a teenager. I guess that's when I became such a loner."

"Really, you felt you were a loner?" Vivian looked surprised. "Here I thought you made friends so easily. I'm sorry, Waverly."

Waverly shrugged. "It's okay. I'm over it."

"But you're right. We were fairly Bohemian," Vivian said wistfully. "Moving about, starting new businesses, taking extended vacations in strange locales. But you did get to see a lot of the world, Waverly."

"That's true. I had a lot of experiences that most kids miss out on. I appreciate that." She smiled.

"So you're basically perfectly fine and normal then?" Vivian peered closely at her. "I don't owe you some big apology for some horrid thing that I can't remember?"

"I don't think so."

"You'd tell me if I did?"

Waverly nodded. "Yes. But I do have a couple of questions."

"Such as?"

"For as long as I can remember, I've called you Vivian. I don't know why or how it started, but I know some people think it's odd. Sometimes I want to call you Mom or Mother, but I stop myself. I know you don't like that—being called Mother."

"You don't think I'd like to be called Mother?" Vivian looked stunned. "I would love it! Whether Mother, Mom, Mommy, Mama, Mummy—anything along those lines would be lovely."

"Really?" Now Waverly was stunned. "Then why have I been calling you Vivian all these years?"

Vivian laughed. "Don't you remember?"

"No."

"I joined a commune a few months before you were born, down near Santa Barbara, and I lived there until you were about four. You had a number of caregivers in the commune, and everyone called everyone by their first names, and because you heard others calling me Vivian, you did too. At first I thought it was cute, but when I tried to get you to call me Mommy, you got mad. You stomped your little two-year-old foot and insisted my name was Vivian. There weren't other children in the commune at the time, so you never heard the word *mommy* being used. So I simply acquiesced and let you call me Vivian. And so it remained."

"Really?" Waverly tried to wrap her head around that. "It was because of me?"

"Oh, I suppose I sort of liked it too. Especially when you were older." Vivian smiled sadly into her coffee cup. "It probably made me feel like we were friends, and I was younger. I suppose it had to do with my rebellion against tradition. But, honestly, if I had that part to do again, I think I'd do it differently. I like feeling like your mother, Waverly."

"So, if I slipped up now and then and called you Mom, you'd be okay with it?"

"I'd be much more than okay." Her smile brightened. "Now you said a couple of questions. What else is on your mind?"

Waverly was unsure, yet she needed to know. "It's about my dad—my biological father." She hesitated. The last time she'd brought this subject up was before she and Neil had gotten married, and the discussion hadn't gone well then. "It's not that I want to make you feel bad. It's just that I'd like to have some idea—even

if only for health reasons—who I'm related to. For instance, what
if I have some DNA issues that I'm unaware of? What should I be
watching out for?"

Vivian nodded. "Yes. You're right. I owe that to you."

"I've even wondered if perhaps there was a sperm donation
involved. And that's why you don't want to talk about it." Waverly
braced herself for her worst fear.

"No." Vivian laughed. "Not of the clinical sort anyway."

"What then? Why the mystery?"

"I suppose I was simply thinking of my own needs. I wanted
to forget about him—to pretend he never existed. But that wasn't
really fair." She paused, as if trying to see into the past. "Your father
was a good man. A very intelligent man." She pointed to Waverly.
"Like you, he was an artist. He was also a musician. He was a very
wonderful person. In fact, since confessions are in order, he was
the love of my life."

Waverly blinked. "My father was the love of your life?"

She nodded.

"Then why didn't you marry him? Or, even if you didn't believe
in marriage, why didn't you just live with him? Why didn't you
stay together?"

"He already had a wife."

"Oh."

"And he had children. He wanted to do the right thing by
them, and I never asked him to do more."

"Did he even know that you were pregnant, that he had
another child?"

She shook her head. "No. I spared him that. Really, what good would it have done? I was able to support myself. I certainly didn't want child support from him."

"You were such a modern independent woman." Waverly wondered if she would be so independent under the same circumstances. Not that she ever planned to find out.

"Anyway, I hear he still lives in Santa Barbara. Same house. Although he's retired. But from what I've heard, he's in good health. I'll be happy to give you all the information, so you can contact him if you like."

"You really don't mind?"

Vivian shrugged. "I suppose I wanted to think that I was enough for you, Waverly. That I'd given you life and freedom and education and experience and that you'd take that and run with it, making it your own."

"And I appreciate that."

"But you wanted more. You wanted a heritage, didn't you?"

"I don't know. Maybe."

"I suppose I was a bit shortsighted—not to mention selfish."

"No, I don't think that." Waverly put her hand on her mother's. "I honestly believe that you gave me the best of what you had to give...*Mom*."

Vivian smiled. "Thank you. And you have grown up into an intelligent, beautiful, artistic, loving, and a moderately well-adjusted person." Vivian studied her. "Though I was concerned for you for a while. It seemed you'd gotten into a rut after Neil died. That troubled me a lot."

"Was that one reason you pried me out of Chicago?"

Vivian nodded.

"I appreciate that. I was in a rut. I was trying to make some small changes, but it wasn't working out too well. Looking back, I suspect I was quite depressed."

"That's understandable. Losing Neil like that…well, it wasn't easy."

"Not at all."

For a while they both sat quietly, looking out over the harbor. Waverly was mulling over their conversation about life and love and parenthood, yet she wasn't upset by any of it. Mostly she felt peaceful and content.

Then Vivian set her coffee cup down with a thud. Waverly turned to look at her.

"Waverly," she said firmly, "I have one more question for you."

"All right. Go for it."

"How do you really feel about Blake?"

Waverly felt her brows arch. "I thought you asked me that before."

"Yes, but you were vague with me. You brought up the business about Janice, I believe, as a smokescreen."

Waverly laughed. "And she was a good one, don't you think?"

Vivian laughed too. "Yes. But now she's not. I know it's none of my business, and you don't have to tell me, Waverly, but I'm curious."

"Well…" Waverly thought about her answer. "I like Blake. He's a good guy. And, yes, I like him."

"But that's it?" Vivian looked disappointed. "You just like him—end of story. That's all?"

"No, that's not all." Waverly took in a long breath, blowing it out slowly. "The truth is I think—I think—I might be in love with him, Mother." She giggled now. "That sounded so strange coming out of my mouth."

"Which part? Being in love or calling me 'Mother'?"

"Both."

"But really?" Vivian's eyes glittered with expectation. "You *might* be in love?"

Waverly nodded. "But it's hard to admit that. I can't help but think about Neil…the vows I made to him. And how I was so certain I'd never marry again after I lost him. Loving someone else feels like I'm betraying him."

"Oh, darling, you made a promise to Neil—until death do you part—and you kept that promise. He is gone. Now you are free to love again. Don't get me wrong. Neil was a truly wonderful man." Vivian sighed. "I really did love him, and I know how much he loved you. But I believe Neil would want what's best for you now. I'm certain he'd hate seeing you being so lonely. I think he'd be smiling down on this new development in your life. In fact, I think he'd be relieved to know that you'd found love again."

"Really?" Waverly studied her mom's expression. "You're not just saying that?"

"I absolutely am not just saying that. I believe it with my whole heart. I think if you examine yourself carefully, you'll find you believe it too."

Waverly leaned over and hugged her. "Thanks, *Mom!*" Now she stood and stretched, shoving her feet into her flip-flops. "But do keep in mind that just because I finally confessed my true feelings for Blake to you doesn't mean he feels the same way about me."

Vivian just laughed.

"Besides, there's Sicily to think about."

"Sicily adores you."

"Yes, as her friend. But one day when we were on the beach together, Sicily told me what her secret dream is." Waverly felt heavy-hearted to remember this now.

"What was it?"

"Well, it's a secret, but I know I can trust you." Then Waverly explained about how Sicily dreamed of getting her parents back together. "Kind of like in the movie *Parent Trap* is what Sicily told me. Except that she didn't have a twin sister to help her out. In fact, I almost got the impression she wanted *me* to help her out. Although how I was supposed to do that was something of a mystery." She sighed. "Even more so now."

"But that's what all children want. I wouldn't be surprised if you dreamed of that very thing when you were little."

"Probably so."

"And Gia is remarried."

"I know." Waverly pressed her lips together. "But I also know that Blake has some strong feelings of guilt. I don't understand all his reasons, but I do know he has questioned his move to the Vineyard. It's not easy for divorced parents to share a child with a whole country between them."

"That's true." Vivian nodded. "In fact, Blake has mentioned that to me as well."

"So," Waverly said as she picked up their empty coffee mugs and things, "just getting me to confess my feelings regarding Blake doesn't change much, Mom."

She smiled to hear that word coming from her own lips.

Her mother smiled back. "That remains to be seen, dear. Time will tell."

Chapter Twenty-seven

....

By the time Blake and Sicily made it back to Vineyard Haven, after the Edgartown parade and stopping for some other sights along the way, the barbecue next door, complete with festive music and laughter, seemed to be in full swing. He'd barely stopped the car when Sicily begged to go over and join in the fun. He told her to go ahead and that he'd put together the plate of appetizers—something he'd insisted on doing—and come over there shortly.

However, he felt torn as he arranged the veggies and dip on a big green platter. Part of him was like an impatient child, wanting to hurry because he was so anxious to see Waverly. Another part of him, also rather childish, was dragging his heels because he was so not looking forward to seeing Janice. But eventually the platter was complete and wrapped in plastic wrap, and he was carrying it down the well-worn path between their houses. As he walked, he prepared for the worst, while hoping for the best.

Judging by the cars spilling from their driveway and out onto the road, there were more than "just a dozen or so guests there." But Blake was relieved since a larger crowd would make it that much easier to avoid Janice.

He was even more relieved when he spied Janice sitting in beach chairs with Reggie Martin and another couple. Thankfully, she didn't see him. Feeling relieved, he hurried inside where he found Louise, despite the fact she'd hired caterers to help, still fussing in the kitchen.

"Oh, there you finally are," she said rather testily. "I was beginning to wonder if you would show at all. But Sicily promised you'd be here." She looked at his platter. "Oh, you shouldn't have. But since we've had a few more guests than expected, I'm glad you did." She leaned over and pecked him on the cheek. "You're a good boy, Blake, even if you did break my daughter's heart last night."

"I, uh, I noticed Janice was with Reggie out there."

Louise laughed. "Yes, and I hope you're not getting jealous, because I fear it is too late for you, dear boy. That ship has already sailed."

Blake wanted to assure her he was not jealous but didn't get the chance as she continued in a monologue that made him wonder if filibustering ran in the Grant family.

"Fortunately, Janice is a resilient girl. Thanks to the way you abandoned her at that party the other night, she has found someone new. Dear Reggie Martin played the valiant knight by rescuing poor Janice and bringing her home. And," she lowered her voice, "they spent the whole day together yesterday. I just hope Waverly isn't too upset by this new development. As I already said to you, don't waste your time being jealous because that ship—the USS *Janice*—has sailed."

Blake had to control himself from laughing. "Don't worry about me, Louise. I'm very happy for Janice's sake. I hope Janice is happy too."

"I should say so." She gave him a mockingly grim look. "Just in case you were worried, I do forgive you."

"Thank you."

"Now go outside and get yourself something to drink."

"How about you?" he asked. "Don't you get to come to the party too?"

She waved her hand. "Oh, don't you worry. I'll be there with bells on."

As he went outside and got himself a soda from the ice chest, Blake felt like a giant boulder had been lifted from his shoulders. He couldn't believe he'd been dreading this harmless little get-together so much. Was he really that cowardly? He took a sip of soda, then spotted Sicily seated at an umbrella table with Waverly and Vivian over on the side of the house.

"This seat taken?" he asked as he joined them.

"It's for you, Daddy." Sicily gave him her *duh* look. "What took you so long anyway?"

"Just puttering in the kitchen." He sat down and smiled at them. "Nice to see you, ladies. You're both looking lovely today."

For a while they made small talk, and he was relieved to hear that Vivian was feeling better. "I told Lou I'd move back here with her tomorrow," she explained.

"And Janice goes home tomorrow," Waverly added with a knowing look.

"I hear that Janice and Reggie spent the day together yesterday," he said.

"Yes," Vivian said. "Louise told me that Janice is already making plans to come back here after Labor Day."

He just nodded.

"And Mom can come stay with me then," Waverly said, "if the beach house is too crowded with Janice there."

Blake was surprised to hear Waverly calling Vivian "Mom," but it sounded nice too. He made a mental note to ask her about that later. "So you plan to stick around that long?" he asked Waverly. "Through September?"

She shrugged. "Sure, why not? From what I hear, Vineyard winters are milder than Chicago—that in itself is something to look forward to. And I can't complain about the scenery here. Plus, I haven't even had time to take up my own painting yet. Winter should be perfect for that. Who knows? I may stay here indefinitely."

"Really?" He tried not to look too pleased about this.

Sicily was nudging him now. "Daddy, will you come play Frisbee with me?"

He looked at her in surprise. *"Frisbee?"* Sicily hated playing Frisbee. Was she feeling well?

"Yeah." She pointed to a basket of beach toys out in the sand. "Louise put some things out for us to use. Come on! It's a party. We're supposed to have fun."

"All right." He stood. "Anyone else care to—"

"Just *you and me*, Daddy." Sicily gave him a very stern look. *"Okay?"*

Feeling a little worried that something was wrong with her, he simply nodded. "I'm coming."

But as Sicily dashed off to grab a Frisbee, he shot Waverly and Vivian an apologetic look, then jogged over to catch up with his out-of-sorts daughter. But after several throws, which appeared to be moving them farther and farther from the vicinity of the party, Sicily came running over to him with the Frisbee in hand.

"That's enough," she declared.

"Enough?" He felt confused. "I thought you wanted—"

"Get a clue, Dad. You know that I hate playing Frisbee. I just wanted to talk to you. Okay?"

"Okay." He still felt off-balance. Had he done something wrong, something to deeply offend her?

"Let's walk," she commanded, "walk and talk."

He fell into step as she walked him yet farther from the party.

"So, you know the other day when you asked me what I really wanted, Dad?" Her voice softened now, sounding more like her normal self. "You know, after you told me that you and Mom would never get back together, which I kind of knew anyway?"

"Yes."

"Well, you meant where did I want to live, didn't you?"

"Maybe." He sighed. "But then I realized that wasn't a fair question."

"Why not?" She sounded slightly affronted now.

He shrugged. "I don't know, sweetie. Maybe it's because kids don't usually get to say what they want in these situations, so it's not fair to ask. But I guess I was just curious. And I suppose I was worried that I've put you in a bad position by relocating myself so far away from your mom. That's not fair either."

"Yeah, maybe not." She picked up a stick and began to drag it through the sand. "Well, I have an idea, Dad."

"An idea?"

Now she stopped and, without explaining herself, started to draw in the sand. He stood and watched as she made a very large heart shape. Then she wrote the word *Daddy* on top of it, which made him smile. Beneath *Daddy* she placed a plus sign. Now he felt worried. Hopefully she wouldn't write *Mommy*. That would break his heart. To his relief, she wrote her own name and looked up at him.

He smiled. "I couldn't agree more, Sicily. You and me forever."

"Meaning you and I can stay together—always? Not just summers or holidays?"

The light went on now—the hidden meaning behind her little exhibition here. "I would totally love it, Sis! It would be a dream come true for me. The question is, would your mother ever agree to it?"

She nodded somberly. "Yep."

"How can you possibly know that?"

"Because I already asked her."

He blinked. "You *asked* your mother if you could live with me? When?"

"Awhile ago."

"Seriously?"

"Uh-huh." She looked slightly embarrassed now.

"Why didn't you tell me?"

"I—I was worried." She fidgeted with the stick, rolling it between her hands. "I, uh, thought you'd say no."

"No?" He knelt down now, taking her into his arms and hugging her so tightly that she dropped her writing stick. "Why would I say no to what I want more than anything else in the world, Sicily?"

Her serious face broke into a huge smile now. "Really, Daddy? You want that more than anything else in the world?"

"Absolutely."

"Cool." Now she extracted herself from his hug and picked up her stick again. With a mysterious grin, she turned her attention back to her beach drawing, making another plus sign under the name *Sicily*. Beneath the plus sign she carefully wrote *Waverly*. Then she looked up at Blake with wide blue eyes. "Daddy plus Sicily plus Waverly...whaddaya think?"

He stared at the heart and their three names inside. "Do you really mean that, Sicily?"

She nodded eagerly.

"You're not just saying that because you think it's what I want to hear?"

She firmly shook her head. "Nope."

"But you didn't seem very enthusiastic the time I brought up my feelings for Waverly," he reminded her.

"That's because I was afraid." She looked down at the heart again.

"Afraid of what?"

She raised her head. There was a slight quiver in her chin. "You want the truth?"

"Yeah, sweetie. It's always the best way to go."

"I was afraid that you'd love Waverly more than me, Daddy."

"Oh, Sis—"

"I didn't want you to choose her instead of me."

"Never, sweetie." He bent down and picked her up in another big bear hug. "Never in a million years. I mean it with my whole heart."

"I know."

After he finally put her down and they were walking hand in hand back toward the barbecue, Sicily got serious again. "But there's still a problem, Daddy."

"What's that?"

"What if Waverly doesn't like you like that? What if she says no?"

"Oh." He nodded. "Yeah, that could happen."

"Will you be brokenhearted?"

He shrugged, unwilling to admit this likelihood to her or himself. "Hey, I'd still have you. How sad could I possibly be?"

She didn't say anything, but as they returned to the party, he wondered how he'd really handle it if Waverly said "no," and he knew that was a real possibility. But he also knew he'd prayed about this whole thing. He'd put it all into God's hands. What would be, would be—and he'd simply have to accept it.

Having just experienced that moment with Sicily on the beach like that—well, it had been even more than he'd hoped for. So he decided to put his worries out of his head and simply enjoy the day.

And that's what he did. He ate good food and visited with people and played some games and spent as much time as he could with Waverly. She appeared to be enjoying herself too. But then, as the afternoon shadows were lengthening and he knew the sun would be down before long, he made a hasty decision. It might also be a crazy decision, but he knew that nothing was going to stop him.

"Care to stroll on the beach, anyone?" he said to Sicily, Waverly, and Vivian, as they sipped cool drinks in the shade.

Vivian declined, and Sicily said "no thanks" with a knowing twinkle in her eyes.

"A walk sounds lovely to me," Waverly said as she stood to join him.

He made small talk with her as he led Waverly down the beach, going in the same direction that Sicily had taken him earlier. Finally he could see it up ahead—the heart drawing was still there, with enough light remaining to make it visible.

"You know Sicily wants to be an artist like you," he said nervously. "You've been a good influence on her, Waverly."

"I'd say the influence was mutual," she said lightly.

"And Sicily actually did some art up ahead, right here on the beach."

"Really?" Waverly cupped her hand on her forehead to see better in the late afternoon sunlight. "A castle? Or a sand sculpture?"

"No. A drawing."

"Well, I definitely want to see it."

So, taking her hand in his, he led her over, stopping right next to the heart. "There it is." He glanced nervously at her, trying to read her expression as she stared with wide eyes at Sicily's heart drawing.

Waverly's mouth was in an odd line, and he couldn't tell if it was a smile or grimace, but she wasn't saying a word. Although he couldn't remember ever feeling this anxious or worried about anything, he knew he was not going to back down. Not now.

"I have to admit," he said slowly, "I was a little surprised when Sicily showed it to me. But I was also deliriously happy."

She turned to look at him. "Deliriously happy?"

"Yes." So then he quickly recapped what Sicily had told him.

"Really?" Waverly's aqua eyes looked misty now. "Sicily said *that*?"

He nodded, swallowing against the lump growing in his throat. "She did. And I have to admit she definitely helped fan the flames already going inside me. But even if she hadn't given her blessing, so to speak, my feelings for you would've been the same."

"The same as what?"

"As what I told you the other night, Waverly, in front of Janice and God and everyone. Although I'll admit my timing was pretty pathetic. Just the same, I meant every word I said…and more."

"You did?" She stepped closer to him now. "And what about that stolen kiss in my apartment the night the stairway fell? Did you mean that too?"

He smiled. Then, gathering her into his arms, he kissed her again. This kiss was more tender and gentle, but just as sincere. As she returned his kiss, the intensity increased—and he knew the warmth and the passion was coming from both of them. It was electrical and amazing—like it was meant to be.

Finally he pulled himself away from her and, cupping her face in both of his hands, he said, "Waverly Brennen, I love you. I think I've loved you since we first met. And even though it hasn't been that long, I know I've loved you more each day since then. The question is, do you love me?"

She smiled into his eyes. "I do love you, Blake. I never expected to experience a whirlwind romance. Not like this. To be honest, my head's still spinning a little. But I do love you, Blake. It's a relief to finally say it out loud. *I love you!*"

They kissed again, for several minutes this time. And when he stopped, they were both a little breathless. He could hear some firecrackers going off somewhere, nothing compared to the fireworks he felt they were experiencing right there on the beach. The sky was already starting to turn periwinkle with pink around the edges. Then, shot from one of the boats out on the Sound, a sky rocket exploded out over the water, sending a starburst of white light into the sky. Just like that, Blake knew it was time. Or maybe he was crazy. But he just couldn't stop himself.

Right there in the gritty sand, not far from the water's edge where more fireworks were being shot out, and right next to Sicily's carefully drawn heart, Blake got down on one knee and looked up at her.

"I don't want to shock you," he said as he took her hand in his, "and it's fine if you need to think about this, Waverly, but I want you to understand that I have absolutely no doubts about what I'm about to do here."

Her ocean eyes were wide, but her lips were still smiling.

"Waverly Brennen, I love you. Will you do me the honor of marrying me?"

She dropped to her knees as well, taking both his hands in hers, holding them tightly. "*I will*. I totally will. I will marry you, Blake. And Sicily too."

They laughed, then kissed again—this time longer than the previous time. Meanwhile more fireworks were exploding around the island—as if all of Martha's Vineyard was celebrating with them. And then, as if jolted by electricity, they both jumped to their feet.

"Let's go tell them!" Waverly said eagerly.

And together they ran down the beach to break the good news to the others.

About the Author

....

MELODY CARLSON is the bestselling author of more than 150 books for readers of all ages, from adult women to teens to children. She has written two previous titles for Summerside Press, *Love Finds You in Sisters, Oregon* and *Love Finds You in Pendleton, Oregon*. When she's not busy writing award-winning fiction and nonfiction, Melody enjoys camping, biking, hiking, and skiing in the beautiful Cascade Mountains surrounding her hometown of Sisters, Oregon. She and Chris, her husband of more than thirty years, have two grown sons and a granddaughter.

WWW.MELODYCARLSON.COM

Want a peek into local American life—past and present?
The *Love Finds You*™ series published by Summerside Press
features real towns and combines travel, romance,
and faith in one irresistible package!

The novels in the series—uniquely titled after American towns with romantic or intriguing names—inspire romance and fun. Each fictional story draws on the compelling history or the unique character of a real place. Stories center on romances kindled in small towns, old loves lost and found again on the high plains, and new loves discovered at exciting vacation getaways. Summerside Press plans to publish at least one novel set in each of the fifty states. Be sure to catch them all!

Now Available

Love Finds You in Miracle, Kentucky
by Andrea Boeshaar
ISBN: 978-1-934770-37-5

Love Finds You in Snowball, Arkansas
by Sandra D. Bricker
ISBN: 978-1-934770-45-0

Love Finds You in Romeo, Colorado
by Gwen Ford Faulkenberry
ISBN: 978-1-934770-46-7

Love Finds You in Valentine, Nebraska
by Irene Brand
ISBN: 978-1-934770-38-2

Love Finds You in Humble, Texas
by Anita Higman
ISBN: 978-1-934770-61-0

Love Finds You in Last Chance, California
by Miralee Ferrell
ISBN: 978-1-934770-39-9

Love Finds You in Maiden, North Carolina
by Tamela Hancock Murray
ISBN: 978-1-934770-65-8

Love Finds You in Paradise, Pennsylvania
by Loree Lough
ISBN: 978-1-934770-66-5

Love Finds You in Treasure Island, Florida
by Debby Mayne
ISBN: 978-1-934770-80-1

Love Finds You in Liberty, Indiana
by Melanie Dobson
ISBN: 978-1-934770-74-0

Love Finds You in Revenge, Ohio
by Lisa Harris
ISBN: 978-1-934770-81-8

Love Finds You in Poetry, Texas
by Janice Hanna
ISBN: 978-1-935416-16-6

Love Finds You in Sisters, Oregon
by Melody Carlson
ISBN: 978-1-935416-18-0

Love Finds You in Charm, Ohio
by Annalisa Daughety
ISBN: 978-1-935416-17-3

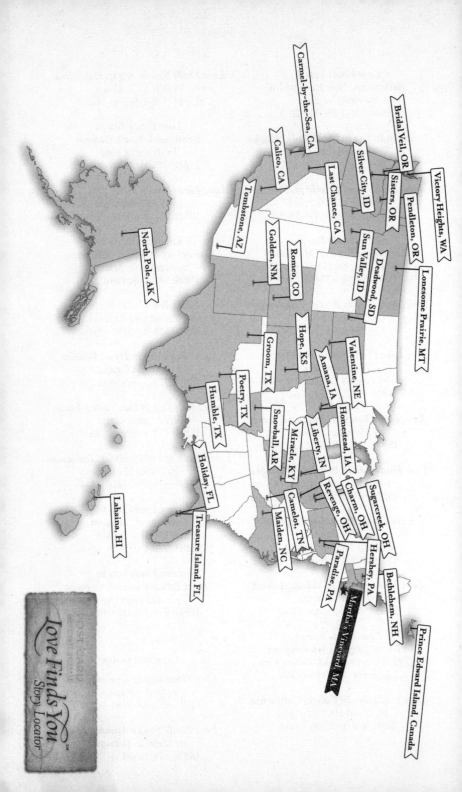